BBC

DOCTOR WHO

HUMAN NATURE

The Doctor Who *History Collection*

The Stone Rose
Jacqueline Rayner

The Roundheads
Mark Gatiss

The Witch Hunters
Steve Lyons

Dead of Winter
James Goss

Human Nature
Paul Cornell

The English Way of Death
Gareth Roberts

The Shadow in the Glass
Justin Richards and Stephen Cole

Amorality Tale
David Bishop

THE HISTORY COLLECTION EDITION

HUMAN NATURE
PAUL CORNELL

BOOKS

1 2 3 4 5 6 7 8 9 10

BBC Books, an imprint of Ebury Publishing
20 Vauxhall Bridge Road, London SW1V 2SA

BBC Books is part of the Penguin Random House group of companies whose
addresses can be found at global.penguinrandomhouse.com

 Penguin
Random House
UK

This book is published to accompany the television series entitled *Doctor Who*,
broadcast on BBC One. *Doctor Who* is a BBC Wales production.
Executive producers: Steven Moffat and Brian Minchin

This edition published in 2015 by BBC Books, an imprint of Ebury Publishing.
First published in 1995 by Virgin Publishing Ltd.

www.eburypublishing.co.uk

A CIP catalogue record for this book is available from the British Library

ISBN 978 1 849 90909 9

Editorial director: Albert DePetrillo
Series consultant: Justin Richards
Project editor: Steve Tribe
Cover design: Two Associates © Woodlands Books Ltd, 2015
Production: Alex Goddard

Printed and bound in the USA

INTRODUCTION

It all began because I got onto the wrong train. I was living in Aylesbury at the time, and I planned to go to London, but instead, with my head in a writer trance as it often is, I ended up heading north. Waiting at the next stop to catch a train going in the other direction, I started having thoughts about what my next *Doctor Who* book could be, and those were suddenly very specific. I'd had three previous *Doctor Who New Adventures* novels published, the last of which had gotten very negative reviews, which were much deserved, it being a shoddy collection of in-jokes and continuity references. I wanted to dig deep again, write something meaningful. What I really wanted to do was give the Doctor a full-blown romance, but I couldn't think of a way to do that that would be acceptable to my editors and to the audience. (It was a different time.) I had in my bag a *Star Trek: The Next Generation* novel, *Imzadi* by Peter David, which did exactly what I wanted to do: broke the perceived rules of the franchise. It suddenly occurred to me that there was an archetypal story shape that did everything I was after, and which *Doctor Who* had never used. Or as the thought was framed in my head: '*Superman 2* works every time.'

Of course, the story of an immortal becoming human is older than that Christopher Reeve movie, as old as belief itself. The details of the plot were much harder to work out. I went to

Australia that year, and spent a lot of time with fellow NA author Kate Orman. As a team, we worked out the shape of *Human Nature* and one of her own books. The villains were a particular problem. At one point they were all thirteen incarnations of the same Time Lord, hanging around together. That would have been pretty hard to write.

Those of you who come to this book having seen the television version starring David Tennant may need a little help. The New Adventures were a continuing series, like the TV show, with their own continuity. As we join the story, Bernice, a companion of the Doctor who I'd created in an earlier book (and who's still going strong in audio dramas), has just suffered the loss of someone she fell in love with in the previous novel, a medieval knight called Guy, and is grieving. That loss could be seen as the Doctor's fault, so he's questioning his actions. There are all sorts of references to the lore established in the books, some of them hidden. I named a schoolboy Clive Ian Alton, for example, to indicate that he might be an agent of the Time Lords' Celestial Intervention Agency, watching to make sure everything happened the way it should. Owls, at this point, were regarded as messengers of the great Time Lord Rassilon. None of it should spoil your enjoyment too much, just be prepared to think 'I wonder what that was about?' every now and then.

The John Smith of the TV version is very much a product of his time, the one of the novel an oddity at the school. The red poppy is chosen in the TV version over the white of the book. These choices and many others are mostly about the difference between a mainstream TV audience and a niche fan one, but some of them are also about budget. As you'll see, there are a lot of similarities also, down to the little girl with the balloon, and in early drafts of the television version we even kept the cricket ball. Russell T Davies, that wonderful man, is certainly responsible for the shaping of those episodes, and, like any great showrunner, wrote some of the best speeches. (Tim's description of the Doctor is entirely his, for example.) However, the misconception has arisen that this was a particularly big rewrite on his part, when it probably wasn't even in the top ten. I hope the reissue of this book helps to balance those scales. Other choices were products of what *Doctor Who* was like in these respective eras: the Doctor of the TV version goes back to Joan to say he *could* be John Smith, the Doctor of the book to say he could *never* be. I'm emotionally attached to both versions.

The character of Alexander wouldn't cause a fuss now, but was something of a departure at the time. Steven Moffat, my drinking buddy, had a hand in John Smith's diary entries (I can't remember exactly how much), and, as you'll see, sort of appears in the book. I figured then that it was the closest he'd ever get to *Doctor Who*. Wolsey the cat, based on a particularly surly animal owned by a friend, continued to appear in print for another eleven years. Those of you who've read Lord Peter Wimsey may recognise the influence of Dorothy L. Sayers on a scene involving John, Joan and the cat. Also to be found here, amongst much pop culture, are references to Kate Bush and the band Saint Etienne which resulted in friendly communications from both.

1995 was a great year to be reading and writing *Doctor Who*. A whole bunch of us, under those brilliant editors Peter Darvill-Evans and Rebecca Levene, were coming up with so many of the ideas that became central to the returning television series. *Human Nature* is still very special to me. I found a way to tell the truth. It wears its heart on its sleeve, and is therefore sometimes completely ridiculous. I'll take that. I never thought I'd be writing about it two decades later. I hope you enjoy it.

Paul Cornell
September 2014

For Penny List

PROLOGUE

'they seem, in places, to address me so directly it's almost uncomfortable'

'either the wallow in the sudden realisation that every single sad song in the world is written for me alone, or the overwhelming, distracting power of a lot of very loud noise'

From the diary of Prof. Bernice Summerfield
Long ago and far away. That's one way of looking at it. But I still sat on the edge of the bathtub and bit my knuckles.

I'm trying to ignore it, and I hope you are as well. An unfortunate episode. If Ace was here, I could say to her: 'Yes, I understand it now, once again. I remember that grief is like having somebody sit on your chest and punch you in the face.' Pain is always forgotten. That's what allows us to have babies. It is a pity she's not here, actually, because now we have so much more in common.

Post-It note covering the above
I will not become maudlin. This is all meaningless. I met someone called Guy, he took on overwhelming odds and then he happened to die. May have died. Did die. Perhaps.

Post-It note covering the above
'These words are not my own they only come when I'm alone'

Post-It note covering the above
Those five minutes… I remember seeing the look on Clive's face when he heard that a dear friend of his had hanged himself. The most frightening thing I've ever seen. Because it was so different. I didn't think that I could make that face if I tried. What was so bad was that Clive had suddenly, in that moment, discovered how to. Now I can do it too.

From the diary of Prof. Bernice Summerfield
'Aren't there any alien monsters we can go and destroy?' I asked the Doctor, on one of the few occasions when I met him in the TARDIS corridors. I mean, granted, I'd been hiding away for a few weeks, and I looked so white that you could put a tail on me and call me Flopsy, but he'd been hiding too. He hadn't followed up on his pledge to take me to Blackpool, or somewhere else exciting. He'd just become sad, at exactly the time I needed him to be happy. Whenever I'd gone into the console room, he'd been absent, and at night I'd just hear the occasional cry from one of those terrible nightmares of his.

'Alien monsters…' he mused now, tapping his finger on the tip of his nose. 'No. They're all gone. Little Johnny Piper – no, sorry, different train of thought. No alien monsters, I'm afraid.' He had that troubled look about his eyes, and wouldn't quite look at me.

I wanted rather desperately to touch him, hug him or something, but everything about him said that that wouldn't be a good idea. He seemed embarrassed about seeing me, which wasn't really him at all. If I didn't know better, I'd say that he was thinking as hard about the last five minutes of Guy's life as I was.

Post-It note covering the above
Summerfield, B.S. Subject: Human Nature: 3/10, must try harder. (The 'Human' is crossed out and then replaced. There is evidence of correcting fluid.)

From the diary of Prof. Bernice Summerfield
We wandered into the console room, me still trying to think of some way to break the ice. One of the many trivial things I'd been doing over the last few days was to try and repair my portable history unit. It's a little screen that lets you access archives while in the field. Or, in my case, while in the bath. Normally you'd need an account with whatever library you're accessing, but, with a bit of help from one of those beardie-weirdie computer experts you trip over in spaceports, I'd put together a program that makes the library think you're a member. The thing broke down, of course, just before Heaven, and I'd been carrying it in my luggage ever since. So, as part of my great campaign to do things, I had hefted one of the Doctor's folding work-tables into the console room and set about dismantling the thing, on and off, with gaps for tea and crying.

As we entered the console room, then, I was surprised to see the unit sitting atop the folding table, complete and repaired. I picked it up and switched it on, while the Doctor glanced offhandedly at various monitors on the console. He'd repaired the unit's hardware, but the programming was all over the place. Travelling through the time vortex isn't the best place to deal in electronic media, of course. It's like trying to follow a soap opera that's being performed on a series of trains as they speed by, while other trains with different stories... well, it's difficult, all right? Anyhow, the Doctor had succeeded in creating some weird protocols, with new files half set-up all over the place, and error messages demanding attention everywhere.

I pressed a few buttons and cleared everything, discovering, to my relief, that the Doctor had got the thing functioning correctly at least. I turned to him, grateful to have something to ask him about. 'Thanks for fixing this up.'

He glanced up from the console. 'I just wanted to work out what it was … how it worked. I reversed the polarity of the communications coil, by the way, so you can write into archives too, but to do that I had to connect it through the TARDIS information processors, because I know how to work with those. So you might get information from the past. Or the future. Which in some cases wouldn't be a good idea, so don't use it when we land anywhere. Please.'

I sighed. 'So you repaired it so well that I can't use it?'

'Repaired? Oh, did it need repairing?'

I smiled, which was good. I got the feeling that the module was a sort of present. 'What have you been doing in the last few days, then?'

'Jigsaws. Chinese cookery. I made clay models. Of the Zygons. I did what I normally do when I'm investigating something … with your unit, I mean. I dived in and messed it up. Threw away the manual, ignored the notes and laughed in the face of Balloon Help.' He left the console, and perched in the wicker chair, his hands folded into a spire. 'That's what I did with the TARDIS when I first got her. You can't do everything for a long time. In the case of the TARDIS, for far too long. But when you do get where you want to go, you've learnt all sorts of useful stuff about the system you're investigating.'

'No wonder your cakes are so awful.' I grabbed a cushion and sat down facing him.

'The ducks like them.'

'The ducks are programmed to like them. Besides, it all sounds rather dangerous to me. You can get terribly hurt, mucking around like that. I prefer to read the manual from cover to cover, hopefully in the bath with a good bottle of Cabernet Sauvignon.'

'Mmmm…' The Doctor frowned again, and jumped up. He started to pace around the console once more, tapping controls seemingly at random. Maybe it was me using the words 'terribly hurt' that had set him off again.

God, *I* was being careful of *his* feelings!

His glance fastened on a monitor and an uneasy grin spread over his features. 'Found it. Good girl.' He tapped a few buttons and straightened up. 'There's a planet called Crex in the Augon system. They have a market there. Would you like to go?'

I had the feeling that saying no would invalidate several days' worth of hovering in the vortex. 'A sort of spacecraft boot sale? Is there something particular you're after?'

'A white elephant. Maybe a pink one.'

'Is this an item or an acquaintance?

He paused for a moment, and then smiled one of his more dangerous secret smiles. 'Both.'

The TARDIS materialised with that noise it has (sorry, I've never been able to come up with a good description) amidst a tight little knot of stalls, under the shade of purple silks and great canopies of striped fabric. The first thing that caught my attention as the Doctor locked the door behind us was the smell, a wonderfully jumbled mixture of spices and cooking scents, a hundred different cultures in one place.

Nobody seemed to bat an eyelid at the TARDIS landing. They must have been fairly used to materialisations. The Doctor raised his umbrella like an aerial, and turned it and his nose until he'd settled on a direction. 'This way.' He walked off in a straight line, tossing a memory module from the TARDIS databanks in his hand thoughtfully.

I followed him through the masses of alien species, both humanoid and otherwise, their bargainings and gestures and laughter merging in one great shout. Felt odd to be out and about, a bit vulnerable. Shrugged it off. The Doctor led the way to a little hillock, its surface once grassy, but now a churned patch of mud. He pulled me after him up to the top of it, and from there we got a good look at the whole market.

It went on for miles, all the way to one cloudy horizon, a brilliant jumble of tents and awnings. The other way, it petered out a bit in the direction of some mountains, and a big dark square with some buildings indicated a rough spaceport. 'It's wonderful,' I opined. 'How did it start?'

'Tax concessions.' The Doctor was still turning like a weather vane. His eyes suddenly focused on something in the distance. He nodded, and then turned to me. 'I'll be gone for an hour. Maybe two. I'll find you.'

'What, in that lot?'

'Back at the TARDIS, then.' He seemed eager to get away, flustered and impatient.

In the middle distance I glimpsed the solution to our problem. 'Tell you what,' I said, pointing. 'I'll meet you over there.'

The beer tent seems to be a universal icon, and one, to paraphrase a recent acquaintance, about which I may write a short monograph one day. The atmosphere's always different to a pub or a bar, slightly edgy and hot under the canvas, relaxed and cool outside. You see more undone buttons and exposed podge outside a beer tent than anywhere short of the Flaborama on Boojus 5. I bought a pint of The Admiral's Old Antisocial at the, thankfully currency-unspecific, bar, and wandered out to the plastic tables.

Now, you may well be thinking: 'Beer? What a terrible idea. That's no solution.' I would reply that you're wrong. It's a solution of hops, barley and yeast, and it is so transcendently wonderful that I long ago made the decision to sacrifice any chance of trim thighs in favour of it.

Company is always an issue at this juncture. There's no point, in my view, in being a solitary drinker. You can do that at home, given a certain degree of sadness which I wouldn't dream of sinking to. Usually. Well, three out of ten times. And it's been a difficult time for me lately. Anyway, there were the usual tables of dangerous-looking space pirates, penniless backpackers with their glasses of iced water, and traders waving their hands and complaining that business wasn't what it once was. Most of them were aliens of some sort.

Therefore, it was with a rather xenophobic sort of glee that I came across a table whose occupants were doubly interesting. They were A: human and B: female. They looked like they all came from different places, and had clustered together out of the familiar realisation that internal gonads are best, actually. So I sat down and introduced myself. Professor Bernice Summerfield, FRAS (Fairly Rotten At Scrabble), current occupier of the Proxima University Chair Of Archaeology (it's in my room, by the begonias), holder of the Martian Gallantry Medal (I found one and thought I thoroughly deserved it). They were suitably impressed. They laughed out loud.

'Jac,' said a young woman with short hair and interesting ear-rings. 'I'm here researching the origins of the market for Ellerycorp. They're thinking of doing something similar.' She introduced the others. There was another short-haired woman with the eyes of a Traveller Priestess, who was called Sarah. I don't think I ever found out why she was there. And there was a feisty-looking woman with tanned olive skin, wearing an assortment of charity shop relics that she somehow made stylish. She was looking at me with a world-weary expression that I found instantly charming, her head propped up on one hand.

'How's it going?' she asked.

For a moment I thought of telling her. But no. 'Fine.'

'Your round, Lucy,' Sarah told her, placing her empty glass definitively down on the table.

'You're not exactly svelte either,' Lucy replied, reaching for the glasses and winking.

I smiled at that, too. 'Same again, please,' I said. As soon as Lucy had departed, Jac told Sarah that the woman was a

Psychology tutor, who'd been here for a month, waiting for an interplanetary lift that never seemed to arrive.

Well, that was a familiar story, and I went on to tell them some of my own history. As regular readers of my diary (if that's you, Doctor, put it down now) know, there are certain portions of my life that I can't readily account for. I tend to gloss over these with a post-it note, but on this occasion I have enough recollections to fill a page, disconnected as they may be. I said all these things, but some of the words may be in the wrong order.

Pint two: I'm arguing with them. 'But that's ridiculous. You can't expect an internal market to operate for any extended period of time –'

Pint three: They're laughing at me. 'There is *not* a God! Listen, if this coin lands on the same side… several times… then –'

Pint four: They're falling over themselves, holding up their hands like anglers talking about the fish that got away. 'Short and stubby. Well, I've only ever encountered five of them, but – what are you laughing at? Did I say something funny?'

Pint five: They're listening intently, nodding every now and then. 'So we had to go away. There were so many of them. I think… I hope it was quick for him.'

Pint six: Sarah is looking at me, concerned and sweet. 'It's not far from here, really. Just a quick hopper ride over the hill. I've got this really great Alcorian wine that you ought to try. And we could, you know, just hang around for a while. Play tennis. What do you think?'

The next thing I knew, a familiar hand was tapping me on the shoulder, and something cold attached itself to my cheek. I was thinking about Sarah's offer, and I tried to swat the hand away like a fly, but then, suddenly –

I was utterly sober.

I unpeeled the medi-patch that the Doctor had slapped onto my cheek and looked up at him. 'What – ?'

'Alcohol dispersion pad. We haven't got much time, and there's a lot you need to know.' He grabbed my hand and pulled me to my feet.

'Hey…' Sarah said foggily, gazing up at me. 'Wait a minute…'

'Leave her alone!' Jac was halfway to her feet. 'Who is this guy?'

'It's all right,' I reassured them. 'He's a friend.' I felt suddenly rather foolish, as if my dad had arrived to pick me up. Rather awkwardly, I shook Sarah's hand. 'Thanks for being so nice. I appreciated the offer.'

She shrugged. 'No problem. I hope it all works out.'

'It will,' I told her. But then I glanced at the Doctor.

'Quickly,' he said.

His pupils were glowing silver.

I got the feeling that it wasn't going to be that easy.

I let the Doctor lead me back to the TARDIS. He was walking quickly, urgently. I glanced back to see if he was being followed, but that wasn't it. He was walking like he was about to explode or throw up, as if something terrible was about to happen and he had to be in a particular place when it did.

'Could I have a few of those patches?' I asked, still banjaxed by my instant sobriety. 'They're already my favourite bit of TARDIS equipment.'

'Yes. No. I don't know, it isn't important!' The Doctor turned a corner, saw the TARDIS ahead and broke into a run. He fumbled the door open and leapt inside, diving at the co-ordinate keyboard and tapping in instructions faster than I could follow. 'Catch!' he called, and threw me a rolled-up scroll. I noted that it was sealed with his thumbprint.

The TARDIS doors closed, and the familiar take-off sound began. The central column started to rise and fall. 'The letter will tell you everything!' the Doctor shouted. 'And pay attention to the list! See you in three months! Eck.'

The last was a little click from his throat, like something switching itself off. The Doctor's eyes flicked back to their normal colour. Then he closed them, and his mouth twisted into a giddy smile.

Then he fell into a crumpled heap.

A red ball rolled from his pocket, and settled in one corner of the console room.

'Doctor?' I ran to his side, and checked his pulses. One seemed to have stopped altogether. The other was racing. My first impulse was to rush him straight into the TARDIS medical bay, but I restrained myself. I broke the seal on the scroll and quickly read the several sheets it contained.

'Oh no…' I groaned when I'd finished, flopping back against the console. I turned to address the unconscious, still grinning, body. 'I may have remarked on this on several occasions in the past, but let me say it definitively this time. You are such a git!'

And, feeling a bit better, I left him there and headed for the wardrobe room.

This adventure was going to require a serious frock.

Diary Entry Ends

A solemn old humanoid with a grey beard stood outside a tent in the marketplace. He put his hand up to shade his eyes against the setting sun. Out of it, from the direction of the spaceport, a hopper was approaching. With a great shouting and a roar of turbos, it descended next to the tent, and the old man walked forward to greet the occupants.

The first of them leapt out, dressed in a long cloak and breeches, his two swords crossed in scabbards across his back. He was a young man, well-muscled and vital. His green eyes flashed in happiness as he embraced the old man. 'Well met, my son! You meant what you said in the message? You finally got one?'

'Indeed I have, Greeneye. It has been a long wait, but a Time

10

Lord finally responded to our signal. I had thought that we hadn't tried enough channels, but—'

'Oh, they heard. They always hear.' Greeneye glanced at the sky involuntarily. 'Are you coming with us, then? You've waited so long, it'd be a shame if you weren't there for the kill.'

'I wish you wouldn't put it like that.' The old man frowned. He brightened when he saw the latest arrival stepping from the hopper. It was a child, a girl of ten or so, carrying a balloon. 'Aphasia, my dear daughter, how are you?'

'I'm not talking,' the girl told him. 'I'm sulking.'

'I told her she couldn't—' Greeneye looked around again, stopping himself. 'Get up to her usual tricks. But quickly now, have you prepared the tunnel?'

'All is ready. Are the others here?'

'We are here!' a hissing voice emanated from the hopper. A dark figure in a wide-brimmed hat jumped to the ground, and pointed a white glove at the old man. 'If you have failed, Laylock, I shall make you suffer. You know I shall.'

'Don't threaten me, Serif. You wouldn't harm your own flesh.'

'Wouldn't I?' Serif glanced at Aphasia, a grin twisting his mouth. He would have said something more, but another hopper was approaching.

It landed, with a swirl of soil, and two more figures stepped from it. One was a big, bearded man, carrying a huge backpack and wearing a belt from which hung numerous weapons. The other was a thin, precise-looking man, his hair neatly backcombed and his cape enclosing an elegant suit.

'Good,' he muttered, looking around. 'We're all here. Into the tent, then, quickly now. We don't want to attract attention.'

They went into Laylock's Emporium, as a sign referred to it. Laylock himself remained outside for a moment, glancing about worriedly, before he followed.

*

Inside, the thin man looked around appreciatively. A polished consultation table, with various computer reference devices atop it, stood at the very centre of the tent, the big roof spar through the middle of it. Brightly coloured canvas avenues led off in all directions, access to the other tents where the real work was done. Gentle music tinkled throughout. 'Very professional. You've gone to a lot of trouble.'

Laylock inclined his head. 'Thank you, August. I've made quite a profit in all this time.'

Serif hissed. 'That is unimportant. The cover story has been successful, that is all.'

'No, no…' August raised a hand. 'I think it's a great achievement. It's not as if our own projects haven't blossomed in this last decade. Now then, I believe Hoff thinks that the Time Lords could be tracking us.'

The big man grunted in the affirmative. 'If they knew everything, they might divert an asteroid, cleanse the whole site.'

'Well, I disagree with that, they haven't the will these days, they'd probably just send an agent. But anyhow, we really should be going. Lead the way, Laylock.'

The old man did so, glancing nervously at the roof.

The cabinet was a rusty old gothic thing, hidden away under a cloth in a corner of Laylock's surgical supplies area. He pulled the cloth aside and slapped a control. The front of the cabinet, previously a metal door, dissolved into the butterfly tunnel of the time vortex.

'Don't stare into it, daughter.' Greeneye hid Aphasia's eyes. 'After a while, you see terrible things.'

Aphasia slapped his hand away. 'I want to see terrible things.'

'The tracer's working,' Laylock confirmed. 'I activated it as soon as he left. There.' A golden thread snaked down the vortex tunnel and spiralled off into the distance. 'That'll lead you to wherever he's going. Estimated travel time… about nine weeks.'

'Yes. Good.' August stared into the tunnel with some trepidation. Behind him, Hoff and Greeneye were bringing in several large packs of equipment. 'We'll need to keep this link open, so you'll remain here, Laylock. That won't be too much of a burden for you, will it?'

Laylock nodded. 'Thank you.'

'Any idea of what he got?'

'No, he brought it himself. They often do, those who think of themselves as composers. He'd been in contact with me for several days, asking for tech specs, wondering if I could really do what I said I could. I had to be discreet; I wondered for a while if he was an Intervention Agent.'

'Opek to a Grotzi he is!' muttered Greeneye. 'If this is a set-up—'

'It isn't, I'm certain,' Laylock told him. 'He was going through real quantum rearrangement effects when he left, at any rate.' He handed August a memory pad. 'This is everything I learnt about him, including a description. I did try to persuade him to give up the Pod, but—'

'That's too much to expect, yes.' August clapped his hands for quiet. 'All right then. This is the best shot we're going to get. Follow me.' He took a deep breath, pinched his nose, and leapt into the tunnel. He shot off into the distance, a doll-like figure, buffeted to and fro until he vanished, his form curling around the path of the golden thread.

'Hey!' shouted Aphasia. 'Wait for me!' And she leapt in too.

Greeneye and Hoff followed, carrying the bundles they'd brought from the hopper. Before he left, Serif turned and pointed at Laylock. 'If you have betrayed us—'

'Of course I haven't, son. Off you go.'

Scowling, Serif leapt into the vortex. A moment later, they were all gone. Laylock patted the cabinet in satisfaction, and threw the cloth back over it. Just the hoppers to hide, and then he could get back to his regular routine.

He just couldn't shake the terrible feeling that he was being watched.

In the long, dark room, all that could be heard was the ticking of a clock and the occasional snore.

Two lines of beds ran along the walls. In them slept boys in their late teens.

But one didn't sleep.

He was sitting up in bed, his hands to his mouth, his eyes staring into the distance. His name was Tim. His mother was dead, and his father, abroad on business, had transferred him to this place.

He'd just had such a dream. A nightmare, full of people and places he'd never seen before. They seemed to address him so directly that it was terrifying.

'I've seen the future,' he whispered. 'And everybody dies.'

She appeared at the end of his bed then, and showed him her skeletal hands. 'Yes,' she whispered. 'Everybody dies.'

Tim screamed.

Lamps were lit, there were cries of alarm and annoyance, and of course she was gone when the light flooded along the dormitory.

From the window came a great beat of wings. Tim spun and stared.

An owl was flapping off into the night.

1
DON'T FORGET
TO CATCH ME

Nine weeks later.

The bicycle sped down the little cobbled hill, the juddering motion making the items in its basket leap about, in imminent danger of falling onto the road.

Bernice didn't care. The sun was up, and, for the first time in weeks, so were her spirits. The little town of Farringham was basking in the glow of a balmy summer day, and the sweet smell of roses was wafting across it on the breeze. 'Good morning, Jill! Good morning, Jenny!' she called as she whizzed past a row of little cottages.

'Morning, Bernice!' the two housewives chorused. Then they resumed their argument across the fence. This time it was about an overhanging tree, tomorrow it would be about barking dogs. They liked to argue, it seemed, and whenever one of them met Bernice, the other would wander up, get involved in the conversation and end up disagreeing with the first.

The bike took the corner at the bottom of the hill far too fast, and she narrowly missed her landlord, Alexander Shuttleworth. He was a jolly, bearded fellow in a white colonial suit and a loud tie, the curator of the local museum. 'Sorry!' she called over her shoulder.

'Charmed, dear girl, charmed!' he boomed back. 'I'll take my medical bills out of your rent!'

Mrs Windrush, her hair bound up in a headscarf and her mouth full of pegs, waved from her garden, where she was putting out her washing. She was proud of her little patch of grass, although she wished that her husband could afford a maid. 'Perhaps next year,' she always said when she and Bernice chatted. They'd been married a year, and Mrs W kept dropping hints about the pattering of little feet, so it was probably just as well that Mr W was up for promotion at his office job in Norwich.

Benny had to wait at the T-junction for Mr Hodges' wagon to trundle by, the horses already sweating in the sunshine. Hodges was a greengrocer, and delivered door to door every morning. His and Benny's routines had become so predictable that they had started to nod at each other, and complain if the other was late.

'Give you a penny for your boots!' he called out this time, winking. Benny smiled back, wondering just how vulgar the catchphrase was. She probably ought to have blushed.

Bernice's target was the Lyons teahouse in the centre of town. A convenient cycle-rack stood on the wall nearby, which she reached, as she always did, just as the town-hall clock was striking its precise twelve o'clock. She dismounted carefully, remembering when she'd ripped the hem out of a skirt by catching it on a pedal. The fashions of 1914 were a lot easier to wear than Victorian gowns would have been, at least. There wasn't any upholstery under the skirt, and no bustle to deal with. Electing to be the paragon of fashion today, she'd chosen a (rather extraordinary) black and navy-blue checked skirt, with a buttoned jacket and lace collar. She had toyed with the idea of a mourning band, to hint that she was well-connected enough to miss the Duke of Argyll, but there was the possibility that somebody would think it was more personal than that and ask about it, and that would be too horrid. She untied the ribbon on her hat, and propped it on the handlebars, shaking her hair extensions to and fro. They still didn't feel natural, but her own short bob would have required some vast and incredible explanation.

The teahouse served a wonderful fruit-cake. Benny ordered a slice with her customary pot of tea.

'Will that be all, madam?' the smartly uniformed waitress asked her.

'Yes, thanks. That's a strange accent, where are you from?'

'Germany.' The waitress giggled. 'I am from Baden Baden, and I am working here for the summer. Mr Condon, the manager, he is my uncle.'

'Oh, right, well, that's… good.' Benny flashed the woman a smile. She curtsied and went back to the till.

The other tables held groups of housewives, maids who'd saved their pennies for a weekly lunch date, and a travelling salesman, his case of samples on the floor beside him as he scanned the racing form in the paper. Benny flipped through a copy of *The Tatler*, making a mental calculation. It was April now, getting really hot and summery. Everybody was talking about holding dances, and whether or not one should offer favours to guests, and if looping the loop in a flying machine clutching two piglets was *infra dig* or not. The papers had scarcely a thought for matters further abroad than Ireland, where the Liberals' plans to give the whole island home rule had the Unionists threatening civil war.

The magazine in Benny's hands complimented the Kaiser's daughter on her grasp of English as demonstrated at various English social events that month.

Benny shook her head and sighed. She put it out of her mind and tipped the waitress generously as she handed her her cake.

'Excuse me,' a voice asked. 'Could I please sit down? There isn't anywhere else.'

'Of course.' Bernice glanced up. An elegantly dressed, painfully thin young woman in a very ornate lace collar was standing there. She could only have been seventeen or so, but her face, as well as being gaunt, was lined with experience. The odd thing was that, a minute before, Benny had been sure that there were lots of places free, on tables across the café. But now all the seats had bags on them. Even the travelling salesman had propped his case on the seat opposite him. A great many people suddenly seemed to be watching Bernice's table.

Oh no, she thought. It's one of *those* people.

So Benny did what she did whenever she encountered somebody who was generally despised. She said: 'Please sit down here, there's plenty of room,' in a rather loud voice.

The woman did so. The German waitress, obviously not understanding whatever cultural malaise afflicted the newcomer, came over at once.

'Could I please have three slices of cake, and a plate of scones, with quite a lot of cream?' the woman asked.

'Hungry?' Bernice asked when the waitress had left.

'I'll say. I'm on the Cat, you see. Got to build myself up.'

'I beg your pardon?'

'The Cat and Mouse Act. I'm on a hunger strike in Holloway. Every now and then, they release me, let me get my strength back. Then they arrest me again, and I go on hunger strike again. I've been in and out three times now. It's getting to be a matter of routine.'

'What did you, erm, do?'

'Stuck a pole through the wheels of the King's pony and trap. He nearly went flying. I suppose that God saved him. I'm a bit of an Emily Davison, you see, only not so brave.'

'Sorry, I'm being a bit dim, I know, but why did you do that?'

'To draw attention to the WSPU's campaign for universal suffrage. I'm an adult woman and thus deserve the vote. Goodness, you're still smiling. You've listened longer than most people do.'

'Because I agree with you. You're going to win, by the way. I'm

Bernice Summerfield.'

The woman shook her hand. 'Constance Harding. I was going to go to my first dance this year, but now, obviously, I can't. When did you come out, by the way?'

A forkful of cake stopped halfway to Benny's mouth. 'Sorry?'

'Your accent gives you away.'

'My accent?'

'Yes, my dear.' Constance sighed. 'Do you know, I was hoping to go cruising before I came out…'

Benny frowned. 'Isn't that rather the wrong way round?'

'I suppose so. My mother was going to come too.'

'Really?'

'Yes, she's very gay.'

'Obviously.' Benny ate her cake thoughtfully. She raised a finger to ask a question, then lowered it again. 'You know, I think we've been talking at cross-purposes…'

Constance glanced up. A plodding blue figure was moving down the street outside. 'Oops. Terribly glad to meet you, must be going.' She took off her hat, dropped the cake and scones into it and ran for the door. 'Do have the cream.' And she was gone.

Benny laughed out loud, once more incurring the displeasure of her fellow customers. She didn't mind paying Constance's bill at all.

After lunch, Bernice returned to her lodgings at Station Cottage. She'd popped into the art shop where Mr Sangster had provided her with some oils that she needed. He'd regaled her with stories of the Boer War, straight, she suspected, out of some cheap paperback he was reading.

Station Cottage, as the name implied, was right next to the level crossing over the branch line. Every two hours, a little train went past, carrying commuters to and from Norwich. The cottage had a little garden with just the right sort of light and facing, and Benny had set up her easel there, intent on painting the gentle hills above the town. Atop one of them was a monument of an old woman, sitting with her basket. This, she had been informed, was Old Meg, who, sometime last century, used to walk all the way to Shellhampton and back every day to sell her small goods. Good to be remembered, Benny thought, for something so everyday and difficult.

She made herself some sandwiches, and wandered out into the garden, putting a hand up to her brow to get a good, distant look at the work in progress. Quite good, really, for a novice.

'It's utterly wonderful!' boomed a familiar voice from the street. Alexander Shuttleworth was leaning on the fence, fanning his florid face with his panama hat. 'You must have been exhibited, surely? Have you sent anything to the National?'

'If I did –' Benny munched her sandwich – 'they would send it back with a note saying that it does not suit their present needs, and there would be a PS asking what it was actually of.'

'Oh, you sell yourself short, Miss Summerfield. I had a lady friend once who was an art lover, and she taught me some of the basics.'

'Really?' Benny arched an eyebrow. 'So do you think it's actually any good?'

'Absolutely topping. Sorry to intrude, by the way. I just popped over because I was bored. There's nothing to do at the museum, young Alec's sitting at the desk, and he's bored too, but I employ him to be bored so that I don't have to be. I wondered if I might watch you paint?'

'It's not exactly a spectator sport, but do come in. It is your garden.'

'Like a malevolent spirit, I can only enter where I am invited.' Alexander opened the garden gate and settled into a deckchair. 'Besides, that's the reason I started to rent the cottage when my sister died. I like meeting new people. Especially those down from Cambridge.'

Benny bit her lip. So far she'd managed to avoid the topic of her supposed studies at Newnham College. 'I'm afraid that I've never been to your old college.'

'King's, it was. They rather disapprove of you roving about, don't they?'

'Rather. Oh, listen, I met a woman on the run from the police today...' And she told the story of her encounter with Constance.

Alexander humphed. 'Damn Liberals! Pardon my French, loved one, but it's really going too far when you're in and out of prison like billy-oh. I don't know why Asquith doesn't just give them the vote, well, for householders, anyway. What do you think?'

'I think that grown-ups should vote, full stop.'

'Good for you. You ought to meet my chum Richard Hadleman. He's chairman of the local Labour group. Young firebrand, just in his twenties. It'll be chaps like him that'll lead us into the next decade.'

'Probably.' Bernice turned back to her painting, not wanting Alexander to see her face.

A great commotion arose from behind the cottage, and the gates of the level crossing were raised. A moment later, plumes of smoke rose from a tank engine as it chuffed past, the warm smell of its boiler drifting through the garden and mingling with the roses. Alexander glanced at his watch. 'Dead on two. The world may be changing, but at least the trains still run on time.'

The scream caused some of the younger boys to look up for a moment.

The Upper School room in Farrar House had two balconies, each one with a cluster of chairs around it. One window was for the boys in general, the other for the Captains, four boys given special responsibilities for their house at Hulton College School.

At that moment, the Captains were beating Timothy with a tarred and knotted rope.

'Gag him, for God's sake,' Hutchinson, a tall boy with cropped fair hair, muttered. 'We don't want Wolvercote to think we're squealers.'

Timothy looked over his shoulder, clutching the cold metal of the radiator which he was bent up against. 'I had a dream, Hutchinson, a nightmare. Death was in it. We all died. We were all killed. The whole of Farrar.'

'We all have nightmares from time to time,' Hutchinson told him, 'but one learns not to wake up screaming. Only four more now. If you can refrain from making a noise, we shan't gag you. D'you think you can?'

Alton wandered in at that moment. He was rather laconic for the Captains' taste, but had passed the tests and pull-throughs designed for the new bugs with startling resilience. Especially impressive was his time on the gym rings, where he'd hung for a whole afternoon without the usual bleating. 'Excuse me, Captain,' he called, 'but the form master's on his way up here. Saw him on the front stairs.'

'What on earth does Smith want?' Hutchinson muttered. 'Oh well, let's not disturb his fair senses. Let the bug up, we'll finish him later.'

Dr Smith entered, his fingers tapping his lip thoughtfully, just as Timothy was skulking back to the boys' side of the room. He was a short, dark-haired man, wearing a brown suit and an outrageous tie. The design of that tie summed up what the Captains thought of their new form master. It was colonial in nature, a swirling and colourful pattern such as one might expect to see on some foreign woman's clothing. As part of a teacher's kit, though, it was frankly inappropriate. The younger boys adored him, because he was homely and full of childish things. That was desperately bad for morale.

Still, the Captains stood to attention and saluted him.

'House master in the Upper!' bellowed Hutchinson, and the boys stood up.

'Who's that?' Smith turned back to the door, as if someone had come in behind him, then, realising they meant him, grinned for a millisecond and waved a distracted hand. He was still wearing his usual bemused expression, as if he was continually missing the point of some joke. 'No, no, sit down. I came to ask… about cricket.' He suddenly pulled a tiny rubber ball from his pocket, and bowled it overarm at a startled lad reading *Boy's Own* in the corner. Gamely, the boy used the rolled-up paper to knock it back.

Smith caught it, grinning. 'Howzat? Oh yes, we'll put you in to bat.' There was general laughter.

The Captains exchanged glances. Hutchinson said, 'If you wanted to ask about the cricket team, sir, you could have summoned me to your rooms.'

'Oh good, do you know about cricket?'

'Yes, sir. I was team captain last year.'

'Only I was wondering –' Smith threw the ball into the air, caught it in his mouth, appeared to swallow it, and produced it again from his sleeve – 'why are there only eleven people batting? Couldn't we include everybody who wants to play?'

'I assume that's a rhetorical question, sir,' said Hutchinson.

In the corner of the room, Timothy was biting his bottom lip, trying desperately not to cry.

'Tell him,' urged Anand, his friend. 'He could stop them. He would.' Anand's father ruled a small independent state in India. He and Timothy were best friends, probably because the rest of the House seemed to hate them equally.

'Yes,' Tim whispered. 'That's the most terrible thing. He would.'

'It seems very odd,' Smith concluded. 'When I was a boy, in Aberdeen, we used to get a couple of planks, knock a ball about.'

'Perhaps we could try that,' piped up Captain Merryweather. 'It might catch on, sir, and they'd all start using planks at Lords.'

Hutchinson glanced at him warningly. His sarcasm had been a bit too obvious. But Smith was grinning that inane grin again.

'Yes… Well, I'll put the team up on the notice-board. We'll start with eleven and work up. Many hands spoil the broth, or not, as my father used to say. Or perhaps he said the opposite. Goodbye.' And he left, tossing the ball thoughtfully.

'Quiet!' Hutchinson called as soon as the door had closed. The laughter that man always left in his wake – what sort of example was that? 'We were in the process of beating Dean, if I recall.'

Timothy stood up, his eyes dark with pain, and stiffly walked back to the radiator. 'It will go the worse for you,' he whispered as he leant against it once more.

'What, bug?'

'I said,' Tim said, in a louder voice, 'it will go the worse for you.'

Hutchinson exchanged bemused glances with his fellow captains. The tone of Timothy's voice was resigned rather than scared. 'Dare say it will, Timbo!' He laughed. 'But you're the one it's going badly for at the moment. Now, where were we?'

In the forest on the hills above the town, a red squirrel looked up, started, and ran.

In mid-air, a shape was forming, a flowing fractal vortex that grew out of thin air, swirling out from a point to become a spinning upright disc, the size of a barn door.

There were five figures in the vortex, in the distance, rushing towards the disc. They were frozen like statues, in leaping postures. They became larger, larger still, and then the first of them fell straight out into the wood.

August got to his feet instantly, letting go of his nose, and caught Aphasia as she fell from the vortex gate. He left her to recover, and slapped the shoulders of Greeneye and Hoff as they stumbled out, carrying their large packs. 'Quickly, assemble the frame.'

The two of them started, with smooth, practised speed, to pull a metal structure from the backpacks. By the time Serif jumped from the vortex, hissing, they'd completed the job. They slammed the final connections together, and a thin metal ring encompassed the fluttering lightshow. Hoff's stubby fingers punched a series of buttons on the base of the ring. The vortex disc flexed, and a single clear note rang out across the woodland. The travellers held their breath. Then the disc stabilised, and a series of reassuring lights illuminated on the control deck.

'Vortex tunnel stable,' Hoff declared.

'Thank my ancestors,' August breathed. 'Now the area. Greeneye—'

'I'm just doing it, Father.' Greeneye turned a slow circle, sweeping a handheld device across the ground. His circle complete, he flicked a control.

A shimmering curtain of light rose from the circle around the group, arched itself into a dome above them, and, as soon as it had become complete, shimmered and blurred into an exact recreation of the woodlands around it. Birds flew across the holographic dome, and the branches portrayed on its surface bent and rustled in the wind.

From the inside, the dome was transparent. August and the others sat down in a circle, paused, and then let out a deep sigh.

'This place smells,' Aphasia declared.

'Indeed!' Greeneye laughed. 'Most places do. But I, for one, am just grateful to be on solid ground, and move my limbs again. We might not have been aware of the passage of time in the vortex, but my bones ache with it. Where are we, anyhow?'

'Planet called Sol 3, in the Stellarian Galaxy.' Hoff was checking the readings on his wrist-scanner. 'Many many library entries for it.'

'Near Gallifrey, then,' breathed Greeneye.

'It is not "near Gallifrey"!' August laughed. 'We're in an arm of Mutter's Spiral, Gallifrey's right at the core. If being in the same galaxy is *near*, then the Sontarans are near the Rutans, for goodness' sake!'

'No harm in being wary,' Greeneye replied, a dangerous glint in his eye. 'You know that those blighters specialise in the stab in the back.'

'You're right, son, you're right. We ought to change anyway. Hoff, activate that media scanner you got on Tauntala, give us a feel for the local culture.'

Hoff fished a screen from the pack and handed out headsets, each of the group programming theirs for their particular interests. Then they set to the business of examining the data that the media scanner was picking up. For some hours, the only sounds that could be heard in the forest were the usual movements of small animals and birds.

Through the bushes crept a great hunter.

He was a tabby tom-cat, and his name was Wolsey. He was far from his own territory, and thus constantly on the lookout for rivals and new things to explore.

The dome was something very new indeed. It was twilight, and he had been about to turn and head home for some food, but the new thing caught his attention.

He approached it cautiously, skirting right round it before venturing towards it. Visually, it was hard to see that there was anything strange there, but Wolsey didn't rely on sight as much as a human would, and he perceived the strange construction as a bundle of strange sounds and absolutely new smells. He stalked right up to the edge of it, and leaned his nose forward until his whiskers were nearly touching the mysterious surface. In a moment, the great hunter would mark the thing with scent from the side of his head, and then it would be his.

A sudden sound.

Wolsey looked up. And jumped.

Aphasia landed right where he'd been, her hands snatching at the air as the cat bounded off into the undergrowth.

The little girl bared her teeth and stood up, brushing the dirt from her dress. 'A cat!' she called to the others. 'It was one of those cat things!'

'A cat?' Greeneye leapt out of the dome, his hand reflexively grasping for the top of his sword. 'A Gallifreyan creature!' He was dressed in relaxed summer whites and blazer, a pristine boater perched atop his newly cropped hair. The only strange things about him now were the two swords still harnessed to his back.

'Would you please relax?' August emerged from the dome behind him, in a dapper business suit. 'You're making me nervous.' He slapped a control on Greeneye's harness and the swords vanished. 'We could only find test transmissions in the radio spectrum, remember? The media scanner had to concentrate on how the locals perceive their print culture. Unless they want to use it as an observatory, I can't see what the Time Lords would want with somewhere as primitive as this.'

'But the cat—'

'There are lots of worlds with cats,' Hoff muttered. He was wearing the medals and uniform of a Boer War veteran. 'Don't let it bother you.'

Serif was still in his long black cape and wide-brimmed hat. He turned his head silently, examining the foliage. 'I will explore with stealth,' he told the others, 'by night.' And he was gone into the forest.

'Serif,' August called after him, but he was gone. 'Oh well, I'm sure he knows best. Hoff—'

Hoff was about to flick a wrist control, but Aphasia jumped up, shouting, 'Wait! Wait! Balloon!'

From out of the square panel that had opened in the dome, a red balloon floated, its string dangling. It hovered to Aphasia's hand, and she grabbed hold of it. 'You can close it up now.'

Hoff did so. The construction hummed with power as a defence shield activated.

'Let's explore, see what we're about,' August decided, pointing vaguely in the direction of town. 'If anybody sees the subject, or this companion of his, then call it in. And there's a TARDIS about somewhere, remember, which is very probably where the target is.'

They set off, Greeneye tossing his boater from hand to hand. Glancing at some animal movement in the bushes, possibly the dreaded cat, he missed, and the hat fell to the floor. He winced, as if bruised, as the evening breeze sent it tumbling across the ground. He halted briefly, concentrating.

The boater steadied itself, and, on some unseen means of propulsion, ran back across the forest floor to Greeneye, hopping back on to his head.

'Whatever this Time Lord's doing here,' he muttered, 'I hope he's enjoying it, because, let me tell you, it's going to be his lifetime's work.'

'Miaow…' said Hoff.

2
Maius Intra Qua Extra

'So…' George Rocastle, MBE, leaned back in his chair and smiled. 'How are things working out, John?'

Dr Smith had plopped down in the chair on the other side of the desk. He pulled at his collar, and grinned giddily. 'Fine… fine.'

'Only I was disturbed by something I heard today. As headmaster, I have to keep an ear out for everything, you know. Why did you venture into Upper School today?'

'It's where the boys were. I wanted to ask them about cricket. Was that wrong?'

'Not… wrong, not as such, no. But there's more of an order to life here than what's in the rulebook. Rather like Great Britain herself, we're proud of our unwritten constitution. *Maius intra qua extra*, you know. *Pars interior ingentior est quam exterior pars?*'

'Ah…' Smith nodded wisely. 'What does that mean?'

Rocastle's moustachioed upper lip quivered, then he controlled himself. 'It happens to be the school motto. If you don't know what it means, I suggest that you look it up.'

'Yes. I will. Do go on.'

'Dr Smith, when I took you on, it was largely on the strength of a superb set of references, possibly the best I have ever seen, from the Flavian Academy of Aberdeen. Your behaviour in the six weeks that we've had you has, thus far, not matched those references. For a start, there's the matter of your hysterical outburst when you sat in on Mrs Denman's biology class—'

'She suggested that the world might have been created in six days. That Darwin's theories were unproven. I had to laugh.' Smith's happy gaze caught Rocastle's disapproving expression. 'Perhaps you had to be there.'

'Then there was the incident over the punishment Mr Challoner had prescribed for Atkins.'

'They were on a cross-country run. The boy was hurt.'

'Mr Challoner's view is that he was slacking. He completed the course twice, so he can't have been too badly injured, can he? Well, can he?'

'No, I suppose not—'

'Listen, Smith, I'll be plain. Your interference in other teachers' lessons is bad for discipline. I've heard that your own History classes run remarkably smoothly. Why can't you let others get on with their work?'

'I...' Smith lowered his head. 'I don't know. I'm sorry if I caused any trouble. I'll try not to meddle.'

'That's the spirit. I admire a man who knows when he's wrong. As for this afternoon's little sortie, well, it's not really done for a housemaster to enter into the personal business of his House. Bad form. I don't know how they did it up in Scotland—'

'My last headmaster, Mr Gothley, was very keen on knowing everyone's affairs.'

'Well, that's the trouble, then. You're just getting used to how we do things south of the border. The Celtic temperament's a fine thing in war. I remember a rather stirring bayonet demonstration given by the Scots Guards at a tattoo when I was a lad. However, the way of discipline and stability is our chosen path, and we do well enough with it.'

'Yes.' Smith nodded. 'I see.'

'Good man. I'm sure we shan't have to talk like this again. Good Lord, is that the time? Not on evening prep, are you? No, well then, I shan't keep you from getting back to the lodge. How are you finding it?'

'I haven't had any trouble. It's always been at the bottom of the drive,' Smith told him seriously.

Rocastle wasn't listening, thumping some papers into shape on his desk. 'Good, good.' There was a knock on the door. 'Enter.'

Joan Redfern entered. She was in her early forties, a science teacher, with an occasional strand of hair escaping from her carefully pinned coiffure. 'Excuse me, Head, and, oh, hello, Dr Smith, I was just wondering if I could use your telephone at the weekend. My aunt in Grimsby appears to be ailing, and I'd like to discover the present situation.'

'Of course,' said Rocastle. 'Will you be requiring any time off, Mrs Redfern?'

'Oh goodness, no, it's not as serious as all that. Thank you anyway. Good day.' She nodded to Rocastle, gave Smith a little smile, and left.

A moment later, when Smith left the Head's study, Joan was waiting for him in the corridor, sitting on the little bench outside normally reserved for quaking schoolboys. 'Sent to see the Head, eh?'

'Yes.' Smith bit his bottom lip worriedly.

'What did he want to see you about?'

'Nothing important. I'm a bad influence. Are you going home?'

Joan stood up. 'Yes. I was hoping that you would walk me to the gate, Dr Smith. If you'd like that.'

Smith stuck his elbow out. Joan raised an eyebrow at it, and, abashed, he took his black umbrella from the coat rack and hung it there.

'I heard that you wrote…' They walked stiffly down the gravel driveway, the crunching of their feet being the only sound in the beautiful blue twilight. A full moon was rising, its surface rippling with the haze of the departing day. Its light turned the rest of the sky into a negative, expectant and shining, the first brave stars appearing over the hills. The school was an enormous dark edifice behind them, a block of shadow which suddenly started to come alive with light as, at once all over the building, prefects turned on oil lamps. In seconds, the light fluttered all over the gothic structure, filling the windows with a sickly glow.

Smith had glanced back over his shoulder, watching as the window of Rocastle's study also slowly illuminated. 'Light…' he muttered. Then he turned back to Joan. 'Sorry. Miles away. What did you say?'

'I said that I heard you wrote. Fiction, I mean.'

'It's nothing. Stories. For children. Magic, elves, you know.' Fireflies were dancing through the trees along the drive.

'I see. Are you a mystic, then?'

'No. Well, not in the romantic sense. I don't believe in sprites or kelpies or boogens or intelligent seaweed.'

'Intelligent seaweed? My, you have an imagination.'

They turned the curve of the driveway so that the school was hidden by the trees. They both slowed to a stop and visibly relaxed, smiling at the similarity of their reactions.

Smith offered Joan the crook of his arm again, and this time, with a wry glance, she took it. 'Go on, then. I need all the support I can get at my age.'

'Why, how old are you?'

'Dr Smith! What a question!' Joan feigned a glare.

'Sorry. I'm forty-eight.'

'Well, I'm—'

'Don't tell me.'

'Younger.'

'Good.'

'Why?'

'Because – I don't know, sometimes I feel terribly old. I need somebody to keep me young.'

'So what did Rocastle have to say to you?'

'He was telling me about some of the unwritten rules. I wanted to ask if he could give me a list, but that's probably the point, isn't it?'

'Oh, that man. He's a complete caricature.'

Smith waved his free hand. 'He's dedicated. He means well.'

'If he was in my class, I'd give him a good telling-off. Far too bossy. He's a… a military twit.'

Smith stared at her for a moment, a boyish grin playing over his features. 'You don't like soldiers, do you?'

'No. Not since my husband, Arthur, died. Let me tell you, John, if I were given the choice again, I wouldn't come here. I had to endure a very harsh interview with Rocastle, and he made my appointment feel like a charitable act on his part, giving employment to a war widow with outdated references. I felt that he was being more of a friend to Arthur than to me. But I needed to make ends meet. And there's, well, there's another factor, which it wouldn't be right to go into.'

'Ah, well, I wouldn't want you to do anything wrong because you were with me. Two heads don't make a right.'

'Two Heads. What a terrible thought.'

'A monster. Like Cerberus at the gates of Hell.'

Joan laughed. 'Well, Orpheus tricked Cerberus, didn't he?'

'He didn't win, though. He looked back to see Eurydice.'

'Thank goodness you arrived. I wouldn't know what to do with myself otherwise. Our talks, our games of whist… I do believe that they keep me sane.'

'Yes.' Smith turned his gaze from the shimmering trail of the Milky Way which was beginning to form overhead. 'I feel the same way.'

'Tell me, have you noticed how odd that boy Dean is?'

'Dean?' Smith was broken out of his reverie. 'You mean Tim? Yes, he is a bit distant. Preoccupied. Like somebody's died.' He grimaced. 'Sorry. Shot myself in the foot. Oh no! No!' He was visibly floundering, letting go of Joan's arm to wave his hands into wild patterns.

Joan was laughing. 'John, don't worry, it was a long time ago. I rather think I've got used to it. I don't believe I've ever heard that expression, shot oneself in the foot. Very descriptive. Where does it originate?'

'I don't know... oh dear.' Looking abashed, Smith took her arm once more. 'You're very understanding. You make everything simple. I like that.'

Joan considered. 'Well, I like the way your face creases up whenever you have to talk about anything emotional, as though it's going to be incredibly painful for everybody concerned. But you go ahead and say it anyway. Tell me, in your past – and please do not feel obliged to answer – was there any great tragedy? A... failed romance?' She saw the knotted look on his face again, and her own smile faded. 'Oh dear. I knew that I should not have asked.'

Smith looked down at the gravel beneath his feet. 'No, no... There was somebody. When I was very young. Her name was Verity. She was a brewer's daughter. We were engaged to be married.'

'What happened?'

'She preferred a sailor. That's the thing about Aberdeen. You get all sorts. Liquorice?' He had pulled a stick of the red variety from his pocket.

Joan snapped off a piece and munched it. 'That's terrible. Did you hear anything of her again?'

'Her sailor fled with a girl he met in a dance hall. That was years ago. I don't know what happened after that.'

'Didn't you offer to take her back?'

'No. Perhaps. I don't know. It's all a blur sometimes.'

They'd reached the old hunting lodge at the end of the drive. Joan, seeing that Smith was uncomfortable, decided not to pursue the matter further, and changed the subject. 'We were talking about Timothy Dean. What do you make of him?' She let go of Smith's arm and watched him fumble for his key.

'Eh? Oh yes. Very precognitive. I mean precocious. Very sensitive.'

Joan sighed, realising that she wasn't going to get any sense out of Smith about this topic. 'Well, perhaps you and I could play a hand or two tomorrow evening. Would you like me to cook?'

'Yes.' Smith, still failing to open his door, turned and gave her a shy smile. 'That would be good.'

'Is there anything you don't like?'

'Burnt toast.'

'Well, I certainly shan't risk that. I'll see you tomorrow at seven then, unless our paths should cross beforehand.'

'Good. Wonderful.' Smith leaned back jauntily on the door.

Which was, of course, the point at which it opened, and he fell inside.

Joan walked off down the lane, waving and laughing.

From the diary of Prof. Bernice Summerfield
That night I had one of my doldrums.

I'd picked up a copy of *Le Morte D'Arthur* from the cottage bookshelf. I wasn't thinking, obviously. Mind you, since one of the alternatives was *A Study in Scarlet*, perhaps I should count myself lucky. I could have found myself on the morning train to London, aiming for a tour of the old folks' homes. Doubtless that would have resulted in me being pursued by a bath chair and its occupant having a heart attack.

I curled up in bed with the bit where Bedivere throws Excalibur back into the lake. When I was a girl, hiding out alone in the forest (and I have spent so much of my life alone, I've just realised that), Mallory and the like were a great comfort. I expected it to be again, and it was, in an odd kind of way, because, almost without realising that I'd started, after ten minutes I found that I

35

was sobbing my heart out. I was crying for a past that had never really existed, some terribly British notion of the previous land, where things were better, and all deaths were noble, and the twilights were presumably golden. My family is British, after all, so I have a right to sob about what was lost. Loss is my heritage. Before the war that took Mum, before all the wars, before the Fall, I suppose, we were comfortable and happy and glad. And then They came, and They had some sort of big plan that We didn't really understand, and just Them being Them made us, who had been all sorts of things, into We.

Same old story, and it is full of its own terrors, and flawed, and has that terrible male triumphalism about it that causes boys to line up and be slaughtered.

But it can still make me cry.

And that night it connected with my own situation, and it affected me, rather.

The night lasted about ten days.

Diary Entry Ends

Dr Smith ignited the oil lamp, settled down at his desk and picked up a pen. He tapped his teeth with it thoughtfully.

It would have been good if Joan had stayed for dinner that night. She was different. Full of life. She made him happy in strange ways. She made him want to write.

He'd always thought he'd had a novel in him, ever since he and Verity had walked down to the shore and they'd danced on the rocks in the moonlight. She'd kissed him then, and whispered something in his ear. Both ideas seemed odd: the whisper and the kiss. He couldn't remember what she'd told him, or what being kissed had been like.

All that was because he'd got his Uppers results that day. It looked certain that he could be a teacher.

He pulled a blank piece of paper from the drawer and stared at it. Very white. Very blank.

He thought for a moment. He could show the story to Joan. She'd suggest changes, they'd work on it together. That would be good.

He put his pen to paper and began to write.

The Old Man and the Police Box

Long ago, and far away, in the reign of Queen Victoria, there lived a silver-haired old man, who had a very good idea. He had thought of a shelter for policemen, with a telephone, so that anybody who was in trouble could call for help. And that was clever, because nobody knew what a telephone was, back then.

Because there had to be a lot of room inside the shelter, the old man invented a way to make a lot of space fit into it. Because the shelter had to be able to chase criminals, he made it so it could disappear and then appear again somewhere else.

The old man was very clever, but very lonely, and so, before he told anybody else about his invention, he used it to go exploring. He visited another world, a place called Gallifrey.

There, he found a tribe of very primitive people.

Smith stared at the paper in annoyance. It had flowed out of him, but he couldn't show it to her. Far too childish. Even for children. And where was it going? He didn't even have a plot.

He'd sleep on it.

He retired, extinguishing the oil lamp on his desk with an irritated jerk of the valve.

As he moved about in the bedroom of the little lodge, a boyish hand silently picked up the first page of the story. After a moment, there was the sound of stifled laughter.

Smith ducked out of the bedroom in his nightgown and cap. He glanced around the place. But all was as it should be.

All that remained of his visitor was a gentle breeze from an open window. It sent the papers scudding to the floor.

Smith retrieved them, and, shaking his head in puzzlement, went back to his bed.

'What do you think?' Greeneye had his feet up against a tree, his back to the hillside above Bernice's cottage. Hoff sat beside him, staring through a pair of advanced binoculars.

The image he was watching was of Benny pacing her room, in blue against white, seen through the wall of the building. 'Native to this planet, a touch of Artron energy, therefore she's been in a TARDIS. Yes, she's the companion. Professor Bernice Summerfield, the subject told Laylock. Sometimes called Benny. There are a few other details in the files.' He pulled a gun from his belt. 'Coming?'

'What? No, Hoff, no! What would be the point of that?'

'We grab her, interrogate her, find out where the Pod is, and we're home before first light. What's your problem?'

'It won't work! She's a Time Lord's human assistant, therefore she must be somebody of particular qualities and abilities.'

Hoff raised his eyebrows. 'Oh yes?'

'She would resist our efforts, try and escape, all of that. No, we must do this in a subtle way.'

'You're attracted to her, aren't you?'

'Well, she has got a nice shape. For a humanoid.'

'I don't believe it. If it's got a corporeal form, you'll cruk it.'

'All I'm saying is, let me do it my way. Tomorrow.'

'All right.' Hoff slipped the gun back into his belt. 'But if it doesn't work, I'll have the hot irons ready.'

3

BOUDICCAN
DESTRUCTION LAYER

The next morning, Smith walked into the classroom, dressed in the mortarboard and gown in which he always looked so awkward. Silence fell, as it always did. The Captains sat at the back, and the boys at the front, and all of them stood to attention as he entered. He caught a paper dart happily, glanced at it, tweaked the wing a notch and threw it back, straight into the hands of the boy who threw it.

'Good morning, class.'

'Good morning, Dr Smith,' they chorused.

'Sit down.' As they did so, Smith opened his briefcase. 'I put a notice up on the board in the corridor. The cricket team.'

Hutchinson held up his hand. 'Excuse me, sir, but weren't we going to talk about that?'

'Were we? I thought we had. Sorry. Oh well, it's only a game. Now, destruction, murder, people impaled on posts—'

'Sir?' Captain Merryweather put his hand up. 'Aren't you going to take the register, sir?'

'Abbot, Andrew?' Smith muttered, flipping open the register. Each boy answered his name, until:

'Alton, Clive Ian?'

'Sir.'

'Dean?'

Timothy was staring out of the window at the terrible

greenness of the cricket pitch. Anand nudged him in the ribs. He looked up. 'Sorry, what?'

'Timothy Dean?' Smith grinned at him. 'I don't know why I'm asking, I can see you're there.'

Hutchinson glanced at the stern looks on his comrades' faces, nodded and stood up. 'Sir, that's not right.'

'What?' Smith peered myopically between Dean and Hutchinson. 'Can't you see him?'

'Missing one's name in a roll call is a disciplinary offence, sir, under the rules of the school. Aren't you going to do anything about it?'

'Why, what do you think I should do?'

'The standard punishment is ten strokes of the slipper, sir. Perhaps you weren't aware of it.'

'Aware?' Smith looked uneasily round the class. 'Yes, I knew that. But this is my form room. Can't I change the rules?'

'None of us can change the rules, sir. Even if we'd like to. If you'd prefer it, I could administer the punishment myself.'

Smith fiddled with the air, thinking. 'Yes,' he decided.

Timothy opened his mouth in horror. Last time Hutchinson had punished him, he hadn't been able to sit down for three days, and couldn't get to sleep for the pain of the bruises.

Hutchinson stood up. 'May I have the slipper, sir?'

Smith was fumbling inside his briefcase. 'I wondered why I had to bring one of these to every lesson. I nearly wore it, but I'd have ended up walking in circles. Ah!' With a flourish, he pulled a fluffy pink slipper from the bag, and experimentally slapped it across the back of his hand. 'Yes... that shouldn't hurt.' He looked up at Hutchinson. 'Ready?'

Hutchinson had walked up to the desk. Now he stopped, stiffly turned and headed back to his place. 'I think we can defer the punishment, sir.'

'Oh good.' Smith looked puzzled, dropped the slipper back into his bag, and smiled at the class. Many secret smiles were directed back at him, except from the Captains, who were staring at him with a mixture of incredulity and distaste. 'Now. Destruction, murder, people impaled on posts. All of these are a feature of Boudicca's rebellion against the Romans, *circa* AD 62.'

Atkins put his hand up. 'Please, sir, do you mean Boadicea?'

'Yes. Boudicca was her real name. She was a Celtic queen, the Queen of the Iceni, who lived around here. She was the widow of Prasutagas. He was the old king. When he died, he left his land to his daughters and the Roman empire jointly. This is when the Romans ruled Britain. He thought that would work. But Roman agents came and tried to take over the place. Why?'

'Because girls couldn't rule a kingdom?' suggested Merryweather.

'That might be what they thought. We don't know if they were acting officially. Paulinus, the Governor, was away fighting in Wales. That might have been the idea. If they'd failed, nobody could blame him. A lot of governments work like that.'

'Not European ones, surely?' Alton murmured, a sly smile on his face.

'Perhaps. In Bosnia – but never mind that. The agents raped the daughters and molested Boudicca herself. So she – what? What's the matter?'

A murmur had rippled round the classroom. 'Sir, what did they do to the daughters again?' asked Phipps.

'Raped them. Had sex with them against their will. Isn't that in the dictionary? Now…' He ignored the murmurings and turned to the map. 'Boudicca's immediate reaction was to do – what to the agents? Hadleigh-Scott?'

Hadleigh-Scott looked up from nudging his deskmate and giggling. 'To make them marry the girls, sir?'

'What? No. Strange. No, she had the agents skinned alive and impaled on posts with their intestines – most texts say intestines – in their mouths. Very nasty. Then, because they'd given the impression they were working on Imperial orders, she called the Iceni to war, and declared that they were free. They didn't have to do what the Governor said any more. The tribe attacked Colchester, St Albans and London, and burnt them all flat. There was so much destruction that archaeologists know when they've got down to AD 62 in those towns, because there's a layer of broken things and ash. Finally, Paulinus returned, got his troops together and defeated the Iceni. Boudicca killed herself. The question is: was this great British heroine, a favourite of Queen Victoria, right to rebel? Hutchinson?'

'Of course. She was fighting foreign tyranny.'

'No she wasn't. Paulinus was the mildest of governors. If she'd have reported the agents to him, he'd have dealt with them himself.'

'But Britain was occupied by the Romans.'

'The people she killed were Britons. Even the legions were mostly local recruits.'

Hutchinson laughed. 'What are you trying to say about Queen Boadicea? That she was some sort of mass murderer?'

'Yes. Of course.' Smith had advanced up the room, staring manically at Hutchinson. 'But was the murder justified?'

Hutchinson squared his jaw. 'Murder is never justified.'

'What about in the Boer War?'

'That was different. That's war.'

'So was this. The Britons she killed were from other tribes. Tribes who had invited the Romans to Britain.'

'Collaborators. They deserve all they get.'

'Years before. They now lived in peace with everybody.' Smith was level with his desk now, glaring down at him.

'Then, no,' the boy blurted, meeting his stare.

'But it was rape. Her daughters. Royalty. Mauled by rabble. Who's right?' Smith lowered his head until it was level with Hutchinson's.

'How can I possibly – ?' Hutchinson glanced away.

'Who's right?' bellowed Smith.

'I don't know!' shouted Hutchinson.

'No!' Smith slapped the slipper across the edge of his desk with a sound like a whiplash.

The boy jumped up out of his seat and stood there, glaring at Smith and panting.

For a moment, the class thought that Hutchinson was going to hit him.

Then Smith turned away, and wandered back towards the blackboard. The slipper had vanished once more.

'No,' he murmured, like he'd lost his place again. 'No, you don't...' He turned and looked at the boys. 'Now, where were we?'

With a mighty effort, Hutchinson sat down. He stabbed the nib of his fountain pen into the paper in front of him, and half wrote, half ripped, a single word:

Later.

The bell rang at eleven, and the class filed out, many of the boys clustering around the notice-board outside as they left. Hutchinson didn't even look at Smith as he marched swiftly by.

Timothy stopped at the desk, and looked nervously up at his form master. Smith was quickly packing his briefcase, ready to get on to his next class. 'Excuse me, sir. Thank you, sir.'

'Oh? What for?'

'You didn't let Hutchinson at me, sir. I wanted you to have this.' There was a quiet intensity, a desperation, to the boy's voice. He pulled a bright red apple from his pocket, and held it out, his hand shaking slightly.

Smith took the apple, buffed it on his sleeve, and grinned at his reflection in it. 'Why an apple?'

'I had a dream. I have strange dreams. I had to give it to you. So you'd remember.'

Smith took a bite and munched thoughtfully. 'An apple a day... saves nine. No, that's not right. What was it that I was supposed to remember?'

'A stitch in time? Keeps the doctor away?' Timothy suggested smiling.

'Probably. Dreams are like that. You never remember the interesting bits.'

Tim took a deep breath. 'I'm… I'm being… It's the rules, I know, and I should just put up with it, but… the Captains, they beat me every day. I only wanted to ask, is it ever going to stop? Does it stop when I'm in the second year?'

Smith put down the apple, and looked around the room, lost for words. Finally, he answered. 'I don't know. Does it? Is there anything I can do? I'll tell them to stop—'

'No! Don't!'

'No, no, then I won't, no…' Smith held up his hands in pacification. 'Does it happen to everybody?'

'No. They do a few things to the others, and they call Anand and Alton names. But it's only me that they give a beating to every day.'

Smith wandered into the middle of the room, biting his lip in concentration. There seemed to be nothing inside him to answer the boy. He'd never been bullied – or had he? If he had, he didn't remember. What would Rocastle say?

'It's part of growing up.' He gazed into the corner of the room. 'It's everyday. Cat eat dog. Survival of the fittest. A place like this – it's full of rules. Full of customs. And they have to be obeyed. It's just the way things are. Discipline. The making of a man. One day, you'll be a captain, and then you can beat who you want. You've got that to look forward to.' He turned back to Timothy and managed to meet his pained eyes. 'Does that help?'

Timothy didn't answer for a moment, looking at Smith almost accusingly. 'Yes, sir. Thank you, sir.' He almost ran out of the room.

Smith stared after him. 'Or you could always burn their houses down,' he whispered to himself.

The door opened and Rocastle entered, beaming. He glanced behind him at the departing Timothy. 'John, I do believe I've misjudged you!'

'Sorry?' Smith went back to his case and finished packing up.

'Well, I was on the way here to give you a bit of a lecture, something mad and racy about Boadicea, I heard. But I stopped to have a glance at the cricket team selection, and heard you giving that strange Dean boy a wonderful talking-to. That's just the spirit! Tell me, would you be interested in helping out with the OTC?'

'The OTC?'

'Officer Training Corps; probably don't have them in Scotland. There's a session tomorrow afternoon. We do it every Saturday. Can't ask you to come along on your time off, but...'

'I'll pop my head around the parade ground.'

'Good... good! Well, keep it up!' Rocastle slapped Smith on the shoulder, and left, rubbing his hands together. He stopped at the door. 'Oh, and interesting team selection, by the way, putting Hutchinson in at five and making Dean captain. I was going to mention it, but, no, no, I think I shall trust your judgement. Good day, Dr Smith.' And he left.

Smith closed his case, picked it up and slowly walked to the door.

All of a sudden, he found himself wishing for evening.

Benny glanced at her watch. Smith was late again. Every Friday lunchtime, they had a regular date outside the Farmers' Arms, and every Friday lunchtime, he was late. The little cluster of tables outside the pub was filling up with customers, and she was sitting there marooned, unable to pop in and order a pint alone. Or a half, rather, or if she was being particularly civilised and non-threatening, a flipping sherry.

She rubbed the bridge of her nose and sighed. The day felt parched and distant, the result of only getting an hour or so's sleep

45

near dawn. The darkness under her eyes was so great that she'd given in to temptation and applied some strategic foundation. Better that than look like a panda. Oh well, only another three Fridays to go, then they could go. Being somewhere else would be good, but being in the future, her personal future, would be better. A year on, and she'd feel a bit more together, and she just wanted to get to that.

For one thing, she wanted to ask the Doctor why on earth he'd done anything as insane as this. If it was some sort of reaction to what she was experiencing, then it wasn't the most useful response in the world.

Benny closed her eyes, wishing that the day wasn't so bright. When she opened them again, Dr Smith was sitting opposite her, a big grin on his face. 'Hello,' he said. 'How are you? And how's your father?'

'I'm fine. He's fine,' Benny replied ritualistically, feeling a great urge to grind her teeth together. 'And how are you, Uncle John?'

'Confused. Happy. Both. I'll tell you in a minute. What would you like to drink? Sherry?'

'Three pints of ESB and a straw.'

'Sorry?'

'Sherry, yes, that'd be lovely.' By the time he'd returned with the drinks, in his case a lemonade, she'd quietened herself a bit. It was just that she would have liked to have had somebody to talk to. It wasn't his fault if he couldn't be that person right now. She made herself sip the sherry instead of throwing it back and banging the glass on the table. 'So, what's confusing you?'

'There's a woman. She's called Joan. She teaches science. I think that she doesn't like me.'

'Doesn't like you? Why?'

'Because she keeps laughing at me. Every time we walk back from school she laughs at me. And she keeps beating me at cards; she enjoys winning. She's going to cook for me, just to show off.'

'This woman who doesn't like you… is cooking for you?'

'Tonight. She disturbs me. Sometimes I can't think about anything else.'

'She'll be stealing your blazer next. Wait a sec.' Benny fumbled in her bag and pulled out the list, which she took a quick peep at beneath table level.

Things Not To Let Me Do

1: Commit suicide, if for some reason I want to.

2: Do physical harm to anyone, if you're aware of it.

3: Eat meat, if you can.

4: Eat pears. I hate pears, I don't want to wake up and taste that.

5: Leave the area, or you, behind.

6: Get involved in big sociopolitical events.

7: Hurt animals, especially owls.

8: Develop an addiction.

9: Anything impossible.

Benny looked up from the document, shaking her head. 'Well, all I can say is, if you're going to do that sort of thing, be careful.'

'Careful? What do you mean?'

'You ought to, erm, make sure you're safe,' Benny whispered, glancing around at the other tables.

'Safe? Oh, I see what you mean. There's no need.'

'Isn't there?'

'No, we never bet much at whist. A wine gum here, a shilling there…'

'I'm not talking about whist!' Benny lowered her voice. 'Listen, don't you think this behaviour, on both your parts, is a bit… odd?'

'Oh yes, that's why I mentioned it. I wish she'd stop.'

'Do you?'

'Well…' Smith's face clouded. 'No, not really. I think I'd miss it if she stopped now.'

'Oh my God…' Benny rubbed her eyes tiredly. 'Are you sure this is a good idea?'

'What?'

Benny sighed and glanced up at the sky. Well, perhaps it wouldn't do any harm. In this era, they'd need to be married a year and have a signed note from both parents before they could even snog, and they only had three weeks. She ought to just let him enjoy the attention. 'Nothing. You're obviously just very good friends and colleagues, and should cook, play whist and disturb each other's emotions as much as you think fit.'

'Oh. Do you really think so?'

He looked so downcast that Benny had to smile. 'Still confused?'

'More so.'

'Your round, isn't it?'

They talked about the cricket team, Smith quickly exhausting Benny's knowledge of this peculiar game in his quest to clarify the rules. He briefly alluded to the Boudicca incident, and Tim's subsequent appeal, but made them sound so everyday that Benny could only mutter about not liking school that much herself. There followed a few questions about her return to Newnham, which she dodged, and about the current health and activities of her father, Smith's brother Jonathan. These she answered with whopping fibs.

'He's gone off to Gallifrey.'

'Gallifrey? Where have I heard that before?'

'It's in Ireland.'

'Rather risky at the moment, surely?'

'Oh, he's in no danger. They're a backward lot, the natives of Gallifrey. Idiots with no dress sense.'

'Yes…' Smith nodded thoughtfully. He glanced at his watch. 'Well, I'd better be getting back to—'

'Joan?'

'School.'

'Same thing. Try not to learn too much.'

He got up, making that gesture he always did with his hand, a strange flutter that Benny took to be a perplexed search for a non-existent hat. That alone was worth a thesis. She'd have so many questions for him in three weeks. 'See you next Friday.'

'Of course.' Benny saluted him with her remaining sherry, and watched him depart. He waved as he mounted his bicycle and peddled off down the road, swerving close enough to the local omnibus to scare the horses.

Benny laughed and drained her glass. 'What the hell. Good luck to her.'

She noticed that, from a table a few feet away, somebody was staring at her, apparently amazed.

It was a tall and handsome young man, with fair hair, dressed in blazer and whites. A boater was perched atop his head. He had halted in the act of eating one of the pub's corned-beef rolls. He broke into a smile as she caught his eye, so she quickly looked away. No thank you. Not wanted on voyage. She put down her glass and reached for her bag, intending to head off for an afternoon's painting and possibly a little sleep.

But the young man had got up from his seat, and intercepted her as she headed for the steps that led down from the raised area of the tables to the street below. 'Excuse me – but it's Bernice, isn't it? Bernice Summerfield?'

'Yes…' Benny stared at the man, trying to place him. She was sure that she'd never met him before. Perhaps he was one of Alexander's friends. 'I'm sorry, have we met before?'

'Hah! Goodness, Professor, the answer's both yes and no. Let me see, this would be the time when, ah, you've just seen me off on my bicycle, haven't you! Oh dear, I'm afraid I did make you worry.'

Benny stared at him, her mouth open. 'Doctor?'

49

'Tenth, actually. I pop back here quite often now. I say, you're drinking sherry! Wouldn't you prefer a… pint of bitter, wasn't it?'

Benny unsteadily sat back down, and the man settled opposite her. 'My God,' she laughed, 'this is a bit of a shock. I'm surprised that this sort of thing doesn't happen more often, really, with time travel and all that. Well, hey, now that you're here, maybe you could explain why you did this to yourself?'

'Made myself into a human, you mean? It was a long time ago, Benny, I'm not really sure that there was a particular reason. I purchased the equipment off of a lovely old chap called Laylock on the planet Crex, a body-smith by trade. But you were there, weren't you?'

'Not quite. I just got to see the before and after comparison. What exactly did you do?'

'You'll have seen the red sphere, the biodatapod? Interesting thing. A near-infinite memory capacity in such a small pod. It uses the fractal technology of the Matrix, I suspect. Well, I went to Laylock carrying a memory module, which contained a fictional persona I'd developed using information from the TARDIS databanks.'

'You'd used the telepathic circuits beforehand, I saw that in the console log.'

'Did I?' The young man pondered, rubbing his chin. 'Now why was that? Oh yes, of course – the telepathic circuits sop up the memories of passengers like a sponge in water. I was using the recollections of previous occupants to create Smith.'

'What, companions like me?'

'Exactly. Including you, actually.'

'Oh dear. I wonder what?'

'Nothing appalling, if I recall rightly.' He reached out and tapped Benny's nose gently. Benny smiled. It hadn't occurred to her, but she rather missed all that hugging that the Doctor went in for. It used to irritate her, but it was typical of him that just when she needed a bit of physical contact, he turned into a chap who felt uncomfortable about shaking her hand.

Well, obviously the tenth Doctor was pretty tactile. Risking the disapproval of the townsfolk, she tapped his nose back.

He grinned. 'Laylock used the character I'd written to program the biodatapod. He stuck it to my forehead, and it sucked all the Doctorish memories and abilities out of me, and replaced them with the fictional ones. It also wooshed thousands of nanites into my bloodstream, and, in about a nanosecond, they transformed my physical being into that of a human, just as I'd wanted. The nanites rushed off with all of the Time Lord cellular information, back into the Pod, leaving me as—'

'Doctor John Smith of Aberdeen, the schoolteacher. I see. And you recovered, just as promised, after three months?'

'Well, Benny, you know that is future information, but...' He glanced conspiratorially upwards, as if to check that the Time Lords weren't watching. 'Of course I did, or I wouldn't be here now, talking to you like this. I put the sphere back to my forehead, or, as I recall, you did it for me, and the process was reversed. I woke up rather shocked, but quite happy.'

Benny nodded, reflecting on her conversation with Smith earlier on. 'I'll bet.' She bit her lip, wondering if she should ask the question that had been nagging at her mind for the last few minutes. She reached out and took the Doctor's hand between hers. 'Listen, you know I've been going through it a bit in the last few weeks. Do I... does everything... turn out all right for me? I'd like to know. Can you tell me?'

The fair-haired man took a deep breath, and the look in his eyes scared her terribly. 'Benny—'

'No! Actually, I don't want to know, I've changed my mind. Don't tell me. Please.' Benny raised her arms in a pacifying gesture. 'I think I could do with that pint now.'

'Benny, relax, nothing terrible happens to you. The last time I saw you, you had, oh, six husbands and three children, and were enjoying being first lady of the court of Cartufel, at the galactic core.'

Benny laughed in relief. 'Six husbands? Really? Goodness, at least I get Sundays off.'

The man laughed with her. He had a pleasant chuckle. 'Would you like to meet my new companion?'

'Of course. Are they here?'

'She's round the back, in the beer garden, playing on the climbing frame.'

Benny raised an eyebrow. 'I think this is going to make me feel very old.'

Aphasia had indeed been playing on the climbing frame in the otherwise deserted beer garden, her balloon tied to her wrist, but then she'd noticed something: a little wooden table on a pole, with bread laid out on it. A sparrow fluttered down, took a bit of the bread in its beak and flew away.

So Aphasia had taken the bread, put it on the other end of the wooden table where she was sitting, and stared at it, ready.

The sparrow had bravely returned for more bread.

A few minutes later, Benny came round the corner of the pub, clutching the pint that her new friend had bought her. He walked with her, having refilled his glass of wine. 'Aphasia, say hello to an old companion of mine, Bernice Summerfield.'

Aphasia made a face, and Benny laughed, sitting down at the table beside her. 'You've got a mouthful of crisps, haven't you? Just like me. I was always told not to eat so—'

A feather sneaked out from Aphasia's lips. She licked it quickly back in.

'Fast…' Benny stared at the semi-dissected bird that lay on the seat beside the little girl.

'Aphasia! How many times have I told you not to do that!' The man in white shielded the bird from Benny's gaze with his boater. 'I'm terribly sorry. She's a little hunter, from one of the lost colonies. Her parents are dead. She survived in the wild until I found her. I'm gradually teaching her the ways of civilisation.'

'Yes, well, don't worry, that's, erm, fine…' said Benny, concentrating on her pint. 'We can say hello when she's finished her lunch. Tell me more about this experiment of yours that I'm taking part in.'

The young man sat down. 'Well, I realise that us meeting now explains a joke you made to me when I recovered. You said that I looked like myself again.'

'Mm-hmm. Sounds like me. I must remember to do that.'

'I've been trying to remember more about the whole situation, but I'm understandably hazy. We hid the datapod with my real persona in it somewhere rather artful, didn't we?'

Benny nodded, smiling ruefully. She put down her glass and took his hand gently between hers again. 'Remember where?'

'Can't say I do.'

Benny let go of his hand and shook her head. 'Well, see if you can before tonight. Bring little Aphasia with the apt name and we'll have dinner. No game, I'm afraid, but I do make a nice vegetarian quiche.'

The tenth Doctor frowned. 'We'd be delighted, but I can't seem to remember where you're staying.'

Benny was getting to her feet, smoothing her skirt. 'Then that'll be another challenge, won't it?'

The man exchanged glances with the little girl, who was finishing up her bird quickly. 'All right. Do you have to rush off?'

'Oh yes. I've just remembered, I left something on the stove.'

'Before you go, please tell me: erm, how do you think I compare with your Doctor?'

Benny glanced at Aphasia. 'Compared to him I think you're rather heartless. See you later.' She reached for her handbag.

Something slashed past the tips of her fingers, and the handle came away from the bag, which went flying.

The man was on his feet, miming holding a sword.

No, not miming. Benny felt, rather than saw, something incredibly sharp cutting the air into ozone in front of her throat. 'Your sense of humour lets you down, Professor. I gather that you checked my pulse and found only one beat. Is that all that gave me away?'

'Hardly. The Doctor's a vegetarian, you see. Add that to the bird-eating companion and the three children, and I was getting rather suspicious. You want the biodatapod, I suppose?'

'That's right. Aphasia –' The little girl was tipping the contents of the handbag over the table. The man glanced at her for a second.

Benny slapped the pint into his face.

The glass spun away in two as it hit the sword.

But Benny was already sprinting for the stile that led into the next field.

The man dived after her, pulling a gun from his belt one-handed. 'Stop!' he shouted.

Benny hurdled the stile, splinters of it exploding up around her knees as a warning burst of silent scarlet energy bolts ripped the wood apart.

Beyond the stile was a ploughed field. She stared at it in horror and dived for the hedgerow.

By the time that Greeneye had scrambled over the burning remains of the stile, his quarry was nowhere to be seen. 'You haven't vanished, Professor!' he called, turning slowly to examine the trees and hedges around him, invisible sword in one hand and gun in the other. 'We only want the Pod. Tell us where it is and we won't harm you.'

Benny didn't reply. She was curled up in the ditch by the hedge, a mass of ferns wrapped around her. She was busy undoing her skirt as quietly as possible. The damn thing had nearly sent her sprawling head first into the stile.

'Very well. Aphasia, it's time for your balloon.' Greeneye gestured to the little girl.

'Should have done it right away,' Aphasia sulked, untying the balloon from her wrist. 'Balloon, find the lady and snuggle her.' She let go of the string, and the red balloon floated up into the air. It stopped, just above head height, and moved in the direction of the stile, until it stopped above Greeneye's shoulder.

Benny had slid out of the skirt, and was trying to remain as still as possible. It wouldn't be long, she reasoned, before somebody from the pub ventured into the garden and saw the burning stile. That might be fatal, since these two, whoever they were, didn't seem to care if they were seen or not. But them being scared off seemed to be her only chance right now.

The balloon had floated down to the level of the ploughed soil, and was making gentle, circular motions.

Suddenly, it halted, and then sped off across the ground, straight towards the hedgerow where Benny sheltered. Greeneye dashed after it, his sword raised above his head.

The balloon dipped down into the ditch.

Benny was amazed to see a red sphere pushing quickly through the ferns above her face, as if shoved by a hand. The thing paused a minute, and then rushed at her.

The surface engulfed her face.

She hadn't had time to take a breath. The skin of the thing tasted warm and organic, not like rubber at all. She started to gag, but forced the reflex down, her hands scrabbling frantically at the balloon. Her fingers couldn't seem to hold on to it, slipping off as they tried to grab it or burst it or something. The red material was trying to force itself down her throat and into her nostrils.

She couldn't breathe.

In a minute, she'd pass out, and they'd have her.

A shadow appeared over the ditch, and in a red haze, Benny realised that her attacker was standing over her, the ozone-stripping blade slicing vegetation with mere gentle movements a few inches from her face.

If she fell now, then the Doctor would be absolutely vulnerable.

So she wasn't going to let that happen.

With an audible yell, she pushed her head straight at the blade.

The balloon hit it.

And exploded.

In the garden, Aphasia started screaming, shrill child screams that didn't stop.

Greeneye snarled, slammed his gun into some invisible holster and reached down with his free hand to grab Benny. He hauled her up to his eye-level by her hair, and shook her until the scraps of balloon, now turning an ugly brown, fell from her face. 'You hurt her!' he bellowed.

'You started it,' Benny told him.

He yanked her head roughly to one side.

Her hair-extensions came away in his hand. He stared at them for a second.

She butted him across the bridge of the nose.

Greeneye fell back and slashed wildly with his sword.

The blade cut a fine line across the blouse material over Benny's stomach.

She turned and sprinted away along the ditch in her bloomers, glancing over her shoulder to see him scramble to his feet, clutching his nose. A little crowd of townsfolk were kicking the stile away. One pointed at her, and suddenly Greeneye was at the centre of a mass of hearty and drunken young men, determined to avenge her honour.

She ignored gallant shouts to return and jumped up on to a gate, then over it.

She landed in a side-road, right in front of Mr Hodges' greengrocer's wagon.

'Whoa!' Hodges shouted, pulling up the horses as they whinnied and bucked. He opened his mouth at the sight of

Benny's muddied and disrobed state, blushed and started frantically to clamber out of his apron. 'What in – ? I mean, by God, girl—'

Benny jumped up beside him and swiftly covered herself up with the apron. 'Home, Mr Hodges,' she told him grimly. 'And don't spare the horses.'

4
GOOD AND BAD AT GAMES

Smith wobbled out onto the pitch, pullovers wrapped around his waist. He took up his place on the little rise beside the cricket pitch. On a distant hillside, a shaft of undiluted sunlight was illuminating the ground.

Smith wished he were there. Only this cricket practice, and then he could go home, change, settle down to dinner and conversation with Joan.

It had been nice to see Bernice. She was like her father in some way, he wasn't really sure which. Jonathan had been in the Navy, broke his nose in Pompey Barracks. Bit of a clumsy so and so. Which was odd, for a sailor. Smith pondered on his image of sailors. He'd known of two, and both seemed very unlike everything he knew about the profession. Everything he'd… learnt.

He glanced down at the woollens wrapped about his waist. He remembered the feel of them. He'd worn one that his mother had made for him, playing in the street with the other children. His should associate them with proud poverty and ambition.

But still, somewhere in a dream, he felt different things about this material. Something about it spoke of sacrifice.

What a strange existence this was, when all that was inside him seemed to contradict the world. Bigger on the inside than the outside, and bursting at the seams.

'Sir? Sir?' Anand was calling. 'We're ready to play, sir.'

Smith started and looked up. 'Yes. Ready. Have you picked teams?' He glanced around and saw that a complete field had been assembled on the pitch, and that Hutchinson and Merryweather had taken up position, doubtless without much debate, with their bats at each wicket. Alton turned his head from wicket-keeping and raised an eyebrow at Smith questioningly. A line of boys were sitting beside him with varied degrees of interest, ready to get padded up and go on. 'I see that you have. Well, go on.'

Anand nodded and turned to begin his run-up. Smith glanced over his shoulder and saw Tim, way out on the boundary, gazing at the infield hopefully. Smith chastised himself. One little mental wander, and the Hulton team captain was sent off to the middle of nowhere.

He glanced back at Hutchinson, the watery sunlight dappling the boy's shirt as he thumped his crease, anticipating Anand's first ball.

And tried to ignore the fact that the boy looked up to smirk at him.

Bernice ran from the cart into her cottage and bolted the door behind her. Hodges had spent the whole journey asking her half-embarrassed, half-salacious questions, and seemed to be on the verge of either calling the police or following her inside when she'd hopped from his cart.

She caught a glimpse of herself in the mirror as she ran into her bedroom, and winced. No time to wash the mud off. She flicked open the locks of her cases, and pulled on some jeans, a T-shirt and some more useful boots than these lace-up monstrosities with heels. Finally, her work jacket with all the pockets. They'd expect her to head straight for the Pod, of course, but if she could do that without them tracking her, then all she had to do was to rugby-tackle Smith and put the thing against his forehead.

She crept quickly downstairs, mentally saying goodbye to the place. Her easel still stood in the garden outside, the painting half-finished.

Everything spoilt, as always.

Aphasia staggered down the hospital corridor, holding her stomach. Her tiny hand clutched for the railing on the wall, and she pushed herself along with it, leaving traces of brown liquid at every touch. That didn't make much difference to the overall colour scheme. The walls were covered with a thin organic paste, green and brown, which was also dripping from the ceiling as a cycle of mist and condensation.

This place smelt. This whole world smelt.

They'd taken her away in a vehicle, when she'd been injured, and they'd tried to make her lie down and put a mask over her face. She'd tried to tell them that she just needed to go and heal herself, but they didn't listen, they just said stupid things to her.

The gas hadn't knocked her out, and when they noticed that, they'd taken off the mask and started talking excitedly to each other. They wheeled her into this place on a trolley.

So she'd opened the pouch in her wrist, and pulled out the bulb, and then they'd started to scream.

Through the haze of her vision, the little girl saw that, ahead of her, a nurse had fallen, pulling over a trolley of instruments as she did. The body lay across the junction of two corridors and was still fairly intact. Aphasia redoubled her efforts to walk and stumbled to her knees beside the body.

The wrist pouch wouldn't close. She'd die if she didn't do something soon and that'd let down all her fathers and her dear son, Hoff.

She reached for the nurse's decaying face, and started to feed.

'Sir!'

Smith, despite his intentions, was deep in *Mansfield Park* when he heard the shout. He waved a hand distractedly –

– and found a cricket ball in it.

The schoolboys applauded and whistled. Smith tossed the ball back to the bowler and bowed exaggeratedly.

'That could have taken your head off, sir!' said Phipps, awed.

'Oh, probably not. Still, someone must be looking after me…'

Smith would have turned his attention back to his book, but the boys became agitated again, a great whispering and the occasional whistle disturbing those sitting beside him.

He looked up to see his niece, dressed in very tight trousers, running frantically across the ground towards him. The batsmen paused as she ran between the wickets, their gaze following her, awestruck.

As soon as Bernice reached the little rise where Smith was sitting, she was offered a flurry of jackets and pullovers to cover herself with, as well as a panama hat from the laconic Alton. She waved them all aside, grabbed Smith's hand and hauled him to his feet. 'Come on,' she said. 'I've got something to show you.'

The boys coughed and muttered things, and a few grins sprang up.

'I haven't time…' Smith looked around in confusion. 'This is Bernice, my niece. Bernice, these are my boys.'

'There's no time for that. You must come with me, it's a matter of life and death.'

'It is?' Smith squared his jaw. 'Very well. Lead on.' He pointed stoically and marched off, then glanced back. 'Shall I bring some of the boys?'

'No,' Benny told him. 'Just bring yourself.'

'Finish the game,' Smith called back to his class as she led him away by the arm, quite a bit faster than he was able to walk. 'Then go in for prep if I'm not back.'

Hutchinson stared after them, shaking his head at the little man. 'Have a nice time, Smith,' he snarled. 'The Head's going to love this.'

*

'Bernice, where are you taking me?' Smith protested, shaking off her arm. They were marching through the orchard that bordered the school, a vast, overgrown river of fruit trees that was part of the Marcham Estate. They had already ventured too far off the footpath for Smith's liking. This was almost certainly trespassing.

'To...' Bernice stopped and turned slowly, pointing at strange red marks on three trees. She settled on the middle one. 'This particular tree. Sit down under it. We're about to recreate a moment in history.'

Smith sat, cross-legged, under the tree, looking rather embarrassed. 'Which one?'

'Newton and the apple.' Benny put her foot up on a low branch and started to climb up the tree.

Smith looked quickly away. 'Those trousers are rather immodest.'

Benny frowned as she climbed. 'I'm not used to you noticing things like that. Ah, here we are.' The crown of the tree was swollen, as if a growth of some kind was inside. Following the instructions in the Doctor's note, Benny had put the red sphere there and watched as the tree's wood had grown to encompass it in seconds. Apparently, Time Lord biodata had that effect on living things, making them a bit like Time Lords. A Time Lord-ish tree wouldn't be as disturbing as a Time Lord-ish person, or even sheep. Benny wondered if the tree's bark rings were forming question marks or something. Indeed, in the brief time that she'd handled the Pod, Benny herself had felt an odd sense of presence to the thing. For the same reasons, the sphere couldn't be kept in the TARDIS. It would mess up the telepathic circuits.

She pulled the TARDIS key from her pocket, and, dangling it over the tree, slapped the swollen wood three times with her hand.

The wood flowed back like liquid, to reveal –

– an empty, ball-shaped cavity.

63

Benny swore six times.

'And is that really ladylike language?' asked Smith.

'Shut up,' Benny snapped. 'Whether you know it or not, we're both in a great deal of trouble.'

Sitting at a little distance from the other boys, Tim sneaked a look at the red sphere in his pocket.

He'd found it when he was walking on his own in the orchard. He'd felt drawn to a particular tree, and sat down in its shadow. Before long, he'd fallen asleep.

When he awoke, the red sphere was sitting on his chest. It looked like it had fallen from the tree.

The thing was hard and shiny, a shine that couldn't be scratched. It looked very like a cricket ball, actually, except there was no seam, no indication of how such a thing might have been made.

He always kept it with him now, because it made him feel a little better. It was like he had a secret, something that made him special. The sphere seemed to tell him things, sometimes, in that a thought came into his mind that he couldn't possibly have thought. The thoughts were always brave and noble.

Perhaps he was a prince, secretly in charge of some foreign land, and this was one of the crown jewels of that place. Just seeing it caused him to remember his true destiny.

'Captain Bug! Are you listening to me, Captain Bug?' Hutchinson was standing over him. 'Our wonderful form master has taken the new balls away with him. Give us that.' He snatched the red sphere from Tim.

Tim stared after the boy as he walked off, idly tossing the sphere in one hand. He took up position distantly then ran in fast to bowl at the small boy who'd taken up his stance in front of the wicket.

Tim jumped to his feet. 'No!' he shouted, and ran forward.

Hutchinson bowled.

Disturbed by the shout, the batsman skewed the ball high in the air, right above Tim.

The young boy stared up at it, silhouetted against the bright sky. He began to shiver terribly.

The ball was whistling as it came down, and the sky had turned dark and ruddy. He heard Hutchinson shouting something.

He raised his hands in a gesture of prayer.

The explosion engulfed them, their whites turning to cinder and their faces jerking back in frozen expressions of pain and sudden surrender.

And then Tim was just standing there, holding the ball.

The other boys weren't screaming, they were laughing.

The batsman was staring at him incredulously.

'Is it possible to get one of your own side out?' laughed Hutchinson. 'Just the sort of leadership we need, Captain Bug!'

In the distance, bells began to ring. The boys picked up their kit bags, and started to file towards the school for prep.

But Tim stayed, looking at the sphere, for a long time.

'But there was something there you needed to see! You have to believe me!' Benny walked quickly after Smith back towards the school. 'Your real name is the Doctor, you're not from this planet. Try and remember!'

Smith glared at her with a mixture of anger and disturbed pity. 'If I'm not from this planet, why do I look and sound like a Scottish schoolteacher?'

'I... I don't know why; you've looked and sounded like a number of Englishmen too.'

'Now I know you're making this up.'

'Look, I can show you a box that's bigger on the inside than the outside.'

Smith closed his eyes, as if struck by a sudden thought, but he just as quickly opened them again and kept walking, not looking at Benny. 'Thank you, no, I've got a dinner appointment.

I mustn't be late.'

'Listen, there are people out there who might want to hurt you.'

'Ah.' Smith turned suddenly and pointed at her, an uneasy half-frown on his face. 'You're trying to distract me. Don't. I'm confused enough. All these…' He waggled the hand irritatedly, searching for the right word. 'All these… fantasies. They're bad for you. They get between you and the real world. This is all there is, Bernice. The school and the boys and dinner. We can't leave it, we can't change it. We just have to live with it. So do that. University seems to have been a bad idea for you. I'll talk to Jonathan about it. And put some clothes on. Good night.'

Benny stopped, and watched Smith march into the school buildings.

When he was out of earshot, she swore eight times.

She returned to the cottage carefully, making her way from hedge to hedge as if this quiet little town was a war zone. She hadn't been followed going to get the Pod, so the man with the sword probably wasn't tracking her now. A fire engine roared past down the street, a fireman on the side ringing its bell urgently as the wooden ladder on its roof rocked from side to side. Bernice noticed that a column of brown smoke was rising from the other side of town. That looked ominous.

Perhaps the lads at the pub hadn't detained her attacker for very long. That was a worrying thought, unarmed humans *circa* 1914 taking on somebody armed with sophisticated weaponry like that. Between them, the man and the little girl could cut a swath through this lot. And there was no Doctor to stop them.

So what was she going to do? There was always the TARDIS. If she could kidnap Smith somehow and get him inside, she might actually be able to persuade him of the truth. She hadn't tried to go into the details of what had happened yet. They sounded pretty ridiculous even to her, but maybe they'd touch a nerve.

She broke from cover and dashed up the path to the cottage

gate then unlocking the door with one twist of the key. If this was going to be a long-term job, or even if Smith really was going to snap out of it in three weeks, she needed to put a pack together. The bloody forest was beckoning again.

Having checked every room, Bernice quickly assembled the basics: camping stove; tent; bottle of rather fine Aldebaran brandy; and shoved them all into a bag. She'd brought them along for outings, but the comfort of the cottage had kept her here.

She crept downstairs. She wanted to warn Alexander about what was going on, but having warned one person, where could you stop? She suspected that, soon enough, the whole town would know that there were aliens about.

'I say!' a voice called, and Benny spun to see Constance knocking on the window. The woman frowned when she saw the way Benny was dressed. 'I say, do let me in, they're behind me!'

Benny swore ten times as she pulled the bolts out, and hauled Constance inside. 'Who's behind you?' she asked.

'Why, the police. What on earth are you dressed like a man for? I mean, I've dared to wear the odd pantaloon myself, but what have you done to your hair? Those trousers are positively obscene, darling.'

'Never mind my trousers, Constance. I might be being chased myself.'

'Yes, I heard. You poor dear. I think that's why they've called in extra police. They arrived in a motor van. We both were heading here, and I managed to put a bit of a lead on with my bicycle when they got trapped behind some sheep, but—'

'You're saying the police are on their way here?'

'Yes, because you were, you know, interfered with. At the pub. Bernice, if they see you in that get-up, they'll have you locked up in an asylum and let that thug who did it off with a warning!'

'They locked him up?'

'No, they're still after him. There were veterans from three different regiments at that inn. They competed over him, but he still got away. I think it was while he was being dragged to the police station by the Dragoons.'

'Sounds nasty. What about the little girl?'

'He hurt her too, didn't he? She was driven to hospital. Out of the frying pan, I'm afraid…'

'What do you mean?'

'Why, the place seems to be on fire. That's where the fire brigade are going. All go in town today.'

Benny shook her head. 'You don't know the half of it. Do you know where I can find a gun?'

Constance looked at her shoes, abashed. 'A gun? Do you mean to shoot him? I understand the urge, but don't you think—'

'I wasn't molested, Constance, at least not in the way you mean. I need to defend myself, and you know where I can find the means to do that.' Benny put her hands on the young woman's shoulders and stared into her eyes. 'Don't you?'

'Yes,' Constance said, after a moment. 'We don't have any guns; we've never had the need to use them, but we are equipped to damage property on a large scale. But the ordnance isn't to be used for—'

'Near here?'

'Very.'

There came a harsh, official knock on the door. 'Come on,' said Benny. 'You show me the way. We'll go across the fields. I'm getting used to ditches.'

Joan carefully lifted the lid from one of the saucepans on the stove and peeped inside. 'Perfect.' She replaced it, and, humming a ragtime tune to herself, popped to the mirror in the lounge to check her make-up.

Well, it would have to do. She didn't look too much of a ruin for a woman in her forties. Like one of those duchesses that surrounded themselves with an army of handsome young men. She'd like to have had her hair done, but her invitation to John had been on such an impulse that there hadn't been time. That was the thing about her job, no time to get anything else done, what with preparation and marking and all that. No time to really live.

She glanced at the clock on the wall, chided herself and dashed back into the kitchen.

Dr Smith wandered jauntily along the lane, glancing up at the darkening sky from time to time. He was dressed in white tie and tails, with a top hat, gloves and a white gardenia in his buttonhole. He was whistling a tune he couldn't place, and wondering about all manner of things he didn't understand. In his pocket was the second part of his story:

> The tribe of Gallifrey thought that the inventor was a god, and started to worship him, but then he told them not to.
> 'I have brought new ideas for you,' he said. 'I want to help you.'
> And so he told them about travelling through time and space, and about the police. He taught them how to build police boxes, and he taught them about law and books and civilisation.

It was progressing, but he still didn't know where it was going.

He stopped beside a tree and doffed his hat to it. 'I wonder, could I have this dance?'

He took the tree by its lower branches and stepped carefully back, moving his feet as if the thing were following his lead. No, his ability to foxtrot hadn't deserted him, so Joan's gramophone wouldn't be a tremendous obstacle; though if she wanted to bunny hug or chicken scramble, he'd be at a loss.

She wouldn't, though, would she? Not in private, anyway.

But there was something else. He looked left and right along the road. There was nobody about.

Carefully, he puckered his lips and touched them to the bark of the tree. He experimented with wider and narrower kisses, finally letting go with a little scowl and shrug. He didn't remember kissing anybody since Verity. Surely there must have been. There'd been somebody called Barbara, hadn't there? In Rome – an Italian? But he'd never been to Rome. He must have read it in a book, probably one of those Arnold Bennetts that were keeping him awake at night.

All in all, it was a good thing that he wouldn't be doing any kissing tonight either.

He spun on his heel and doubled his speed along the road.

Joan opened the door of her little house to him and took his hat, popping it on the peg in the hallway. 'What a K-nut you look! It's nearly ready,' she told him. 'I hope you like fish?'

'I don't know,' Smith grinned. 'What sort of fish is it?'

'Cod in a white wine sauce, new potatoes and mixed vegetables. I am not exactly Rosa Lewis, but—'

'I'm sure it'll be fine. How was your day?' Smith wandered about the room, examining the pictures and ornaments that decorated the front room. He took off his gloves and put them down on a bureau. As Joan turned back to the kitchen, he raised a small display case that seemed to have fallen over on the mantelpiece, saw that it contained three medals and put it back down again.

'Fine,' Joan called. 'Lab all afternoon, and you know boys and chemicals, they love mixing things up and making clouds of smoke. Talking of which, did you see the fire in town today?'

'No.' Smith settled into an armchair. 'Cricket practice. What was burning?'

'Mr Blum the fishmonger says that it was St Catherine's. We will have to see what the paper says tomorrow.'

'The hospital...' Smith pondered, hefting a gunmetal paperweight in his hands. There was an insignia of some kind

70

stamped in the metal, a few numbers and letters. He quickly put it down as Joan came back into the room.

'It's ready,' she said. 'Come on through.'

The meal, as it turned out, was excellent. Afterwards, Joan set up a little table in the front room, and they played a few of their customary hands of whist, at which she was supreme, as always.

Smith threw up his hands and let his cards fall to the table. 'You're too good for me. Is there another game we could play?'

She arched an eyebrow. 'You sound like a young rake.'

'I erm, ah, well, I was wondering if you played chess?' Smith fumbled with his collar and succeeded in unfastening a button.

'Not very well, but I do have a set.' Joan exited for a moment then returned, blowing the dust from a fabric-bound board. 'Under the bed, and rather distressed.'

'I'll only distress it more. Which side do you want?'

'Black.' She sat down, pulling her chair around to face his.

They began to set up the pieces. 'That's odd. Most people choose white.'

'I suppose that I like other people to make the first move,' she murmured, not looking up.

'I'm just the opposite.'

'Are you really?'

They played for a few minutes, then Smith seemed to break off thinking about a move. 'My niece came to see me on the cricket pitch today. She's down from Newnham College. She was dressed in trousers.'

'Oh, a suffragette. Silly things. We'll get the vote sooner or later, just as Mill predicted. I don't think there's much point in burning things down.'

'No,' Smith agreed. 'There's always a way to talk yourself out of a situation. She dragged me off into the orchard.'

'You did say niece?'

'Yes. My brother's daughter. She's called Bernice. You ought to meet her. I'm sure you'd like each other.'

'Quite possibly. These bright young things take my breath away, with their motor cars and their vortexes.'

'Sorry, their what?'

'Oh, you know, Wyndham Lewis and all that. It is as if all the rules about art have been torn up. All very exciting, but they do make me feel quite old.'

'Oh, Bernice isn't that young. Thirty-two. I think.'

'Your brother must be much older than you.'

'Yes. He's a sailor. Got his nose caught in… She wanted me to see a tree.'

'Why?'

'I don't know. She tried to find something there, but couldn't. She told me it was very important.'

'Oh dear. Do you think that she could be in trouble?'

'Perhaps. I don't know. She seemed to think that I was.'

'Hmm. I could imagine you getting into trouble quite easily, but I think you would be able to get out of it, also.'

'That's not usually the way.'

'I can see you as a prefect or something, running about organising things. Where did you go to school?'

'Well, that's complicated… An old woman taught me how to read, at my father's hearth. Her name was Sarah McLeod. She died at Culloden.'

'Oh, I'm sorry. A classical place for a McLeod to die, though.'

A sudden image had rushed into Smith's mind, contradictory to anything he could express: an old lady on the end of a bayonet. 'She was old,' he whispered. 'And then I went to a little school in London. I carried the Oxford English Dictionary in my left blazer pocket and a bag of marbles in my right. No wonder I started to lean to the left.'

Joan laughed. 'You seem to have lived several lifetimes. Like Whitman, you contain multitudes.'

'It feels that way, sometimes,' Smith agreed, missing the reference.

'Whitman also said – Oh, hello, Wolsey.' The tabby tomcat had wandered under the table, put up a questioning paw against Joan's leg and then hopped up onto her lap. 'Are you a cat person, John?'

'Yes,' said Smith, still looking as if he was trying to organise several different thoughts that were buzzing randomly around his head. 'May I?'

Joan paused only a moment. 'Yes, of course, Wolsey loves attention. He arrived after I'd moved in here. He's a wanderer. I'm not sure how long he's planning to stay.'

Smith got up and made his way to Joan's side of the table, the chess game forgotten. He squatted beside her and gently put his fingers on Wolsey's chin. Wolsey had his eyes closed as Joan stroked his stomach, but now he opened them and rubbed the scent glands on the side of his head against Smith's fingers.

Smith trailed the tip of one finger round the back of the cat's ear as it curled itself on the white material of Joan's lap, stretching its back to be stroked. Joan ran her fingers down its back, letting Wolsey feel the tips of her nails, as Smith rubbed it under the chin with his thumb, smiling as the cat stretched its jaw forward in pleasure.

'Look, he likes this,' said Joan, her voice low. She took the base of the cat's tail gently in her hand, and smoothed it all the way down, letting go of the end with a little reflexive twitch. She repeated the action many times, shifting her weight to give Wolsey more room to turn and twist in her lap. The cat was purring loudly and unrestrainedly, opening itself up to the two pairs of hands.

While Joan smoothed its tail, Smith was running the tips of his fingers along its stomach.

'My goodness,' Joan breathed. 'You must be good at that. He normally grabs people who do that and tries to bite them.'

'I'm good with cats,' Smith muttered. 'They run right up to me as if they know something I don't.'

'And do they?'

'I don't know.'

'They must feel safe in your hands.'

'They aren't. I don't keep things safe. I used to. Perhaps. I can't keep all the plates spinning. I drop some.'

Their hands collided across the soft expanse of Wolsey's stomach. Smith's hand swept right over Joan's and she kept that hand still, accepting, the tips of her fingers gently playing with the smallest swirls of the animal's fur.

A moment later, Smith's hand swept back again and she looked at the top of his head as the hand passed over hers, delighting enormously that he didn't look up and meet her gaze with something terrible and shattering like a smile.

'Well, that is always the risk, if you're a plate, isn't it?' she whispered, letting her fingers catch his cuff, but keeping her eyes firmly fixed on the fine hairs at the back of his neck. 'If you want to be spun, then you must accept the possibility of being broken.'

Slowly, his head came up to look at her, his gaze flicking uncertainly over her face, as if in search of a sign. His pupils were bigger than she'd ever seen a man's be, and she'd seen several.

'And do you –' he gruffed, seeming to have such difficulty with the words, but with no difficulty at all in the sudden certain strength of his stare, 'accept that possibility?'

Joan paused for a moment, feeling Wolsey squirm at the sudden lack of their hands. She wetted her lips and willed herself to form the sound. 'Yes.'

He bent his head to her, and like a little boy just discovering this, took her face in his hands. They were warm and still against the skin of her cheek. She felt that, more than she'd felt anything for years. She closed her eyes. The distance between then and now hurt inside her, and she let go of the breath she'd been holding, letting herself breathe deeply and fast, remembering all the things about being married that she'd enjoyed and let herself forget. Her heart was pounding like a dance, but he was studying her, like a painter, from a distance. She opened her eyes again, and saw that he was terribly afraid.

'Yes,' she insisted. 'Yes.'

'Yes,' he said. And brought her mouth onto his.

After a moment, a minute, they parted again. And kissed again, exploringly this time, now that that terrible uncertain thing was dead and they were delighting in the knowledge that this was what they both wanted to do.

Finally they stopped, and Joan let her head fall onto his shoulder, and, in a kind of unlikely stumble, they got up and shuffled back to sit together on the sofa. Wolsey fell off in disgust and stalked into the kitchen.

'May I sit on your lap?' Joan asked. 'I feel, oh, I'm blushing, like a young maid, and, I must admit, I'm rather enjoying it. You don't think me forward, do you?'

'Oh yes…' Smith giggled. 'Forward. As opposed to reverse. I've got all my gears mixed up.' He helped Joan as she got up, smoothed down her skirt and settled back onto his lap.

'This is so ridiculous,' she said, not being able to catch his eye as he awkwardly put an arm around her waist. 'I've been married, I shouldn't feel all nervous like this.'

'I'm, erm, nervous too,' Smith muttered. 'I don't feel as though I've ever done anything like this before.'

'I'm glad you feel like that, because I'm terribly afraid,' Joan whispered. 'You do mean you're my sweetheart, don't you, John? I'm far too old to be ruined. Not that I have been ruined yet. I mean at all. I mean—'

Smith's face hardened. 'Stand up,' he told her.

'Oh no, John…' Joan's voice sounded utterly lost. 'No, please don't. You won't tell, at least say you won't tell, I'll give you anything—'

'Hush.' Smith sternly walked into the hall and picked his hat from the peg. He positioned it carefully on his head.

Joan ran to the door, and pushed herself between it and him. She'd had time to become angry now. 'How dare you use me this way!' she demanded. 'To think I trusted you! I may be ruined tomorrow, but I'll tell you what I think of you first!'

'And what's that?' Smith grinned.

'That—' Joan frowned. 'That… what are you grinning at?'

'I'm grinning at time. At circumstances. At my sweetheart.'

'You mean—'

He tipped up the brim of his hat, and, against her slight protest, kissed her again. 'I won't tell anyone, because I don't tell people things I can't believe. You can tell me all about it again tomorrow. And tomorrow. And tomorrow.'

Joan laughed with relief and kissed him again, longer. 'So why are you going?' she asked. 'I mean, you could stay for a little while longer at least.'

'I could – but I wouldn't want you to think anything was ruined. Least of all you.' He put a finger to her nose and opened the door. 'Good night, Joan.'

'Good night, John. Oh—' She stopped him. 'I just realised. Smith and Joan.'

'Well,' said Smith, kissing her knuckle, 'that does sound like a double act.'

And then he was gone, off into the night.

Joan gazed after him until he vanished, him turning and smiling back at her at intervals.

Then she closed the door and leant on it. 'Oh my goodness,' she exclaimed, putting a hand to her breast. 'I think I just started getting younger.'

Smith skipped down the lane, his hands in his pockets, whistling a tune that the Isley Brothers hadn't written yet, a grin that was unwipeable spread across his face.

Up ahead, he glimpsed a street lamp that hadn't ignited, the last one on the corner before the darkness of the countryside swept in. He looked up at it and raised a hand, intending to tap the pole. In romantic stories, the gas filament would then ignite.

He tapped.

Nothing happened.

Still indomitable, he shrugged, turned and made his way off down the lane.

Behind him, a little corner of light sprang up.

He glanced back at it and nodded. 'Yes.'

5
HURT / COMFORT

Excerpt from the writings of Dr John Smith
So for what season or circumstance was I built? My thumbs are useful, my appendix, which hurts sometimes as if newly made, is not. Sometimes it feels as if I'm bigger on the inside physically, too. Joan told me that the Latin I failed to understand referred to that. The school motto refers to the relative dimensions of books. I like that. If you could see information, a book would be like a pincushion in your hand.

Still haven't found Gallifrey on the map. Maybe I made it up?

Excerpt from a letter written by Joan Redfern, date unknown
I'd forgotten. It was like a sleeping tiger, and it was suddenly awake and upon me again. And it was beautiful.

As darkness fell across the valley below, Benny and Constance were walking up a narrow lane, past badger sets and through thickets of stinging nettles that Benny had to swat aside with a stick taken from an old elm. They were climbing up to the wooded hillsides, Benny realised, heading in the direction of the statue of Old Meg.

During the walk, while Constance was silent, Benny had come close to despairing. There'd been no sign of the aliens, if that was what they were. Perhaps the reason that the Pod was gone was that they'd found it and gone too. She and the Doctor would be trapped here, and she'd have to find a way to survive when the money ran out. Perhaps Alexander would give her a job. At least she could sleep in the TARDIS. If the aliens had the Pod and hadn't left, mind you, the only option was to get it off of them by force. Now, that would be really difficult.

'Have you got arms dumps all over the place?' she asked Constance.

'Yes. Asquith doesn't show any signs of budging, so we're going to start blowing a few more things up.' The young woman had struggled valiantly up the hill, hitching her skirts as they went.

'What if a war starts and other people start blowing things up?'

'A war? With whom? I mean, it looked as if the Germans were going to have a pop a few years ago, but that's all calmed down. Churchill's started to dismantle the Navy, and they're doing likewise. No, it's only now, now that there are no more wars to be fought in this world, that we can really do something about our situation. Asquith thinks he can sleep easy, bar Ulstermen or Anarchists, but he hasn't reckoned with us.'

They'd reached the top of the hill. Benny helped Constance step over a stile, and they walked over to the statue. The old woman sat proudly on a stone chair, her bag clasped in her stone hands, looking down at the valley.

While Constance started to examine the back of the chair, Benny glanced down at the town below. Comfortable lights had popped up all over and the smoke of evening cooking was drifting from chimneys. A line of white steam marked the passage of a train along the branch line; she could just hear its sound in the distance, the regular beat of humanity at peace.

She thought of scarlet explosions, for a moment, of beams bursting across the valley, reducing the town to rubble in seconds. Actually, now that she'd got that picture in her mind, something about the valley fitted. A slow trail of brown smoke was drifting from the hospital, which still had a fire engine standing beside it. She shivered.

Constance was examining the base of the statue. 'We'll need a lever of some kind. What about your stick?'

'I can do better than that.' Benny unfolded a lightweight plastisteel crowbar from her jacket, pushed it into the thin gap between one of the stone panels and the surrounding masonry, and heaved. After much shoving, with Constance's help, the panel came away and fell to the ground.

Inside the block were a number of sticks of industrial dynamite, packed in straw with long taper fuses. 'If only Ace were here,' said Benny, frowning at the primitive explosives.

'Who?'

'Absent friends.' Benny reached inside and grabbed a bundle. It was sticky. 'I know nothing about this kind of thing, but this doesn't feel very safe. How long have you had it here?'

'Ever since I stole it from a quarry. The first time I was let out of prison and came down here on holiday, that was, oh, eighteen months ago?'

Benny sucked in a breath, and carefully put the dynamite back. 'I think that's going to be more trouble than it's worth.'

'As you wish.' Constance watched as Benny replaced the panel at the statue's base. 'Is your motive for seeking a weapon purely revenge?'

'Hardly. A friend of mine's in trouble. I have to find a certain object to help him.'

'And where is this object?'

'Ah, that's the question, isn't it? I have a terrible feeling that I know who's got it. In any case, I'm in a bit of a pickle.'

Constance checked the edges of the replaced panel of masonry and straightened up. 'You're not in a pickle at all. Where were you planning on staying this evening?'

Benny knew the answer to that instantly. She'd steeled herself for another night in the woods, already welcoming the idea of being alone like a boxer welcomes the first punch. But Constance gave her a little more heart. 'Perhaps there is somewhere. The house of a friend. If I tried to take that little lot down there, I think I'd explode on the way.'

'I'll go with you.' Constance took Benny's arm and carefully allowed herself to be led down the hillside. 'If I cannot provide you with weapons, at least I can manage moral support.'

'The court martial will come to attention.' Hutchinson banged the gavel on to the three bedside tables that had been lined up in front of him. Tim stood on a bed facing him, a horrified expression already on his face. The other boys stood in a circle around him. 'The case is the crown against Timothy Dean. The defendant is charged with being a bug, and allowing his just punishment to be ignobly deferred by a master. How does the defendant plead?'

Tim stared at the circle of boys. 'I... I don't.'

They laughed. Hutchinson banged his gavel. 'Guilty or not guilty?'

'I'm neither. Or both.' His voice was a whisper, but it seemed to echo from every corner of the dormitory. 'If you're trying me, then you'll decide, won't you?'

'Then another charge is added,' Hutchinson decided. 'Contempt of court and of British justice. Let us first hear from the prosecution.'

'My lord,' Merryweather stood up, a dish rag on his head, clutching the lapel of his blazer, 'the prosecution's case is that Dean, through the extraordinary protection of one Dr Smith, managed to get out of a simple slap with the slipper. This can't be allowed to pass. The implications for discipline are terrible. I move that Dean suffer the fullest possible punishment, and will prove that this is most deserved. I call no witnesses, since I believe my case is proved by one look at the defendant's bug-like features.' He sat down.

'And now the council for the defence,' said Hutchinson. 'Let us hear from Dean's best friend, Darkie Unpronounceable.'

Anand looked up from his uneasy place in the circle. He'd kept his gaze to the ground previously, embarrassed that he was part of this idiocy.

'Darkie Unpronounceable!' Hutchinson repeated, looking searchingly around the circle. 'If there is no defence, then we shall proceed straight to the sentence.'

Anand heaved a heavy sigh. 'I'm—'

'No!' Timothy cried. Suddenly, all eyes were upon him. 'There's nobody here called that. I'll defend myself.'

'Very well!' Hutchinson beamed, thumping down his gavel. 'What do you have to say for yourself?'

Timothy paused, considering. When he spoke, his voice quivered with fear. If only he'd let Anand defend him. Lately, his thoughts seemed to be full of danger like this, leading him into all sorts of awkward corners. 'I'm sorry that I didn't hear Dr Smith yesterday. It won't happen again.'

'Well, that's all very well,' began Merryweather, 'but there's the matter of—'

'It's just that I've been having these dreams,' Tim continued, oblivious, his voice a whisper that echoed around the wooden corners of the dormitory. 'They distract me. They're with me all day. I see you all die, over and over again. You're screaming, Captain Hutchinson, because you know that something's about to fall on you. Merryweather's only got one leg. Please… does anybody else have dreams like that?'

Hutchinson glanced at the other boys, a wide grin spreading over his face. 'I think we're made of different stuff to you, bug. You can't scare us.'

'I'm not trying to scare you. I'm just saying that I see it all the time, and it distracts me. That's my defence.'

Hutchinson nodded. 'Very well. What's the verdict of the jury? Hands up for guilty.'

All the boys put their hands up but one. Anand. Timothy smiled at him.

'So, guilty it is.' Hutchinson banged the gavel again. He reached behind him, and put a black square of the material used to repair school uniform on his head. 'I sentence Dean to be hanged by the neck until dead. Is the executioner present?'

Phipps raised his hand. In it was a noose made from gym rope. Timothy stared at it.

'You're joking, of course?' said Anand, looking between Timothy and the rope. 'You can't go through with it.'

'Shut up, darkie. Take him to the window.' The boys rushed forward, pulling Timothy off his feet and carrying him towards the window. Somebody pulled it open and propped it up. The noose was thrown around Timothy's neck, despite his weak protests. The other end of the rope was tied around the foot of a heavy wardrobe.

Anand turned and ran for the door, but a couple of boys grabbed him before he got there and sat on him, stuffing a handkerchief into his mouth.

Hutchinson leapt up on to the bed, swinging the cloth excitedly around his head. 'Executioner, do your duty!'

Phipps supervised the frenzied dragging of Timothy to the window-sill. The boys grabbed his arms, and aimed him like a battering ram for the gap between the window and sill. Chill winds blew in from the darkness outside. The rope swung from Timothy's neck, and he went limp, giving up his struggles.

Let them, the voice inside him said. Hang me, cut me down, spread my blood on the field. End my life. I'll return.

With a great rush, the boys threw Timothy out of the window. The rope unreeled after him, and then snapped taut.

They piled to the window and gazed out. Far below, Tim's body hung limp, swinging in the breeze, his arms dangling by his sides.

'He doesn't seem to have grabbed the noose...' Merryweather whispered.

'No,' Hutchinson agreed, his face absolutely still. 'He doesn't.' Then he yelled with sudden violence: 'Reel him in, for God's sake! Before somebody sees him!'

Benny and Constance stood outside the little red-brick museum. Benny was busy throwing stones at one of the windows above, not wanting to ring the little bell on the front door.

'So you are a friend of Mr Shuttleworth,' Constance whispered. 'I know him by reputation. He has some associates who are very active in the Labour movement, and they've been supporting our cause. Oh, there he is!'

Alexander, clad in a bath-robe, had angrily pulled up the window and glared down at them. 'What the devil? Oh…' He broke into a smile. 'Pardon my Greek. Be right down.'

They waited, crouched behind the hedge, for quite some time. Finally, Benny pulled out her watch and glanced at it. 'What's he doing in there?'

'He boasts, people say, of his several lady friends. Mr Shuttleworth seems to share Mr Wells' opinions on free love. What do you think?'

'Erm, I'm certainly opposed to paying for it. Should I feel nervous about staying with him?'

'Oh…' Constance seemed to consider for a few moments. 'Well, I have never heard of him doing anything actually improper.'

'What do his girlfriends say?'

'I haven't met any of them. He's apparently very circumspect.'

From the other side of the hedge there came the sound of tapping footsteps. Benny and Constance crouched down further.

Of course, it was just at that moment that the door opened and Alexander, now in smoking-jacket and trousers, stepped out onto his doorstep. To his credit, he didn't even glance in the direction of the fugitives in his garden, noting Bernice's anguished hand signals out of the corner of his eye. Instead he smiled at the young nurse who was standing in the road beside his gate, her head turning this way and that as if sniffing the breeze. 'Good evening, nurse. Can I help you in any way?'

The nurse turned and looked at him suspiciously. 'No, no, I was merely waiting for somebody. Perhaps you may have seen her. A lady of around my age in a checked skirt, perhaps in a state of some disarray.'

'Would she be…' his gaze flicked down into the garden, 'muddy?'

'Yes, that's her. She fled from the blaze at the hospital. I've been sent after her.'

'Yes, I was wondering what the to-do was over there. Is everybody all right?'

'Oh yes. A blanket caught fire, and it spread. The fire brigade quickly extinguished it. Now, I must hurry you. Where did you see the lady?'

Benny sneezed.

Alexander sneezed. 'Still a chill in the air. Sorry. I saw her pass this way about an hour ago. She went, erm, that way…' He gestured vaguely down the road. 'She was running.'

'Thank you.' The nurse lifted her skirts and dashed off in the indicated direction.

Alexander glanced down into his garden. 'You can come out now,' he called softly. 'A policeman I could understand, but how does one end up being chased by a nurse?'

Benny patted his shoulder as he showed her in. 'Wouldn't you like to know?'

Smith leaned back in his chair, his arms behind his head. His writing was getting better. He hadn't wanted to go to bed when he came home. He was so full of emotion and energy. He felt reborn. He'd gone straight to his desk and started to scribble page after page of his children's story. He was rather proud of it.

The Gallifreyans eventually made a wonderful world for themselves, with towers and cities, lords and ladies. The inventor watched over them and advised them on how best to make their world as civilised and law-abiding as the England that he'd left behind.

But as time went on, he became discontented with the place. The Gallifreyans had taken his ideas far too much to heart, and they'd become boring and stuck-in-the-mud. He invented a way for them to start another life when they died, and gave them another heart, hoping that this would make them joyful and happy. But they were just as dull, and now they lived longer. Worse than that, they no longer had children, so there was nobody noisy around the place to ask questions. Finally, he could take no more of it. He took one of the police boxes and headed back to Earth. The Gallifreyans would chase him, he knew, because he'd broken one of the laws that he'd invented.

But he'd decided that being free was better than being in charge.

There came a clatter from the window. He hopped up and opened it, and was surprised to see an owl sitting on a low branch outside, regarding him with disdain.

'Hello', said Smith. 'And who are you?'

'Woo,' said the owl.

'How do you do, Mr Woo?'

'Who.'

'Who? You, Woo.'

The owl, looking as flustered as an owl can get, opened its wings wide and flapped up into the air. Smith flinched and the bird flew past him through the window, settling on the mantelpiece of the cottage with a proprietorial air.

'Oh no,' Smith sighed. 'You can't stay here. There's no room. Why do you want to stay in a house, anyway?'

The owl didn't say anything. It just closed its eyes and turned its head away.

Smith looked at it for a few moments, wondering if he should try and lift it outside. The claws looked rather fierce for that.

Finally, he just spread some newspaper under the mantelpiece and left the owl to sleep.

He returned to his writing table, and was just about to pick up his pen again to edit what he'd written, when there came a knock at the door. 'Could you get that, Merlin?' he asked the owl. No reply forthcoming, he went and opened it.

The door was slammed out of his grip.

Something dark launched itself through the gap and landed on his chest, pinning him to the floor.

'Silence!' it hissed.

Smith frantically reached for a poker that stood by the fireplace, but the lithe dark figure snapped a hand out. It caught Smith's fingers and wrapped them in its own gloved fist.

It wrenched Smith's left hand up to face level and the little schoolteacher caught a glimpse of glittering eyes and white teeth under the brim of the hat.

'Pleased to meet you, human!' snarled Serif.

Then he bit the end off Smith's little finger.

Benny and Constance sat in the little back bedroom of Alexander's rooms above the museum. A heavy curtain hung over the small window. When Alexander had popped out to make the tea, they'd heard footsteps going downstairs. Unfortunately, the window was on the wrong side of the building to see who might be leaving.

'I'm getting positively used to hiding,' Constance sighed, leaning her head on Benny's shoulder. 'I wish, sometimes, that I could change the way I look, just magically transform into a bird, or a cat. Wouldn't that be wonderful, to change what you were just by thinking about it? Wouldn't you like to do that?'

'Not really.' Benny was wondering if this place had a bath. The mud was dropping off her and getting the bedclothes dirty already. 'I just want to be me and do that as well as I can.'

'But you could get into any dress you liked or be a man for a day and go out carousing.' She started to twirl the ends of Benny's hair absent-mindedly. 'You could do whatever you wanted. This sullied flesh could melt and resolve itself into a dew.'

Benny rubbed her brow, wondering why everything in her life seemed to happen at exactly the wrong time. She plucked Constance's hand from her hair and patted it comfortingly. 'That's a lovely idea, but it doesn't help me at the moment. Right now, I need to find this object I'm looking for.'

'Well, if you know who's got it, then in the morning you can just go and get it off them, can't you? I know all the back ways and side roads. With my help, it won't be hard at all.'

'I suspect it may not be as simple as that, but, yes, I'll meet you in the morning and you can give me some idea of the territory.'

Alexander bustled back in with glee, handing them each a mug of steaming tea. 'Goodness me!' he exclaimed. 'What excitement! Why was that nurse after you, do you think?'

'I have no idea.' Benny took a long swig from her mug. 'I don't know any nurses. Perhaps she's another one of this lot who are hunting me.'

'As you say. I mean, terrible for you, being pursued, but this is dreadfully exciting. Oh, I say, it's only just occurred to me. Bernice, you're wearing trousers!'

'Many people have already noted that, Alexander. I don't suppose you've got a bath, have you?'

'Oh yes,' said the effervescent curator. 'By sheer chance, I, erm, already had the boiler on. Was going to have one myself, after my lady friend had left, but your need is greater.'

'Wonderful.' Benny drained her mug in one lengthy gulp. 'Now, Constance, will you be all right getting to your own lodgings?'

'Of course.' The young woman finished her tea and stood up. 'I shall see you here at eleven, and then we shall reverse the roles we have so far played. Your persecutors shall be the prey, and we the hunters.'

'You know,' said Benny, 'when you say things like that, you almost make me feel confident.'

The dark man swirled in and out of Smith's vision, a fluttering phantom above him.

Pain was shouting distantly. Smith clutched his hand, astonished at the new shape of it. That was the thing about taking a wound, the unreasonable fact that a bit of you had gone.

Serif had chewed on the finger thoughtfully for a few seconds as Smith had screamed, and then swallowed it. He put a hand to Smith's temple, and suddenly the little schoolteacher found that he couldn't scream any more. Some part of him wanted to reach down the creature's throat and take the lost part of him back, but most of his thoughts were consumed by a sickening, flattening, terror. He noticed, as his vision swirled randomly around the room, that the owl seemed to have gone. Perhaps he'd only dreamed it. Serif spent several minutes just sitting on his chest, concentrating. Finally he spoke.

'I can taste who you think you are. Laylock did his work well. You are full of nanites, and if I had eaten more of you, they would start affecting me. This person you have made for yourself is quite fascinating. Shall we dig a little deeper?'

The gloved hand again touched Smith's scalp.

He and Serif were standing on a shale beach beside a cold sea at night, watching the beam of a lighthouse cycle round and round in the mist. 'This is the home that you fled?' Serif asked.

'Aberdeen, yes.' Smith took a deep breath of sea air and looked at his hand. It was whole again. 'Who are you? What do you want with me?'

'You don't know where the Pod is. I wonder if it has been destroyed. Laylock is sometimes very fallible, and on occasion… untrustworthy. If the Pod has failed, we may at least discover some important information about you. I know they have a lighthouse on a place called Gallifrey,' Serif murmured. 'Tell me, does Aberdeen have defences?'

'A sea wall, that's all. To stop the flooding. There's no soldiers here. Nothing special about the town at all, except for the rock—'

'Ah yes, the radioactive granite, so conducive to mutation.'

'No, the rock with "Greetings From Aberdeen" written through it. Very tasty.' Smith glanced up at the headland above the beach. 'Oh my God! Verity!'

Serif followed his gaze. A young woman with a moonlike, innocent face was staring down at them from the shore.

'Ah, so there is beauty in truth. Who is she?'

'A girl. We used to be together. Now we're not.'

'What does she mean to you?'

'She's what I'm always just missing. We met here once. We were very different, from opposite sides of town.'

'Are some of the citizens of Aberdeen better off than others, then?'

'You could say that. There's a poor house, run by the Church. That's where I was brought up.'

'Really? What was the name of your teacher? What did he tell you of the sea wall?'

Smith opened his mouth, and suddenly found himself convulsing. He fell to the ground, his hands grasping frantically at the pebbles. It was as if something huge had given way inside him. 'No! No!' he shrieked. 'Can't tell!'

He reached out a hand piteously as the woman on the shore turned and walked away. 'Verity!'

'So you know there are certain things you should not say. Interesting.' Serif raised his gloved hand and clicked his fingers.

Smith found himself back on his own living-room floor again, paralysed. The pain flooded back into his finger. He struggled to breathe, and managed to gasp regular, shallow gulps of air as Serif got up and wandered over to his bureau. 'You've been writing fiction,' the dark man whispered, picking up a page from Smith's story and glancing at it. 'In fiction, we reveal our deepest unconscious thoughts. Would it be of any use to me to read this? You may speak.'

'Unconscious?' Smith gasped. 'How can thoughts not be conscious?'

'Hah! What a primitive world this is you've found for yourself. Why, these humans must think of themselves so simply, as straightforward animals who think and do, decide and set about. Well, I know better, and so should you, as that deep-set defence mechanism I just uncovered indicates.' He squatted back down beside the prone teacher. 'My name is Serif. Unlike my fellows, I have specialised in matters of the mind as well as the body. I've often had cause to unpick the programming of a personality, rewrite certain aspects. I do this by regressing the subject right back to the moment of birth and then working forwards. In your case, of course, that's not really appropriate. However, we can make some progress. In doing so, we may learn all sorts of incidental things about dear, ripe Gallifrey along the way. Do you think that's how we should proceed?'

Smith snarled a response. A vast roaring of blood filled his ears and the pain from his finger was terrible, as if some healing machine was trying to start its work and failing. That failure was filling his senses with agony, and he couldn't decipher what on earth his assailant was saying.

'It was a rhetorical question,' Serif told him, and placed his hand back on Smith's head.

Smith stared at the woman whose head lay on his shoulder, her straight, backcombed hair warmly touching his skin.

They were both dressed in togas, lying on a lounger in the courtyard of a villa. The only sound was the gentle trickle of a fountain.

'There,' the woman said. 'That wasn't so bad, was it?'

Smith was about to reply, but then he was staggering back from a door, dropping his briefcase and clutching his nose, shouting all manner of colourful swearwords.

'It's one of these new automatic jobs,' a voice said. 'Still some teething troubles, what?'

But hadn't his brother told him about that? Funny how close to you some stories got, as if they were memories.

He was waltzing with a woman in a flowery dress, pleased at how her movements matched his. Around him men in uniform were all dancing with their partners. 'Perhaps we could go on somewhere?' he asked.

Under an orange sky, a group of dark figures stood around a singing structure, a million fine chords sighing in the wind. Information was flowing down the chords, being woven together in the mesh they were forming between them. Spirals of microscopic data had been flowing into the loom for days. Now something was due to emerge.

The woman walked forward and touched the chords.

Something shaped itself into her arms. A male child.

'Again?' said the child.

'Again?' said Serif.

There was a crash, a thump and the orange sky became plaster-white again.

A woman was looking down at Smith, the remains of a heavy vase in her hands. Serif was lying on the carpet, his hand an inch from Smith's head, a surprised look on his unconscious face.

'Have you seen an owl?' Smith asked the woman.

'Yes,' said Joan. 'How did you know?'

Smith was barely aware of Joan leaving again to run up the driveway to the school. She left Serif, who showed no sign of waking up, roughly bound by a sheet. She woke Mr Moffat the bursar up, and demanded to use the school telephone, shouting at the night operator that this was an emergency, a burglar had been caught and the police must be summoned.

A Black Maria stopped outside the cottage and Sergeant Abelard, an old man with a white Kitchener moustache, helped his two constables to lift the still-unconscious Serif into the back of the van.

'An anarchist, by the look of him,' said the sergeant. 'One of these Russian fellows like as did Sidney Street. Perhaps it was him set off the poison gas in the hospital.'

'Poison gas?' exclaimed Joan.

'Sorry, madam, I didn't mean to alarm you. It's all dealt with now, the papers will be full of it tomorrow.'

'What happened?' asked Smith. He was wrapped in a rug, a cup of tea in his right hand, his left little finger bandaged up by Joan. She'd winced as he did as she'd bathed the end of it in alcohol.

'Somebody set off what we think must have been a gas bomb in St Catherine's. We wired Whitehall and they said to have the fire brigade hose the place down. They've been at it all day. Some of those lads got a look inside the place, and what they describe… well, sir, I wouldn't like to repeat it in the company of a lady. There's a convoy on the way from Clapperton. We'll hand the matter over to the army boys when they arrive. Bit of a feather in my cap to have apprehended somebody, though. What did he want here, do you think?'

Smith stared at him. 'He must have been a burglar. He cut off my finger. Perhaps he was looking… for a ring? No, I don't wear a ring. He knocked me out. And there was something about an owl…'

The policeman flipped his notebook closed. 'I don't think he'll be much help to us tonight, madam. It's understandable. Could I ask you both to call at the police station tomorrow morning?'

Smith and Joan agreed, and thanked the police. The van drove away and Joan pulled up a chair to sit beside Smith, who was still staring vacantly into space.

'It is odd that you should mention an owl,' she said. 'I was about to go to bed, when I was disturbed by a great clattering at the window. I looked out, but only saw an owl flying away. I glanced down and there were your white gloves. You had left them behind on the sideboard. I had an odd fancy to return them to you. Nothing bold, I was merely going to post them through your letter box, with a note about seeing you tomorrow. When I got here, the door was open and you know the rest.'

'Do I?' Smith smiled gently. 'I'm very confused. I seem to have been dreaming, but I don't quite know where the dream ended and waking up began.' They talked for an hour or so more, and gradually Smith began to feel stronger, the fear of his attack draining from him and reality reasserting itself.

'Do you want me to stay?' Joan asked. 'I am capable of sleeping on a chair.'

Smith bit his lip and a slow grin chased the chill from his face. 'No,' he decided finally. 'You get home to bed.'

'All right,' said Joan. She got up and quickly kissed him. 'Bolt the door behind me.'

'Will I see you tomorrow?'

'That was the plan, but since you are now injured—'

'I can't think of a better cure than looking at you. What'll we do?'

'I shall make a picnic. We'll go along to the police station and then find some quiet spot to eat it, hopefully out of the range of poison gas.' She stopped on the way to the door. 'Oh my goodness, how will we know if our spot is safe?'

'Anywhere that birds still sing,' said Smith, 'one can have a picnic safely.'

6

A DEAL WITH GOD

Alexander knocked on the door of the bathroom. 'Bernice, have you drowned?'

There came a satisfyingly loud splash from inside and then a tired mutter: 'Fell asleep. What time is it?'

'Nearly midnight. I've made up the back bedroom for you. Would you care for a cup of cocoa or perhaps some Scotch?'

'A double, thanks. I'll be out in a minute.'

When she came out, white, soggy and wrapped in a rather good silk kimono that Alexander had given her, he was waiting in the parlour with two glasses and a bottle.

She poured and they clinked glasses.

'So, may I ask as to the nature of your current troubles?' Alexander began, rolling the whisky around his mouth. 'You're proving to be a most exciting tenant. You are not, I take it, actually down from college?'

'No,' Bernice admitted. 'I'm not. Do you want the vague, generalised, believable version, or the absolutely ridiculous specific one?'

'Oh, the latter, definitely. I've been following the affairs of Constance and her like long enough to know that, once embarked upon, rebellion is a positive opiate. I mean that in two ways. Firstly, it's addictive. Secondly, it opens up whole worlds full of new dreams. Do tell me yours.'

'Right.' And, without sparing a detail, Bernice told the whole story of her life and adventures with the Doctor, right up to the present. Alexander's eyes grew wider, and his whisky consumption grew faster, every moment. 'And so, here I am,' she concluded, with a big smile. 'Do you know, I've always wanted to tell somebody all that. I'm sure I'm breaking some sort of rule. What do you think?'

'This knight of yours—'

'No, no, I mean, do you believe me?'

'Do you really want me to?'

Bernice finished off the last glass and reached for another bottle with a swift wipe of her lips on the back of her hand. 'Yes. Rather terribly, actually.'

'Well, what proof can you offer me? What happens in the next ten years?'

Bernice shook her head. She'd anticipated the question. 'I don't think I ought to talk about that. Tell you what, wait a minute.' She hopped up and rummaged around in her pack. She returned carrying her portable history unit and handed it to Alexander. 'There.'

He stared at it then punched a few buttons. 'Now how does this work? There's a roller behind this little frame, operated by clockwork, and the words on it appear...' He fell silent. After a moment, he gently put the unit down on the table, and stared at it.

Then he started to laugh. The laugh grew bigger and bigger. He leapt up and swung Bernice around the room in a happy arc. 'It's true! It's true! You're from the future!'

'Yes, yes...' Bernice found that she was laughing too. 'Now put me down. We still have dizziness in the future.'

'Oh dear...' They slumped into armchairs. 'So, these people who are after you – are they from the future too?'

'Yes. Or at least, I think so. I think they've taken the object, the Pod, which could make my friend himself again.'

'Well, we must try and get it back. I could raise quite a good gang, if I tried.'

'No, you mustn't do that. These people have weapons which could level this place. We need to sneak up on them.'

'Understood.' Alexander crunched up his face with joy, hanging on to his chair like a boy on a roundabout. 'This is fascinating! What a strange predicament your friend's got into. Why do you think he wanted to be human?'

'I'm not sure. I think he wanted a change, to have a holiday from being him.'

'Maybe there were things that he could only do if he was human. You describe him as a friend. Are you and he husband and wife?'

Benny laughed. 'No. He doesn't really do that sort of thing. He surrounds himself with female company, mind you, quite innocently.'

'And male company?'

'Occasionally. Equally innocently.'

'Well, perhaps he wants to fall in love.'

'He couldn't have thought of that when he did it,' Benny protested uncertainly. 'But you might be right.'

'Oh, I usually am,' muttered Alexander. 'God, I'm in danger of keeping you up all night. Listen, tomorrow the three of us, you, me and Constance, will go and find this Pod thing, all right?'

'Does Constance have a young man?'

'Well, my chum Richard says so. Not him, but I think there are a few in the Labour group who worship her.'

'Oh. Odd.'

'Hmm?'

'Nothing.' Benny got up and stretched. 'I'll see you in the morning. I gather that I should put a chair up against my door.'

'Dear girl, why should you?'

'Constance said that you believed in free love.'

'Not with those in distress, loved one! Or those in mourning.'

'Yes...' said Benny. 'Good night.'

After she'd gone, Alexander reached for the history unit again, turning it over and over in his hands. 'My God,' he whispered, 'I'm glad I lived to see this.'

A little circle of boys had gathered around Timothy's bed, staring down at the body.

They'd tucked him in and told the Prep master that he was feeling ill. Then they'd turned off his bedside lamp and prepared the cold body for bed, folding him into his pyjamas like they were dressing a flaccid, awkward mannequin.

Anand had been locked in a chest and declared ill also.

Phipps stared at Hutchinson's stoic features. 'We can't go on with this, Captain,' he said. 'They'll want him for OTC tomorrow. They'll come and see him.'

'Died in his sleep?' suggested Merryweather.

'They'll see the rope marks on his neck, for Christ's sake! And what about the darkie?'

'You could kill him too,' murmured Alton, seemingly amused by the whole business.

Hutchinson glanced up from the body, as if woken from a dream. 'I don't know what you're all talking about,' he said. 'He'll be fine in the morning.'

'Hutchinson,' Merryweather hissed, 'he's dead!'

'He's not dead,' Hutchinson fixed the younger boy with a glare, 'until I say so. Any objections?'

Phipps put a hand to his mouth. He'd been looking ill all evening. 'No, Captain,' he mumbled.

The others replied the same, one by one.

'Good,' said Hutchinson. 'That's decided. I suggest we all retire.'

Somewhere outside of time, in the white void.

'Who are you?' Timothy asked Death.

Death glared at him. 'I'm the sister of Time and Pain and several more. We're the dreams of Time Lords. We leak out across the universe, and occasionally somebody like the Timewyrm gives us form. Certain Time Lords, in their nightmares, or in states like you're in, make sordid little deals with us. We might even take them on as our Champions. We make them pay a price.'

'Does that mean I'm dead?'

'Don't ask that too loudly. I'm waiting here for somebody particular. I don't have to deal with you. Do you know what a respiratory by-pass system is?'

'No.'

'That's all right then. You've just got one.'

Tim woke up and reached for his neck. He pulled the collar of his pyjamas aside and found the red marks where the rope had bitten him.

'I'm alive!' he gasped. Then the gasp became a shout. 'I'm alive!'

Phipps was the first one to wake, smothering a scream with his bedclothes when he saw Timothy sitting up in bed.

The others ignited their bedside lamps, and, seeing the miracle that had occurred, ran to surround the boy again. 'But you were dead!' Merryweather cried. 'You'd stopped breathing, there was no pulse!'

'I died,' Timothy told him. 'And then I came back.'

Hutchinson pushed his way through the crowd and glared at Timothy. Timothy met his gaze evenly.

After a moment, the Captain turned away. 'As I said,' he murmured. 'A lot of fuss about nothing. Don't forget it's OTC tomorrow, Dean. Make a man of you.'

The others hesitantly followed Hutchinson's example and returned to their beds, many of them still staring at Timothy as they did so.

After the lights had all been extinguished again, Tim flexed his fingers experimentally, staring at his young hands. 'Too late…' he whispered.

Serif opened his eyes. 'I don't believe it!' he whispered.

He was in a tiny, white-brick cell, with a solid metal door. One small barred window looked out on the darkness. The only light was that which washed under the door. On the floor in front of him sat a tray with some bread and cheese on it.

He jumped to his feet and hammered on the door.

After a few minutes, a tiny slat at eye-level slid open. 'Oi,' said a voice. 'Be qui-et. Silencio. Get my meaning? You'll wake the other prisoners.'

'You—' Serif rammed his hand at the little gap, but the slat slammed shut again before he could touch whoever was outside.

It was inconceivable, but somehow the ex-Time Lord had outsmarted him. He turned back to the interior of the cell and paced up and down, considering his options. He didn't carry any of the extravagant weaponry that the others favoured. If they'd only given him some meat…

Serif finally came to a bitter conclusion. He concentrated for a moment, then pulled off one of his gloves.

He put the revealed chalk-white hand up to the window and concentrated again. It took an hour, but, finally, Serif was convinced that he'd released the correct molecular messages into the air. Directing them would take longer still.

He just hoped that Greeneye wouldn't smirk about it.

Sergeant Abelard carefully closed the partition and wandered back behind the desk of the small police station.

'You've been back and forth to that door all night, Sarge,' said Constable Bickerston. 'And you've been on the go all day. Shouldn't you be getting home?'

'No, Alfie, I'm not a happy halibut. Army lads'll be through here any time now. I want to know what's going on. We might be at war tomorrow.'

'War?' Bickerston looked up from his newspaper. 'What, you reckon it was the Germans did that to the hospital today?'

'Germans, perhaps. Austrians or Russians, more likely. You didn't see what that gas did, Alfie. Most of the patients and staff in one of the wards just vanished, melted like they were made of chocolate on a hot day. But it was the ones at the edges that had the worst of it. There were bits and pieces of them everywhere. I've persuaded Geoffrey down at the newspaper not to mention it tomorrow, not until we can find all the relatives. But there'll be no holding him if the news gets out to London. What with that, that business at the pub and our anarchist down in the cells...'

'You reckon they're all connected?'

'Well, I'll be damned if it's a coincidence, a gas bomb, a violent robbery and an assault on the same day. That, what, triples the crime rate for April in one go? No, I think we've got our man, but it'll be down to the Army how they treat him. I hope they – oh, hello, miss, what can we... do for you?'

A nurse had wandered into the police station, carrying a red balloon. Abelard and the constable exchanged glances.

'Excuse me, officers,' the nurse began, 'but I was wondering if you might have chanced upon a friend of mine. He's a tall rather sinister gentleman in a large hat.'

'Are you a relative, miss?' asked Abelard.

'Why, yes, I'm his daughter.'

'Come now, miss, you can't expect us to swallow that.'

The nurse laughed and her voice changed. 'You said something funny. I'm tired of talking in that stupid way, so I'm going to talk like me now, all right?'

'That's absolutely fine, miss. Would you care to sit down for a while? Perhaps we could have a little chat.' Abelard opened the partition and showed the nurse towards the row of chairs that ran along the edge of the room. 'Now, were you in the hospital this afternoon when… when something awful happened?'

'Yes!' The nurse hopped up and down, smiling at him. 'I was because I did it!'

'Did you really, miss?' Abelard reached for his notebook, suddenly wondering if he ought to put in a call to the constables from Berridge, who were still helping to clear up at the hospital. No, this girl was obviously round the bend. 'What was it that you did, then, exactly?'

The nurse let go of her balloon, which floated up to the ceiling, and unbuttoned her cuff. She showed Abelard her wrist. 'Watch! Nothing up my sleeve, just like a real magician. And now… ta-dah!'

The inside of her wrist split open like a piece of meat on a butcher's rack. There was no blood, just a black capsule that plopped neatly out into her hand. The wrist swept shut again.

Abelard stepped back, astonished. 'How—'

'Now, here's the clever part…' The nurse began to unscrew the cap on the capsule.

'Sarge!' shouted Bickerston. 'That's the gas, it must be! Stop her!'

Abelard dived forward and wrenched the black capsule out of the nurse's grip. He stared at it for a moment.

She glared at him, her hands on her hips. 'Oh!'

'For goodness' sake, hurry up, can't you, Aphasia?' August wandered in and shot Abelard through the head.

As the body slid down the wall, he turned his gun towards Bickerston, but the constable had already dived under the counter, grabbing the telephone as he went.

'Balloon,' Aphasia sighed, recovering her gas capsule from the bloody wreck on the wall. 'Behind the desk.'

The balloon swept down from the ceiling and dropped below desk level, from where the sounds of frantic dialling issued.

'Hoff's back at the dome,' August told Aphasia. 'Have you seen Greeneye?'

'No, but I got a message from him.' The dialling had stopped, the receiver slammed back down again, and now the sound was a violent thrashing and muffled shouting.

'Did he say where he was?'

'No, but he said he had a new plan.' The sounds from behind the desk grew quiet, and then stopped.

The balloon floated back to Aphasia's grasp.

'That's all we need,' August sighed. 'If it's anything like the last one, we'll all get injured this time.'

The telephone behind the desk began to ring. 'Go and get Serif, would you please?' August asked. 'Oh, and kill anybody else you find.'

As Aphasia ran through into the interior, he opened up the partition and squatted down. He nudged the body of the constable aside and plucked the receiver from his fingers.

'Hello? Yes. Yes, Major, I see. Very good. All right. See you then.' He replaced the receiver just as a ragged alcoholic scream came from one of the cells.

Serif stalked out into the duty area, Aphasia skipping behind him merrily. He glanced at the carnage against the wall. 'What took you so long?' he mumbled, and carried straight on out of the doorway.

August smiled at Aphasia. 'He could at least have said thank you.'

They marched up into the forest to the dome, Serif keeping his distance ahead of August and Aphasia.

Hoff was looking up at the moon, idly picking twigs off the trees and eating them. He spun round as Serif stamped into the clearing, levelling his gun at the dark figure.

'Don't be so melodramatic,' Serif grumbled, opening the dome.

'Look who's talking.' Hoff smiled at August as he and Aphasia arrived. 'Should have left him there. Any problems?'

'No, except that I answered a communications link to an approaching military convoy. Quite wisely, they've come to the conclusion that events at the hospital were somewhat extraordinary and are on their way to investigate.'

Hoff shrugged. 'Could nuke them. One mini-missile would do it.'

'Yes,' August tapped his chin, 'but that would quickly bring the whole country down on us. At the moment, we're free to search for the Pod, but things would really slow down if this becomes a battle zone. That, and Greeneye's fears could come true. The Time Lords might notice a major conflict. No, I think we should just seal the place off. What have you got?'

'Heat barrier?'

'Bit showy.'

'Fear barrier?'

'We want to minimise panic and confusion, not create it.'

'Time barrier, then. Wall of temporal displacement. Two layers, each with time on one side a second earlier than on the other. You can walk through one from either side, but not through both. Anybody short of a Time Lord who tries to go through, it's like they're walking through a wall. If they keep trying, all sorts of bizarre effects start happening, many of them fatal.'

'Good.'

'Glad you escaped the hospital.' Hoff patted Aphasia on the back, and the nurse's body went flying, landing on the humus a few feet away like a thrown paper dart. Hoff laughed. 'Sorry. Should have realised that body wouldn't be very dense.'

'Well, I'm getting rid of the ugly thing!' Aphasia yelled. She leapt to her feet and ran into the dome.

'Invaluable as always, Hoff,' said August, following her. 'Oh, and could you check the security systems on the dome? This search of ours is going on far too long.'

'Perhaps Greeneye's found something.'

August sighed. 'Perhaps cats will fly.'

So it was that in the early hours of the morning, a thin linear ripple appeared in the air on the other side of the hill, an impossible shifting of reality that gave off an atomic twinkle. It arced right over the town like a rainbow, and then fanned out, expanding in a circle to form a dome. Then another layer swept out in the same way, following it exactly.

The walls of it swept round the outskirts of the town, slicing straight through trees and foliage, creating marks in wood that would still be visible decades later.

A flock of pigeons were caught by it, and one of them spiralled to earth, its wing spinning off on the other side of the airknife.

An owl, hovering over a meadow in wait for prey, sensed the thing coming, and ceremoniously flapped town-wards to escape it.

Those that were awake to see the dome's sparkling progress, at the farms and dairies and post offices, thought that it was the aurora and smiled at it. It completed its arc, sparkled again for a moment, and vanished.

The town was cut off from the world.

The first person to notice was Mr Hodges, whose horses suddenly stopped and whinnied in the middle of the road in the darkness before dawn. He got down from the cart and quietened them, and told them that they had to get to town for market, give the stallholders time to unload the produce. But they wouldn't go any further.

Hodges took his cap off and scratched his head. It was like there was something in the road that was scaring them. He knew that sometimes even the smallest animal in its path would cause a horse to startle. He took his walking stick from the seat and walked forward, knocking it along the ground to scare off anything that was lurking in the bushes. A fox maybe, or one of Mrs Deel's dratted dogs. In the back of his mind was the thought that perhaps it was the man who'd attacked that saucy young thing Bernice. But Hodges was a practical man, and he didn't get scared by unseen things in hedgerows.

The stick hit something with a resounding chime.

Hodges stepped back, and swung it again, struggling to comprehend the idea that… there was a big sheet of glass here? He reached out a hand and touched it, unable to see anything. His fingertips passed through something, a light chill, and then encountered a smooth surface.

He leapt back. A memory had heaved itself into his mind: his Kitty, dead for ten years now, holding up little Albert for him to see. Everything had been clear, like a waking dream, but it was fading now… He looked round, horrified, expecting to see St Peter or someone in the dark roadway, but all that there was was the approaching dawn and the distant cry of lambs.

Shaking, Hodges reached out for the barrier again.

Morning. Dr Smith woke at the sunshine through his curtains and winced at the pain in his finger.

He got dressed and wandered into the washroom. The events of the night before seemed like a nightmare. If he'd had a whole little finger on his left hand, he'd have written them off as that. What sort of burglar bites the end of your finger? He'd ask Joan to check the bandages today. Probably a good sign that it was still hurting.

He stared at his face in the mirror then felt the stubble on his chin. Holding his damaged hand awkwardly away from the sink, he managed to wedge the pot of shaving foam in a corner under the mirror and worked up a useful amount of foam one-handed. He wasn't going to see Joan with a rough chin.

Oh, and he'd told bloody Rocastle that he was going to go to his OTC meeting today. Well, he could just manage without him. It wasn't in his contract to work on Saturdays. He shaved, being even more careful than usual with the big cut-throat razor. He remembered his first real shave as a boy, the barber on Espedair Street who smelt of tobacco, and kept talking about running away to sea, for some reason. His skin had felt wonderful afterwards, but very hot and red, and he'd woken up the next day with a face covered in acne. That always happened, his dad had told him. The girls would understand. Well, the Duchess – Verity – had, at any rate.

He splashed some water on his face, wiping the foam away one-handed.

He pulled out the big metal tub from the cupboard and filled it with jugs of hot water in the lounge, picking up the local newspaper from the doormat on his way into the kitchen. There was no word about the hospital at all. They must have gone to press before it happened.

Odd. He clenched his teeth and glared at the absence. It was as if gears inside him were trying to engage but missing their wheels, an inch up the hill and then always a jerk back. This must be what Sherlock Holmes felt like when he was thinking about a problem... Good, actually, if Conan Doyle would write a couple more stories now, he could ask *The Strand* whatever fee he liked. Or perhaps this was just the common feeling of people now, that they were bloody missing something.

A finger, actually, That was the whole of it; he was still a bit shocked and the emptiness inside was a measure of that. A man in love shouldn't be blue.

A man in – God, enough time for foolishness later. Bath'd be good for shock.

He threw the paper across the room and dropped his dressing-gown over the back of a chair. Gingerly, he stepped into the hot water and, settling into it, sighed.

He watched the ripples of his arrival flow from his body to the sides of the metal bath, then bounce back again.

Yes, this mood was probably something biological, a funk caused by losing one's finger and all the fingery functions associated with it.

'Oh well,' he sighed. 'It could have been worse.'

The dark mood stayed with him as he walked into town, despite the fresh sunlight of the Saturday morning. The market was setting up its stalls, and the Romany Punch and Judy man had parked his cart beside the oak on the green. The ice-cream boy with the cool cabinet on the front of his bicycle pedalled by, crying his wares. Smith stopped at the edge of the market square and folded his arms around himself, looking at all the people.

He could barely remember most of the rubbish that his attacker had come out with. None of it had really made sense, but it had still felt as if the madman was talking directly to him, as if there was some other essential John Smith that one might talk to and yet which John himself wasn't aware of.

He shook his head. Nonsense. He should stop reading lurid books and join in with the boys' sport a bit more. Exercise was the solution, and it might help his aching hand, too.

There was a bakery, Caldwell's, on the other side of the town square. Smith made his way to it, keeping his left hand carefully up against his chest and shaking his head at the barkers for the various stalls as they tried to sell him fish or vegetables or ice. A lot of the stalls seemed very empty this morning, and one or two of the owners were sitting behind empty displays, glancing impatiently at the road that led out of the square.

A wonderful smell of newly baked bread always permeated from Caldwell's, and that was what brought Smith there every morning before work, in search of his regular steak and kidney pie.

Well, that and Fiona. Fiona was a small, red-haired girl who always seemed to be smiling. She was second-in-command at the bakery, beneath the beaming Mr Caldwell, who, when he saw Smith, would always warble something in a thick Arbroath accent that Smith affected to understand. Fiona and Smith said three sentences to each other every day; they were always good sentences.

Today, she stood patiently waiting as Smith hovered by the pastry counter, his finger moving to and fro over the pies. He was the only customer at the moment, the midday rush not having started yet, so he could afford to take his time.

'Not having your usual then, Dr Smith?'

'No. I wanted something… Oh, I don't know, Fiona.' He looked up at her appealingly. 'I keep wondering… I wonder why I wonder why. I wonder why I wonder. I wonder why I wonder *why* I wonder why I wonder…'

Fiona looked from left to right, went to the door and glanced outside, then went back to Smith and hugged him carefully like you'd hug a teddy bear.

Smith hugged her back, rather abashed, for a moment.

Then Fiona brushed down her pinafore and went back behind the counter.

'Do you feel better now?' she asked.

'Yes,' he muttered, amazed.

'And do you know now?'

'Yes,' Smith grinned. 'Could I have a muffin, please?'

Munching his muffin, and feeling a little better, Smith headed for the police station. On his way, he passed the gate of the little churchyard of St Anthony's, then paused. He glanced at his watch. He had time.

The inside of the church had that polished smell and the light scent of new flowers on top of it. No vicar about. Smith walked to the altar and looked up at the ribs of the roof that met overhead. His parents had been Presbyterians, very strict and conventional, and thus he'd grown up without religion.

Sometimes, it would be nice to have some.

So he tried. 'God?' he asked the roof. Something in him expected an answer. 'What is it inside me that hurts so?'

'Can I help?' asked a voice from the vestry. A kind-looking

vicar was smiling at Smith, extending his hands welcomingly.

Smith glanced ruefully back at the ceiling. 'No,' he muttered. 'I was just a little lost.'

He doffed his cap to the priest and left.

So, what was left was Joan.

He turned the corner beside the police station, hoping to see her there immediately, but instead there was a cluster of police vans, and an ambulance crew carrying stretchers out of the place.

Smith stayed where he was, watching. He should go forward and declare himself, say he had an appointment, ask if there'd been an accident. But he didn't want to get involved.

'Got you!' Joan said, tapping him on the shoulder. 'How is your finger?' She was carrying a picnic hamper.

Smith took one of the handles, resisting the impulse to embrace her. 'Getting better.' He nodded towards the police station. 'I think we've come at a bad time. Shall we go?'

'Well, no, we cannot. Not really.' Joan frowned at the confusion before them. 'Come on, let's explain ourselves and get it over with.' She led Smith towards the policeman with the most insignia. 'Excuse me. We were due here this morning to give evidence.'

The policeman took their details, and was suddenly interested when Smith revealed his identity. He took a full description of his assailant and went over certain aspects of it with him.

'I think that's right…' Smith pondered. 'Why do you want a description? Can't you see for yourself?'

The policeman flipped his notebook closed. 'I'm sorry, sir, I'm not at liberty to say any more. The station will be fully staffed again by midweek, and if you could return then, I'm sure they'll want to go into the more general matter of the break-in. Good day to you.'

As they walked away, Joan frowned at Smith. 'He's escaped.

That's what's happened, isn't it? He must have hurt some policeman doing it.'

'Oh? Oh no!' Smith turned round urgently. 'But what if he—'

Joan took his arm reassuringly. 'Don't worry. Why should he come back? You said yourself that he was a burglar. That sort never visit the same place twice. And if he was one of these Balkan anarchists, he must have picked you quite at random. You've got no connection with middle Europe, have you?'

'No.' Smith still glanced over his shoulder at the ambulance. 'But why are they keeping it a secret? They didn't say anything about the hospital in the paper, either. It's as if something terrible's happening. They won't tell us about it.' He squirmed electrically, wringing the air with his hands. 'I feel like I should do something.'

'I'm sure they've got it all in hand. If you can do anything, they'll ask you. Now come on, I know the perfect spot for a picnic. Or don't you want to have a picnic with me in a quiet little meadow?' She raised a flirtatious eyebrow.

Smith patted her arm. 'That's one thing I'm still certain about.'

'I am rather glad you lost your finger, as a matter of fact,' Joan told Smith as they negotiated the hamper over the stile. 'I became so uncertain last night, that's why I wanted to drop a note off with your gloves. Suddenly having to look after you made it all so much easier.'

'You did more than look after me. You rescued me.'

'I suppose I did. Do you mind? I'm sure you'd have won the contest eventually.'

'Mind?' Smith helped her down into a meadow filled with dandelions, an old oak tree at its centre. The white seeds of the flowers scampered over the grass in the gentle breeze, and small birds chirped as they swung to and fro in the sky, snatching for the first bees to wake in the approaching summer. 'I owe my life to you. How could anyone mind that?'

'I'm glad you see it that way. I just could not stand to see you being beaten.' She turned aside, leaving the hamper on the stile for a moment. 'The truth is that I'm feeling rather overwhelmed, John. To have a sweetheart again. It's been a long time. I think I have forgotten some of the words.'

'Then close your eyes.' He went to her, and put a hand on each of her shoulders. 'And listen.' He did likewise.

They stayed like that for a while, listening to the sounds of the birds and the distant calling of animals, and feeling the sun on their faces. Joan held his hand on her shoulder.

'Do you remember now?' he finally asked. 'They're singing this for you.'

'Is this our song, then? The call of birds?'

'Why have only one song?' Smith whispered. 'We can have them all. Do you remember how to be kissed?'

'Yes,' she said, and turned, pulling Smith to her, delighting in the feel of his hand in the small of her back and the complete contact of their bodies and strengths. Their mouths met and played with each other for a long time.

Finally, she let go, laughing. 'I think I've picked up several verses now, as well as the chorus!'

'You're blushing.'

'Am I?' Joan went back to the hamper and gamely picked it up, smiling all over her face. 'Jolly good.'

Bernice woke up refreshed and quickly got dressed, ready for the morning's expedition. She wandered out into the little kitchen of the apartment area, wondering if Alexander was awake yet, and was surprised to see him at the kitchen table, snoring loudly over it. It looked as if he hadn't gone to bed. An empty whisky bottle sat on the table, beside the portable history unit.

'Been there, done that…' Benny murmured, plucking the unit up from the table.

She froze when she saw what was on the screen.

The Somme: Casualty Lists, Located and Missing.

One name was blinking away on the list beside a map reference, a regiment and an identification number.

Richard Hadleman, Cptn Dd, psn gas.

'Oh my God, Alexander… What have you done?' Benny sat down and deactivated the unit. She reached across to Alexander and gently shook him, waking him up.

He grunted, and then stared at her for a moment, bleary-eyed. 'How dare you?' he asked, gently and rhetorically. 'How dare you allow me to know?'

'I didn't even think about it. I'm so sorry.'

'This war. Can't you do something to stop it?'

'I'm marooned, Alex. I'm virtually helpless. If the Doctor was himself…' Benny stopped, stood up and went to the window. She looked for a moment at all the ordinary things outside, and remembered a dream she'd had that night about mud and armed men. 'No. No, I don't think he'd do anything either.'

Alexander stood up. 'The only reason for this war is so that modern capitalism can destroy the great empires. It's just a great shedding of men who would otherwise need jobs! Isn't anybody going to see that? Isn't anybody going to say that killing half the world over Serbia is insane?'

'No.' Benny squared her jaw at him, finding herself defending history as if her pet dog had savaged a sheep. 'They all dive in like it's a great relief to them.'

'What if I went to Sarajevo? Shot the man who kills the Archduke?'

'Somebody had a go a few streets earlier. Somebody else would be around the next corner. Besides, it isn't really down to him, is it? As you say, the industrial world is waiting for this war. A way would be found. I'm just sorry you had to find out about it.'

Alexander sat down slowly. 'We could push for a revolution now, declare a workers' state. I always thought it could be real now, that it could be done. But there's no time. Damn it, if only you'd told me earlier! I have to get to a telegraph, there's only a few weeks before it all starts, I have to…' He found that he was staring at his hands, and suddenly burst into great sobs. 'Poison gas? How can they contemplate *poison gas*?'

Benny went to him and held him. 'I'm so sorry. What have I done to you?'

'Did it to myself, loved one,' he said, quietening after a while. 'God, what do I say to Richard when I next see him?'

'There's nothing you can say. I don't want to raise false hopes, but it may not happen. His death, I mean. I don't know what records you were accessing, but if they're ones from the future, then all sorts of things may have happened in between. Time's very big. We don't get to see it all. That's all I can say, really.' Bernice was rapidly starting to feel as if she'd killed Richard Hadleman herself. 'Damn it, Alexander, I wish you hadn't looked.'

Alexander pulled out a big spotted handkerchief and blew his nose, quickly wiping his tears away, though a hard emptiness remained. 'Why, if I may ask, did you and your friend decide to visit us here?' he asked. 'Are we morbid zoo creatures, on the brink of extinction?'

Benny leant on his shoulder. 'Wasn't my choice. He wanted to come here and suffer a bit, I think.'

The doorbell chimed. Alexander rose and visibly pulled himself together, buttoning his waistcoat. 'I'll have to go through all that business of going to prison,' he muttered. 'I might be too old to be conscripted, though, at least initially. What a winter it's going to be for us all.'

As he wandered downstairs, Benny grabbed the unit, and tapped out a request.

Shuttleworth, Alexander: No records.

She leant back and switched the thing off, hiding it in a deep pocket. She had already broken several laws of time before breakfast. Oh, and ruined somebody's life. She was definitely going to have words with the Doctor about this.

Assuming, of course, that the Doctor ever existed again.

Constance strode merrily into the room, wearing green velvet pantaloons. 'Put on my bloomers,' she explained. 'And how are you both this morning?'

Benny glanced at Alexander's deathlike face as he stamped back up the stairs. 'We've been better.'

'So, are we going to go and get this thing of yours from whoever's got it?' Constance asked as Alexander led them through the darkened corridors of the museum, refusing to open any curtains.

'That's the plan. Alexander says he has something to help us,' Benny whispered, wondering why she was whispering. Despite everything, Constance's chirpiness was raising her spirits too.

'I do indeed, loved one!' Alexander boomed, overhearing. He was taking deep breaths, being immensely brave. They'd come to a locked room, for which he produced a vast and assorted bunch of keys to enter.

The room was a musty, wallpapered storage area, containing everything that the museum didn't see fit to display. Benny wouldn't have minded an afternoon cataloguing the stuff; there were certainly a few pieces of old metal that might have been worth the trouble, but Alexander went straight to a packing case, and pulled out two revolvers and several boxes of ammunition. 'Belonged to an uncle who was at Spion Kop.' He glanced at Constance. 'I would have told your comrades of them, but I didn't want knocks on my door at all hours from maidens wishing to be armed.' He handed her one of the pistols. 'I couldn't face handling one; perhaps you can.'

'We have never used firearms,' Constance told him, slipping the gun into the pocket of her bloomers. 'But I shall not hesitate to do so in defence of my life. I should have you know though,

Bernice, that we may commit arson and explosion, but have not murdered anyone. We are sincerely moral campaigners.'

'Fine. One day, I'll learn to talk like that, too,' Benny opined, checking the sights on one of the pistols. She spun it, loaded it and dropped it into a pocket. 'Busy day. Now, shall we—'

An explosion came from upstairs. Dust detached itself from the roof in a solid layer, then fell.

'Oh my God!' Alexander yelled. 'Quickly, the back door!'

They ran through the museum and Alexander swiftly unlocked the door.

Benny put a hand on his shoulder. 'Calm down. Don't run.' She stepped to a window, and took a quick glance around the frame. The backstreet was empty. 'Now I really wish Ace was here. I should think they're firing some sort of heavy weapon from the field opposite. If we pop down the street and along the hedge, we might be able to get up to the forest without being seen.'

A trail of dark smoke was already drifting from the upstairs rooms. 'How do you think they found you?' asked Alexander, the door handle gripped in his hand.

'Probably a tracer of some kind. Beyond your ken, Alex.'

'Excuse me,' asked Constance. 'Do I take it that we are being fired upon?'

'Yes.' Benny grinned at her over her shoulder. 'Sorry. Happens to me every other week.'

'What an exciting life you must lead.'

'I have considered learning to type. All right, Alex, let me go first. Constance, when I say go, run as fast as your bloomers will carry you.'

Alexander opened the door and Benny hopped through it, glancing quickly left and right, the pistol up to her cheek. The little cobbled backstreet ended in a rough track that ran along the edge of a field. Big hedge, luckily. Behind it, she could see the glint of metal.

A purple sphere rocketed from the field and burst through an upper window of the museum with a tremendous flammable thump.

'Go!' Benny called. 'Quietly!'

Alexander and Constance ran with her to the hedge, and, crouching, they raced up the muddy track.

Benny had that familiar sick feeling in her stomach again, imagining bullets snickering through the hedge and slicing them up. She really hated combat, hated the people who did this for a living and got close to enjoying it.

Well, there were exceptions, of course.

She'd been too cold with Alexander. Despite, no because, he was in the same boat as her. Except he'd only lost a friend.

They ran flat out for a hundred yards, hedge to the left, backyard walls to the right, and broke out, thankfully, into a small copse at the edge of the woodlands. A chalky path wound upwards into the hills, and they followed it for a while, finally collapsing behind an uprooted tree trunk. Through the trees down-slope, a tiny length of fence was visible. In the field beyond it, strange figures were attending a silver cylinder. 'Another two of them,' Benny muttered. 'I wonder who they are?'

'You mean you don't know?' Alexander glanced behind them and forced a smile. 'I say, look, we're not alone on the barricades. It's Mrs Redfern's cat. Wolsey, isn't it?'

Wolsey was staring at the three humans from behind a tree. He had something in his mouth. Constance looked at him nervously. 'Do shoo it away,' she said. 'I can't stand cats. Now, Bernice, shall we find this object of yours, now we are free? Who is it that has it? Some friend who is keeping it safely?'

Benny sighed. 'I haven't been clear about what I've got you into, have I? I thought that the two who attacked me had got hold of it. I was planning to nick it back off them. Unless the ones with the cannon are a different bunch, then they still must think that I've got it.'

'What is that in your mouth?' Alexander asked, holding out a hand to the cat. Wolsey stepped forward, watching Constance as he came. He dropped the thing in his jaws as he rubbed his head along Alexander's hand.

Alexander picked the muddied scrap up. 'Bit of lace collar.' He glanced up at Constance. 'Just like yours.'

'Goodness, so it is!' Constance turned to look, slipped the pistol from her pocket, pointed it at Wolsey and fired.

The shot just missed, and the cat leapt away, bounding off into the forest.

Benny jumped to her feet, but Constance jumped with her, shoving the revolver into her neck. 'Damned cats,' she muttered. Then she whistled.

From higher up the slope, two armed figures appeared, running quickly downhill and covering Benny and Alexander with their weapons.

'Allow me to introduce August and Hoff,' the being that had been Constance told the others.

'You're—' Benny shook her head in frustration. 'I should have realised.'

'Not at all,' said Greeneye. 'I thought we were getting on rather well. Resolving as a dew and all that. Tell me, do you prefer me as a man or a woman?'

'Do you do amphibians?'

Alexander looked between the three aliens. 'If this is a disguise, what have you done with the real Constance?'

'Stew,' August told him. He clapped Greeneye on the shoulder and took the revolver off him while Hoff disarmed Bernice. 'Now, since it seems that neither of us have the prize we're after, I think you ought to come back to our base with us and have a little chat, don't you?'

7

FRIENDS
AND OTHER LOVERS

Rocastle stood in the middle of the rear playing field, his back straight, his chest proudly inflated, his swagger stick tucked under his arm. He wore his old uniform, the one he'd worn in the Transvaal, his campaign medal ribbons on the breast.

The boys stood before him in a square, at attention. Hutchinson, Merryweather and the other Captains stood at the front, their OTC uniforms neatly pressed and clean. The outfits were a light tan. Nobody would mistake them for the real thing, but they did give the lads a soldierly air. 'All present and correct, Captain Merryweather?' he asked.

'One absentee, sir. Dean, sir.'

'Does anybody have a reason for Dean's absence?'

Inwardly, Anand flinched, but he kept his gaze straight forward, not saying a word. When the house had woken that morning, there had been no sign of Tim. He suspected that he'd run away, which was jolly well the right thing to do in the circumstances. If it wasn't so far, he'd have gone, too. He had written to his father explaining the circumstances of his misery last night, and expected him to arrive next week to take him away.

After a moment's silence, Phipps blurted out, 'He's still ill, sir!'

'Very well, then. He's going to miss out on having a go at the Vickers gun then, isn't he?' Rocastle was pleased at the smiles of

121

anticipation from the boys. 'The Regiment has kindly lent us one such weapon for the next month. Now, stand by for inspection.'

Rocastle slowly walked along the rows, noting an undone button here and an unpolished rifle there. This was the part he enjoyed most.

Timothy had spent most of the night in the tree in the orchard, the one he'd been sitting under when he'd got the Pod. He thought he knew why that had happened, now, because he'd actually been up this particular tree quite a few times before, tapping the wood with his fingers, getting a rhythm going, trying to be a ragtime drummer. The tree knew who he was, and had trusted him with what it contained. Or at least, that was what the Pod said. Since he'd died and come back to life, Tim had been even more certain that his prize talked to him, told him things. Told him he could do things.

It was with him while he sat in the crown of the tree that night. As the hours went by, he watched snails unfold and struggle across the grass and bats flicker through the trees. He heard the distant rustle of badgers in the darkness and the sharp cries of foxes mating.

He wasn't cold. The burns on his neck had healed and vanished. As well as watching the world around him, he was watching himself and trying to understand all he was. He kept looking at his hands, marvelling at what complex things they were, how much time was inscribed on them. Every now and then, he felt a burning desire to find a mirror and see his face. He knew that it was the same, but he also knew that it would seem different.

He wasn't just here in the tree, either. He was wandering over the fields and watching the others in their beds, walking down the aisle between them. He was a baby lying in the arms of a woman who was the nearest thing he had to a mother, with stubby limbs that he could barely move. He was a slender enchanted sword, he was the rain in the air, the light of the stars, a word on a page in a book that he also was.

He found himself speaking words that he had both read and invented: 'I lived as a warrior before I was a man of letters. I wandered, I encircled, I slept in a hundred islands, I dwelt in a hundred forts.'

The words seemed good to him. Definitive. He put his hands to his chest and felt the beat of his hearts.

'Timothy Twice Born. Timothy Two Heart. Dead and then recovered.'

He had stepped down from the tree towards dawn, shaking the dew off of his shoulders.

There was a whole world to explore.

'Charge!' bellowed Rocastle, and the boys set off across the field, bayonets fixed on the end of their (fortunately unloaded, because at least five of them were squeezing the trigger as they ran) rifles.

They impacted the stuffed sack targets, each tied into the shape of a man. Most of them carried through very well. A few made a cursory stab then ran off again, and a few got carried away, attacking the stuffing again and again. That wouldn't do in battle. While that was going on, another man would be on them.

Alton, for some reason, had spun his rifle and slashed his target across the head. Remarkably agile, but still not quite the thing. He'd have to take him down a peg for that.

He took a moment to glance at his watch. Where had Smith got to? The man had made a promise to be here. Do his standing in the eyes of the boys a power of good.

'And halt!' he shouted. 'Now then, let's see what we can do with that Vickers gun, shall we?'

Smith and Joan were lying back in the sunshine, elbow to elbow, looking into each other's eyes.

'I have to ask you,' said Smith, 'about Rocastle. You said there was some other problem with him. What was it?'

'Oh, nothing terrible. He only asked me to marry him.'

'What?'

'Yes, early in our acquaintance, he thought that he would take the burden of widowhood from my shoulders. I told him that it was a very charitable thought, but that I could never love another.'

'Do you still feel the same way?'

'Of course.'

'Oh…'

Joan looked at him seriously for a moment. Then she burst out laughing. 'Your face!'

Smith's frown left him and he returned a nervous smile. 'So you were lying to Rocastle?'

'Of course. He's hardly love's young dream, is he? And I had to let him down very gently, because he could have declared that it was too embarrassing for both of us and sacked me on the spot. As it turned out, he became very noble and left with a terribly brave and tragic look on his face. You could have cut butter with his chin. He turned at the door and told me that he thought my love for a departed hero was quite admirable, and that he would gladly sacrifice his own happiness for it. I do believe the man is looking to sacrifice himself for something continuously. I had to stuff a handkerchief in my mouth to stop myself giggling until he was out of earshot.'

Smith had been staring at her. 'You're brave.'

'They say that about people who are dying. Like them, I do not see that I've ever had any choice to make.'

Smith folded her into his arms and kissed her.

A shadow fell over them. Joan opened her eyes, then suddenly jerked away from Smith, frantically brushing down her blouse. Smith looked up.

Timothy was standing there, smiling down at them.

'Ah, Timothy, we were just –' Smith looked at Joan, who was

looking away, quickly munching at a sandwich again – 'having a picnic…' he finished weakly.

'I saw you here. I wanted to ask you something,' said the dishevelled boy. 'They're learning how to be soldiers, back at the school.'

'Shouldn't you be there?' Joan asked, relieved that the boy seemed not to have noticed the kiss.

Timothy sat down, his legs crossed, on the edge of the rug. 'That's what I wanted to ask about. I wanted to ask, don't most soldiers get killed? Especially when there are machine guns involved? Isn't this a bad thing to teach them, in that case?' His blue eyes stared at Smith, who fumbled with his tie awkwardly.

'Questions like that, they're too big for us…' he muttered.

'You see, my father said I would be a soldier, but I think that means I shall die. Or worse, that I shall kill other people. I don't want to do it. What should I do?'

'There's a passage in *Henry V* that I could recommend. It's not a sin to kill people if your sovereign's ordered you to do it, because the decisions of war are between him and God. It's not your fault if you're obeying orders.'

'So the murders are his fault?'

'Well, in war it's not exactly murder. There are bigger things involved. King and country, duty to your fellows. That sort of thing.' Smith glanced at Joan, only to find that she was looking at the sheep in the next field, ignoring him. 'Perhaps you could ask the vicar for some more help?'

'Perhaps,' sighed Timothy. 'I think I know what he'll say, though. He'll say I have to be a soldier.'

'Well, that's not true, is it?' Joan interrupted, her voice sharp. 'There are lots of things you could do. You don't have to be a soldier.'

'I don't have to be a soldier.' Tim rose to his feet, nodding. 'Good. Thank you.' He turned and wandered off again, vanishing back into the forest. Smith stared after him, impotently raising a hand with a half-formed intention of telling him to go back to school. Finally, he turned back to Joan. She was still avoiding his gaze. 'That might have been the wrong thing to say.'

'Oh, might it?' There came a distant rumble. Then another, a moment later. 'That sounds like thunder. Perhaps we should pack up and go, Dr Smith.'

'There aren't any clouds. Perhaps it's Rocastle playing soldiers.'

'Playing soldiers?' Joan hadn't yet made any move to begin packing. 'Well, that is a fine turn of phrase from somebody who seems so fond of the military. Or perhaps you have one word for me and another for the rest of the world?'

'What? No…' Smith bit his lip in frustration. 'What else could I tell him?'

'The truth? That being a soldier is all about being killed and being afraid of being killed? It seems that you and Arthur share some of the same illusions.'

'No! I mean –' Smith knelt up, gesturing frantically. 'I don't know anything about the army. I learnt all this from other people. I wouldn't know what to do with a gun. I used to lose every fight in the playground. There was a boy with an early beard, and you know how bad they are. He used to put me in a headlock and upset my experiments. But Tim's in my class. When he asks his teacher a question, he has to tell him something or… or the world breaks down; the art and the science and the society have no meaning.' He gazed around him, as if seeing the countryside for the first time. 'We'd be so alone, without the thoughts of past people. Making the world. Making this place for us to inhabit. We'd be… meaningless.'

Suddenly he stood up, turning away from Joan. He clutched his wounded fist with his other hand and stared at it. 'No. That's wrong,' he whispered. 'Those aren't my lines. What am I missing?'

'John?' Joan had got to her feet also. 'John, please don't be so upset. Are you all right?'

Smith stared at her, clutching his hand as if it were the last plank of the ship he'd been wrecked with. 'If you said "fly", I'd grow wings.'

'I know. I'm sorry. Would you have me change my ideals?'

'No.' Smith let his hand drop to his side. Whatever he'd been trying to remember, it had been swept away. 'I'd rather I changed mine.'

Benny and Alexander were being manacled by the wrists to a pair of upright metal sheets in the aliens' dome. The metal was stained with old blood and showed the signs of heat and hard impacts. Benny took the chance to look around the dome. A central woven green mat, presumably where these people slept, lay in front of a metal frame covered by a sheet. Bags of equipment and ordnance lay scattered about on the leafy soil floor and sensor equipment stood around everywhere. The dome itself was obviously some kind of a field; there must be a generator somewhere. The place had an offhand aura of violence and the smell of a slaughterhouse.

'You can ask me to talk if you like,' she told the occupants. 'It's one of my things. The trouble is, as you've fortunately discovered, I won't be able to tell you anything useful.'

'Yes, I'm aware of that,' August told her. 'You thought we had the Pod, we thought you had it. Since Dr Smith doesn't seem to have it either, what we've got to find out is: who has got it?'

'Beats me. Don't take that as a hint. Who are you lot, anyway? Why do you want the Pod?'

'Typical Interventionist training.' Greeneye stepped out from behind a screen, back in his normal form again. Aphasia, similarly transformed, followed him. 'We tie you up, you get us to explain the plot.'

'Well,' Benny glanced at her boots, 'I haven't been trained by anybody, as I have to remind myself at intervals, and I had in mind a sort of a deal. I rather like it here. The Doctor's fallen in love and is blissfully happy. I don't call all that a fate worse than death, to be honest. If you can find this bloody Pod, you're welcome to it. I'll even help you find it. But I do like to know who I'm dealing with.'

'Now she's pretending to side with us!' laughed Greeneye. 'This is classic!'

'Yes, but I think we should observe the formalities.' August indicated the others. 'We are Aubertides, Professor Summerfield, from the planet Aubis. We're shape-changers, as you may have gathered. We can eat anything organic and can duplicate the appearance of anything that we take in that has its genetic material reasonably intact. If we have so much as one complete cell, we can take on the memory of what we eat, also.'

'Wonderful, isn't it?' Greeneye took a pinch of Bernice's hair in his fingers and sniffed it. 'We are what we eat, as I'm sure you were about to observe. Haven't you ever looked in the mirror and wished to be different: thinner, stronger, more beautiful? Or met somebody and wanted to be whatever they needed, old or young, man or woman?'

Benny looked at him cheerfully. 'Sounds like hard work. I wouldn't change one lovely inch of me.' She glanced at the strand of hair in his fingers. 'You know, if you eat that, you'll have terrible trouble with split ends.'

Greeneye let go.

Benny glanced at Alexander standing beside her. He had a solid look of anger about his face, his gaze fixed ahead, as if he were waiting for a chance to express his rage. It might not be a good time to ask this next question, but she wanted to know.

'Did I ever meet the real Constance?'

Greeneye concentrated, then nodded. 'Yes. In the tea-shop, that was her.' He licked his lips. 'She was delicious.'

'You bastard!' shouted Alexander suddenly, his face reddening.

'Hardly,' said Greeneye. 'August's my father.'

'Father to all of them, actually,' August explained, clicking a button on the wall. Alexander opened his mouth to shout again and found that he couldn't. 'Aubertides bud. I produced Greeneye from a pouch that had grown on my back. He then gave birth to one of our family who didn't come with us, who in turn produced Serif. Serif produced Aphasia—'

'With certain... improvisations of my own,' whispered Serif.

'And Aphasia produced Hoff, the baby of the family. That was a difficult birth, I can tell you.'

'It was yucky!' Aphasia spat.

'Now, normally, that would be it for an Aubertide. The genetic material gets drawn too thin, and six family members is all you get. The Grand Circle on Aubis was made up of thirty-six members, for example, six complete families. That's not really enough for us, which is why we're here. We've devoted our lives to the pursuit of power and pleasure...'

'Thrown off of Aubis, conquered six solar systems in the local area using biological weapons, used the proceeds of their economies to fuel new weapons research and conquered several more,' Greeneye explained, as if reeling off an old story. 'The trouble is, a sort of lethargy sets in.'

'We have no political or sociological goals beyond our own pleasure,' Serif hissed. 'Which means that we swiftly reached a point where we had no goals left at all. There are only six of us. We have already returned to Aubis to conquer it and slaughter our former tormentors. It does not take a dozen planets to serve our greatest desires – even Greeneye's perverted sexual appetites.'

'Oh yes?' Benny raised an eyebrow.

'I have... an attraction to other species,' Greeneye told her.

'So I noticed. I suppose budding must get boring. Especially when you can't do it any more.'

'Well, that's just the point,' said August. 'We encountered a Time Lord on the planet Apertsu, which we were contemplating as our next acquisition. The Apertsians are a race of flying rodents, and he was acting as a security consultant for them, setting up various defence barriers which would have presented us with considerable problems. Now, you hear a lot of rubbish about the Capitol not interfering in the affairs of other races, and at the time we were rather surprised to see him there, but it seems they do this sort of thing quite often when they feel that they might eventually come under threat. They're quite keen on interbreeding the humanoid races, for one thing, directing genetic drift by introducing genetic material from one biosystem into another. One surmises that they're looking for a way to ease their periodic infertility.'

'We kidnapped this Time Lord,' Serif hissed, 'intending to see if I, who have gained mastery over the depths of the mind, could pry any of the secrets of regeneration from him. I could not. His consciousness was as labyrinthine as any of the barriers he planned to set. So we took a biological sample and consumed it between us, intending to take on the ability to regenerate genetically. Nothing happened save a fever that nearly killed us. While we were in this weakened state, our subject was able to escape and return to his TARDIS. Moments later, we were time-looped.'

'It was horrible!' Aphasia added. 'Like being on a roundabout all the time!'

'He must have returned to the Citadel and convinced the Interventionists to take us on,' August continued. 'We were only saved by Greeneye's intuition that you could outrun a time loop by completing the action spiral faster and faster. Time Loops are creatures, after all, and any creature can be fooled. We fled the planet as quickly as we could, but the whole adventure had given us a new aim in life, a plan that would provide us with ambition and future purpose. We want to take on the attributes of a Time Lord, the ability to regenerate included. As our research proved, our genetic matrices are similar enough to theirs so that each of the thirteen incarnations of an Aubertide Time Lord would be able to bud, and each newly budded descendant would be able to regenerate twelve times itself and have a child each time. So an individual Aubertide would be able to have thirteen children, and each of those thirteen, also.'

'You should be careful,' Benny mused. 'You're trying to reinvent the Grandparent. Christmas will never be the same again.'

'We're extending our family to the size of an army. With Serif 's skills at influencing a child as it develops in its parent, we'll be able to create individuals suited to particular tasks. The Aubertides, once ignored as a race, will become a major force in galactic affairs.'

Greeneye saw the piteous look on Bernice's face and shrugged. 'Don't knock it, it's something to do.'

'So,' Serif continued, 'we set up one of our family as a body-smith. He turned out to have a natural affinity for the job, restructuring the bodies of the rich to suit their desires.'

'It was nearly as lucrative as looting and enslaving,' Hoff muttered.

Serif continued the story. 'We let it be known that he was in a position to give a Time Lord whatever form or mind they wanted. That's a particular dream of Gallifreyans, as I knew from wandering through that young Interventionist's mind. They regenerate and find themselves to be much the same, and every now and then they dream how wonderful it would be to be able to fly or be of the opposite sex or have a child. That last is a very common dream, for children on Gallifrey are very rare.'

August twirled on his heel. He seemed to be enjoying telling the tale. 'We sent out a call along the subtler back streets of electronic dispatch, the frequencies listened to by Interventionists and assassins. After months of waiting, stuck on one planet while... our brother... went about his work, finally the call came. It was your friend the Doctor, with a great sadness about his shoulders. He wanted to be human, had even written a fictional human memory print for himself. Now, this was ideal for our purposes. Had a Time Lord arrived wanting wings, we would have attached our Biodatapod to his forehead, and he would have found himself with said appendages, but without the genetic information that made him a Time Lord. That would be contained, carefully edited and programmed, and then made ready for our use, by the most complex nanite processors ever designed, in the Pod. He'd be rather surprised by that, so a degree of force would have been necessary, particularly if he was on a mission from the Capitol.'

Greeneye nodded. 'Interventionists have several backups. We were ready, when we thought up this plan, to fight our way to the vortexgate, ready for the double-cross. Since the Pod takes days to make the genetic information usable by an Aubertide, we thought we'd have to run somewhere quickly with it.

'We didn't have to go through all that, thanks to the Doctor,' said August. 'His offer seemed so perfect that we spent days checking the incoming path of his TARDIS, watching for others around it, scanning the market area for other Gallifreyans. But there were none. We thought he would take the Pod off to a primitive civilisation, forget he was a Time Lord and probably just leave it lying around somewhere for us to pick up. There was no need for any large-scale action of the kind that those with Time-Space Visualisers tend to notice, no need for any violence at all. Of course we said yes, and he arrived several days later. Everything was going as planned until—'

'You arrived here and couldn't find the Pod anywhere.'

'Precisely. It's not in his house, it's not in his clothes or baggage. We've even searched the schoolroom where he teaches. Tell me, why did you think we had it?'

Benny shrugged. 'Because it's gone from the place where I was told to hide it.'

'A tree?' Serif asked.

'As a matter of fact, yes.'

'Yes, that's clever of him. Time Lord biodata can hang on to organic matter quite invisibly, though the data can start to affect the host form.'

'Good thought.' August clicked his fingers in Hoff's direction. 'Scan for any unusual vegetation in the area. Now, Professor Summerfield, do you have any other ideas as to who might have taken the Pod?'

'Not one. As you know, I'm as in the dark as you are. Which is great, incidentally, because you've got absolutely no reason to torture me.'

'Very true,' August agreed. 'We'll kill you both quite humanely before we eat you. Oh, and, Greeneye, do you want to—'

Greeneye nodded.

'It seems he does. So that's something to look forward to at least.'

Benny kept her tone level. 'I thought we had an agreement.'

'You have absolutely nothing to bargain with.' August gestured to his family. 'All right, we'll do a sweep for unusual bioactivity right across the area.' He glanced at the two captives. 'And be back in time for tea.'

Smith and Joan had finished their picnic and had walked idly with the hamper for a while, crossing from one field to another. Smith suspected that they were both trying to get out of range of the military noises which had been coming from the direction of the school. They largely walked in silence, him glancing at his hand from time to time and wondering if he'd scared her with that sudden outburst.

How odd. The large things inside him shouldn't come bursting out at awkward times like that. He didn't want to scare her. 'I'm not like that,' he said.

'Like what?'

'Like you think I am.'

'And how's that?' At least she was smiling.

133

'I don't know. But I'm not like it. You make me lose the ability to communicate. Like there's sometimes a huge gap between us.'

'I feel the same way, and that is rather frightening. Odd to find that one's sweetheart disagrees with one on something so central.'

'But I don't!' He was about to start on another huge explanation when she put a finger to his lips.

'Hush. I don't know why, but it seems to me that you are just discovering what you think, like a little boy being influenced by great men and heroic stories. That makes me feel like I'm being romanced by a young swain, and I suppose I quite like that, but I do wonder if it's good that you should be such a blank slate. Any other woman, I suspect, would want to feel that she would be the one growing wings if asked to fly.'

'That's not because I'm special. It's because you are.'

'Thank you, sir.' She put her arms round his neck. 'I dislike it when you're very manly, yet I wonder who else but me leads you.'

'Another woman?' He frowned.

'Rocastle. Or some other general.'

'Ah, but he was just as led by you. You're my general's general, so I owe you ultimate allegiance.'

'But is that good?'

He put an unwounded finger under her chin. 'Is that important?' And kissed her again.

She pulled away after a moment. 'Very manly.'

'Too manly?'

'No.'

'Will you marry me?'

Joan froze, staring at him. 'I… Could you give me… a few days to think about it?'

'Of course.'

Joan grinned, looking happy and lost. 'I hate to be so

conventional, but could I have a ring or something? Then if I say yes, you could… see that I've said yes.'

'Oh, yes.' Smith fumbled in his pockets, putting the hamper down on the grass. 'I hadn't anticipated this.'

'You mean you hadn't planned it?'

'No.' He switched pockets, searching in his waistcoat. 'But I mean it. Completely. Utterly. Ah…' He pulled out a ring with a purple jewel set on it. 'A little gaudy. Don't know where I got it. Perhaps I wore it once. Will it do?'

'Yes.' She took the ring and stared into the jewel. 'And I was complaining of you being easily led. Goodness, I can hardly catch my breath.' She grabbed his hand and held the ring up to his finger. 'Wait a moment – this doesn't fit you! Heartbreaker!' She laughed, trying to fit the ring over his finger, much to Smith's discomfort. He started to hop, holding his wounded hand to his head and looking away as if to ignore the pain.

'It was mine, I'm sure. Maybe I changed? Ow!'

They fell into a pile of limbs, Joan's legs tumbling round his very immodestly, and kissed excitedly in such a jumble. Finally, they unwrapped themselves, Joan blushing thoroughly again. 'We're not married yet, John Smith. Do you like blackberry jam?'

'Jam? I don't know. I wonder if I've tried it?'

'Well, I make some every summer, so let us keep our hands to ourselves and see if we can find any early blackberries.' She hopped up and picked up her hat from where it had fallen. Instead of replacing it on her head, she upturned it and headed off for the hedgerow.

Smith followed, his hands in his pockets, whistling a jaunty tune. He bent to pick a poppy and fixed it to his buttonhole.

'That's good!' she called, wandering along the hedge and plucking at the occasional early berry. 'What is it?'

'I'm not sure.' Smith tried to remember the lyrics. 'This old heart of mine… is weak for you… That's the title, but I don't know who sings it.'

'Some harmony group, probably. We must go to London and see one, if we save up, and have a meal in some terribly precious café.'

'Yes.' Smith winced. His hand had contracted again for a moment then, as if something else had jarred. 'I'll just walk to the fence…' He set off up the field, wishing that he could identify what it was that was curling him up inside. Perhaps it would get in the way of his marriage. Marriage! What a leap! How had he done that?

Ahead the field broadened out into a meadow with a few trees. At its end, up a light slope, was a wooden fence. And around the fence wheeled a flock of swallows. That was an odd sight at this time of day, there'd be no big concentration of insects for them to catch. And they were very low.

Something was shimmering in the air, a heat haze on a day too cool for one. It was actually getting closer, too, as he approached it, which was as impossible as walking through a rainbow.

He reached his wounded hand out to touch the phantom.

The shock rushed up his arm and thumped straight into his head.

A cat pinned down on a table, its skull open to show its brain. The folds of its head were pinned back and bloody white, like the skin on a roast chicken.

It was alive.

'Who's going to intervene?' a woman shouted. 'Who can save them now?'

He stepped back in fear and lost the vision. His hand plucked the poppy from his lapel and he sniffed it absently, his mind racing. There was a wall here. A real wall. Walls meant a prison. A prison meant guards. But what did the vision mean?

Joan wandered up to his shoulder, her hat full of blackberries, and he bounced the poppy off her nose, still frowning.

'Tell me,' he said. 'When you first met me, did I have an umbrella?'

8

EVERYTHING CHANGES

Alexander slowly turned his head towards Bernice and coughed experimentally. The noise echoed around the little dome. He opened his mouth and shouted something, but no sound was audible. Finally, he tried a whisper:

'I didn't understand a word of that. Are they Martians?'

'No. We could do with a few Martians right now. They'd sort them out.' Benny closed her eyes, trying to stop the feeling of panic that was welling up in her stomach. If the fear overwhelmed her, she wouldn't be able to think. 'If I could reach to get the laser cutter out of my pocket, we'd also be better off. Alex, can you think of a really clever way to get out of this?'

'Not at all.'

'Because neither can I, and I really don't want to think about what's going to happen when they get back. So what do you want to think about? Women?'

'Women? If I'm about to be killed, loved one, that's the last thing I want to think about. Were you in love with your knight, Bernice?'

'Oh yes. No doubt about it. Full-scale romance. We nearly got there, too. Another few feet, and – oh, sod it!' She started to pull at the manacles, her wrists chafing white against the cuffs. 'I will not die like this! There's so much more to do! Do you hear me, Alex?'

'I hear you, loved one,' Alexander whispered.

Benny strained her hands against the manacles until her thumbs started to dislocate with the force of it. If your life depended on it, couldn't you just ignore the pain and wreck your hands?

She gritted her teeth.

Probably not.

Then the metal sheet thumped her in the back.

She waggled her hands to let the blood flow back into them, and the sheet fell backwards, nearly pulling her off her feet. She pulled forward and took the weight of it on her back. At the base of the sheet was a churned-up clump of soil. Two thin metal spikes that had fixed it into the ground had snapped in half.

'I pulled it out of the soil! I bloody pulled it out!' Benny shouted. 'Quickly, Alex, heave!' She hefted the sheet of metal on to her back, still manacled to it, and stamped around behind Alex to lean all of her weight on the back of his sheet. Together, the weight and his efforts snapped the supports on that one too.

'My God, how do we get out?' Alex stumbled forward, tortoise-like, carrying his sheet as Benny carried hers.

'Which button was it? I think that's it…' Benny stamped up to a piece of machinery and angled the bottom corner of her sheet at it. She swung the metal deftly and the corner hit a button dead centre.

A square opening appeared in the side of the dome.

'Come on!' Benny called. 'Run!'

The two awkward fugitives scrambled out into the forest and jogged away as fast as they could manage doubled up.

'At least we'll be safe if they start shooting at us,' murmured Alexander.

'Now these–' Rocastle held up a smooth, shiny-jacketed bullet pulled from the belt that fed the Vickers gun – 'are for enemy armies. Austrians, we might assume, Serbians or Germans.

These will go right through the body and leave a clean, decent wound or kill instantly, as such noble enemies deserve.'

The boys were clustered around, listening intently as Rocastle sat on a sandbag behind the machine gun, their imaginations racing across landscapes of cavalry charges and courageous squares of men in uniform. He held up another bullet, a square, sharp-edged one. 'This is for tribesmen, rebels and those whose creed is unchristian, thus disallowing them from the basic brotherhood of all professional soldiers.'

'Please, sir.' Merryweather raised his hand. 'Did you use those in Pretoria?'

'Well, ah…' Rocastle stroked his moustache thoughtfully. 'What can I say, Captain Merryweather? Mixture of both. Brother Boer doesn't always behave like a serious soldier. Most of them were farmers with knives between their rotten teeth. Not our decision to make; anyhow, use of weapons is down to the C.O. Anyhow, enough stories. Shall we give it a go?'

'Yes, sir!' chorused the boys.

'All right, then. Phipps, you've seen how to pass the ammo belt. Pay attention, boys, you'll all get a chance to fire her. Stand clear now. Don't get near the cartridge ejection.'

The boys hurried behind the machine gun as Rocastle trained it on a row of straw figures in the middle distance. Phipps got down on one knee and grabbed the belt of ammunition that fed into the side of the gun.

'Is the line of fire clear?' asked Rocastle ritually.

'Yes, sir!' shouted Phipps.

'Stand by to fire.' Rocastle slipped the safety catch off. 'Fire!'

The noise of the bullets ripped up the air, hot cartridges spinning out of the gun. The boys took a step back, gritting their teeth against the urge to put their hands over their ears or to cry. The targets spat straw everywhere, buffeted as they hung as if they were being torn apart by some invisible monster.

'Sir! Christ, sir!' Phipps shouted. 'Stop!'

'What did you say?' Rocastle bellowed, referring to the blasphemy rather than the sound. Then he saw it himself, and let go of the trigger.

Behind the targets, a dishevelled figure was pushing through the hedge, its school uniform in tatters.

'Tim,' whispered Anand.

The figure wandered up to the targets and touched them gingerly, as if examining them. It turned to look at the group of boys around the machine gun, and grinned at them.

It was wearing poppies in its hair.

Rocastle stood up, the sudden fear he'd felt when his finger was still on the trigger boiling into rage. 'Captain Hutchinson, I am going to my study. Bring that boy to me. The rest of you are dismissed.'

Hutchinson and Merryweather dragged the unresisting Timothy along the polished corridors to Rocastle's study. 'You're a disgrace to the school uniform,' Hutchinson told him, pulling the flowers from his hair. 'You look like a girl.'

'Really?' Timothy asked. 'A pretty one?'

Hutchinson punched him hard in the stomach and left Merryweather to straighten him up as he knocked on Rocastle's door. He waited for an answer, then stepped inside and saluted again. 'Prisoner and escort, sir.'

Rocastle looked up from his desk, resisting a sudden impulse to tell Hutchinson that this wasn't a playground game. No. The boy was following proper form. 'Let the, ah, prisoner, in, Captain. You needn't escort him. Then you're dismissed.'

Hutchinson nodded, led Timothy into the room and left, closing the door behind him.

The boy immediately limped over to Rocastle's bookshelves and started scanning them. He didn't even seem to notice the Head, who had begun writing again to give the boy some sense of scale. After a moment, he realised that he was being ignored back, and something snapped inside him. He leapt to his feet. 'Dean! How dare you ignore me!'

'Sorry.' Timothy raised his hands in a gesture of pacification. 'I thought you were busy, sir. That's an early edition of Darwin on your shelf. I thought you—'

'Never mind the bloody books.' Rocastle matched each hissed syllable with a stride round his desk and made the last one into a slap that sent the boy flying into the corner. 'You could have been killed this afternoon! What were you playing at? What *are* you playing at?'

'I'm not sure, sir,' Tim sighed, staying where he'd fallen. 'I see so many strange things. I think I've grown up.'

Rocastle laughed bitterly and dragged him to his feet. 'Like hell you have! I've heard enough about your illnesses, your cissy ways, and now the flowers in your hair! A fine miss, you are, boy! Now, are you going to pull yourself together and join in with this outfit? Are you?' He shook Timothy harder and harder, until his head swung from side to side sickeningly.

'Don't—'

'That's sir!' Rocastle bellowed, his face red.

Timothy closed his eyes as he was shaken, drew in a breath and stuck out a finger.

The finger caught Rocastle in the centre of the forehead.

He stared at it. Then he crumpled into a heap.

Timothy staggered back, staring down at the body. Then he started to laugh, wiping his mouth on the back of his unbuttoned sleeve. 'You'll die in pain, in ten years, with a tumour on your bowel,' he told the unconscious figure.

Then he turned and ran from the room.

Mr Hodges had been kneeling in the middle of the road, praying, when the army convoy rolled up. An officer had hopped out of the first of the dusty green vans, introduced himself as Major Wrightson and asked what the trouble was. Hodges told him

141

that he'd had a vision up ahead and been called upon to change his ways. He asked the major to leave him alone, and, with a nod and shrug to his comrades back in the van, the soldier did so.

They drove around him, with great care, and picked up speed as they returned to the centre of the road.

That was when the first van compacted, its front flattening like it had hit a wall. The cap on the radiator blew upwards in a blast of steam. The other two vans braked before they ran into the back of the first.

Mr Hodges had stood up to watch the soldiers scramble out and stare at what was in their way: nothing. The front of the crashed van was rapidly rusting, a thin red layer rising to smudge the air around its bonnet. To Hodges, it made the soldiers look like they were just figures in a painting, staring at a puff of paint that had fallen across the canvas. A smell of passing thunderstorms suddenly filled the air, but this was a clear spring morning.

Some of the men, those who lived through the next few months, claimed that they'd smelt something sulphurous in that suspended red cloud, but the recollections everybody had of the spring of 1914 were full of portents after the fact.

The major had clambered out of the cab and started shouting at his driver to back up. He probed the red cloud with his baton. With a sudden crash, the whole front end of the van gave way and the cloud grew heavier. It was following a gently upward slope, describing the perimeter of something invisible that the major measured by walking along it, slapping the air with the baton.

The air made a fearful series of echoes.

One soldier had opened his eyes full wide then, and ran to a bush to be sick. His fellows calmed him, and he told them later how the noises had reminded him of something big and terrible, like being buried under a pile of metal and hearing faint voices, the language of which you don't understand. They all felt lonely at the echoes, even Wrightson. He was an Eights enthusiast, and the clash of his stick on the air only made him wonder why he was here, why he wasn't scudding across some bright, flat lake in the sunshine. The echo was like being lost at sea, a little shape rolling in waves that reared like mountains alongside you.

'That's the voice of God, that chime,' Hodges had sighed, his gnarled old face beaming in the first real rays of the morning sun. 'He's coming back today.'

'You may well be right.' The major watched as what had been the bonnet of his van dissolved into an oxidising cloud. He turned to the man in charge of the following truck. 'Gas masks!'

The soldiers ran back into the trucks, emerging a moment later wearing the grotesque masks with their dangling filters. The major spent a few moments trying to persuade Hodges to wear one too, to no avail. 'All right. Stanley, Torrence, with me. Let's see how far we can get through this thing.'

Two soldiers shouldered arms and ran to Wrightson's side. They walked up to the barrier, hands outstretched, and touched the smooth surface of the air. 'Wonderful,' Wrightson breathed. He'd been chosen for this job because he'd been part of the only unit in Britain to have been training under gas conditions. If this was the war he could look forward to… well, it was different, anyway. 'Try and push through it,' he ordered. The three men advanced, heaving against the barrier, their palms feeling the slight warmth of it.

'Sir!' called Stanley. 'Look!'

A soldier was running towards them on the other side of the barrier, waving his arms urgently. 'Ah, good, now we'll get some answers,' muttered Wrightson. 'Hey there, who are you with—' The thought died in his mouth as he recognised the Royal Artillery shoulder flash. Somebody from his own regiment in fact…

'Oh my God,' Stanley whispered.

The man on the other side of the barrier was Stanley too.

'Don't touch it!' he was shouting. 'Don't—'

The Stanley on this side of the barrier thought of himself for a moment, and then he was the dome, stretched across the countryside in an arc, and glad to be everywhere the dome touched at once. He resolved himself into being a hundred yards down the road, and saw his former self, that silly old thing, trudging up to the barrier. He ran forward, shouting for him not to touch it.

Torrence, who was a lot less of a churchgoer than Stanley, found that he'd lived in the past and would live in the future. He saw the view from the longhall in Dublin and felt the bones of a roe deer between his teeth as the sun rose over Ethiopian plains. He saw Torrence continued, his name and his cell memory, across generations. He saw that he would have children and that they would prosper. And here he was, as yet unmarried.

He fell from the barrier, his mind blinking off like a speck of static, dead.

Wrightson flashed upwards through the atmosphere, yelling as he encompassed the globe of the Earth inside his body.

Suddenly he stopped. Great stellar teeth flashed at him. 'Is it time?' enquired a surprisingly soft voice from a bright star that flashed past. He was left stumbling in its trail.

'I don't know. Is it?'

Whatever was associated with the object turned, and Wrightson caught a look of agonised imprisonment from it… from her. And then she was gone.

Earth returned like a knot in his stomach. He took his palms off the barrier, and looked down to see Torrence lying there. He would have done something, but Stanley was running towards the barrier again.

This time he wasn't alone.

A young man was holding his hand.

The soldier and the boy ran right through the barrier. Stanley collapsed into Wrightson's arms.

Timothy looked around at the soldiers. 'More of you? Well, don't do anything rash.'

'Now, wait a moment,' Wrightson began, 'what—'

'Actually,' Tim interrupted him, 'don't do anything at all. Especially to this wall, whatever it is.' With a grin of accomplishment, he turned on his heel and ran back through it.

The soldiers watched him go. Wrightson got a stretcher party together for the unfortunate Torrence.

'Sir,' said Stanley, grabbing his superior by the forearms, 'did you see it? Is it the Lord, sir?'

'If it is,' Wrightson spoke loudly, so his men could hear, 'then he's got the Artillery here to guard him. We'll form a perimeter round this thing, one man every hundred yards. Keep an eye on your neighbour, don't touch the wall. Meanwhile, I'll try to get a wire through to HQ.' He lowered his voice again and disengaged from Stanley's grip, patting the man gently on the shoulder.

They shared a long release of breath. 'In short,' muttered the major, 'holy flaming cow.'

Benny and Alexander ran through the forest, carrying the big metal sheets on their backs.

'How far is it to this blacksmith of yours?' Benny panted.

'It's over the hill.'

'So am I. This is the sort of thing they tried to make me do when I was in military training.'

'You were going to be a soldier? Do they let ladies do that in the future?'

Benny was about to reply with something apt, but then she saw a figure standing behind the trees in front of them and a surge of fear swept through her. 'Alex, look!'

As Alexander swung his burden to see, the lithe figure broke from cover. It was a schoolboy, Benny was relieved to see, albeit a very messy one. He stood watching them for a moment.

Benny noticed that he was holding something. Was that a

cricket ball? Then she realised. Just as Timothy turned and ran.

'Wait, stop!' Benny yelled. 'He's got the bloody Pod!'

She tried to run after him, but fell, halfway up the slope that Timothy had scrambled away up. Alexander hobbled over, and with much effort, got her back to her feet again.

'We, loved one, are in no position to take part in a chase.'

'I know, damn it,' Benny sighed. 'But unlike everybody else, we now know who's got what we're looking for.'

Nathan Bottomley was a blacksmith, farrier and metalworker. He was known to everybody in Farringham from those occasions when he'd come into a house and bash the boiler with a spanner, listen to the chime and then mutter: 'No, that's absolutely ridiculous. You were hoping for hot water at Christmas?'

He was currently attending to the first of a pair of new shoes for the old Lucas mare, hammering the red-hot metal against his anvil, holding it in the clamp. An edition of *Sons and Lovers* was propped open by a metal doorstop beside him. He had opened up the big doors to his workshop by the stream to let the cool breezes in, but it wasn't as satisfying a day as he had expected. It wanted to storm, but couldn't. A bit of rain would be a relief.

'Nathan!'

Bottomley looked up at the urgent call and saw a bizarre sight trudging into his yard. Alexander Shuttleworth and a girl in trousers, with dirty great sheets of metal on their backs.

'Nathan…' Alexander leaned heavily on the wheel of a threshing machine that was in for repair. 'Help…'

Hoff looked up at the sky and shook his head. 'That dome's doing bad stuff with time.'

The aliens had taken up a place in a cluster of trees above the town and were training a variety of scanning devices on the valley below.

'Oh?' August looked up for a moment. 'I thought you had the

technology sorted out?'

'I thought so too.' Hoff shook his head again, and was silent.

'This is a complete waste of time.' Greeneye was pacing back and forth, twirling the dials on his particular scanning unit randomly. 'The Pod isn't showing up as a mutation agent or broadcasting on any electromagnetic wavelength. We'd need to be psychic.'

'That,' hissed Serif, grabbing the scanner off him, 'is one of the things we shall be, if we can find the Pod!'

'Greeneye's just hungry!' Aphasia teased. She didn't have a scanner. She'd just narrowed her eyes and was turning her head in an imperceptibly slow arc.

'She'll still be there when we get back,' said August. 'I just hope that you do your business behind the screen or something.'

'I want to watch!' moaned Aphasia.

'You can.' Greeneye ruffled her hair. 'Tell you what, you can have her pancreas afterwards.'

'I've got the pancreas, I've got the pancreas!' sang the little girl, glancing up at Serif. 'And you haven't, and you haven't…'

Serif raised a dangerous eyebrow and stalked off.

'Got something!' Hoff stabbed a stubby finger on to his scanner unit. 'A source producing rapidly decaying particles in negative time. Way beyond the technology levels here.'

'Could be an effect of the time shield?' August glanced at the figures. 'Except – it's moving! Come on!'

The Aubertides ran downhill towards town, Serif pursuing them with broad strides in an attempt to catch up.

'So, what do we do now?' asked Alexander.

Bernice was gritting her teeth as Bottomley hammered a sharp metal tool into the fastening of her left manacle. 'We find that boy with the Pod, and help out with his, admittedly so far rather successful, plan to hide it. How would he have got hold of the thing, anyway?'

'Well, the orchard where you say you left it is part of the Marcham estate, old Mrs Marcham's place, but it's notoriously ill-tended. She doesn't get out much, and so her staff leave the fruit to rot. It's a huge area, and it snakes right round the forest and the school, with all sorts of secret places. The place is therefore beloved to wasps and boys of Hulton College.'

'Where Dr Smith works. I see.'

'And, of course, schoolboys love to get hold of mysterious things.'

'So I remember.' Benny triumphantly broke free of the first manacle and waggled her hand to get the blood circulating again. 'Your average fifth former's got his finger in more pies than Mr Kipling.'

The blacksmith glanced between the two manacled figures propped up against his workshop wall. 'I'm astonished. You've met Rudyard Kipling?'

Benny burst out laughing and used her free hand to pat the man on the shoulder. 'No,' she assured him. 'But I know a man who has. Hopefully.'

Bottomley shrugged and continued his work.

Dr Smith had placed a ladder against the wall of the cottage and climbed up it, while Joan held it steady. He undid the catch on a hatch in the ceiling and opened it, then climbed up into the loft. A moment later he called: 'Come up here and see!'

Joan gingerly climbed the ladder, and John helped her step out on to the beams of the little loft. He'd lit an oil lamp hanging on a hook, which gave the wooden space a gentle lemon hue. It had started to rain outside, and the sound of raindrops formed a gentle patter on the roof. The gaps between the beams were only plasterboard, so the two lovers took care to step only on the wood. Mouse-eaten cardboard boxes, orange crates and suitcases secured by belts were piled around the cool stone arch of the walls.

Smith squatted, lost his balance, waved his arms and was only saved from falling by Joan putting a hand on his shoulder. 'Thank you,' he said. He started to untie one of the suitcases.

'So what is it about this umbrella that so intrigues you?' Joan asked. 'I thought we might get on with the business of jam.'

'It's just –' Smith opened the first suitcase and began to sort through the items he found there – 'I remember a strange umbrella, but I don't. I know I had one, but I don't remember carrying it… using it… getting it.'

'How strange. I do like this attic of yours, it reminds me of Christmas. A wonderful darkness and light at the same time.' Joan sat on a packing case and looked around primly. 'When I was a girl, we were the first people in our town to have a Christmas tree. My father saw the big one in London that Prince Albert had brought over, and thought that it was a good idea. At first, visitors would comment on how strange it was to have a tree inside the house, but then they all started to have them, so Father felt vindicated.'

'My father wasn't that sort of person.' Smith glared at a pair of juggling balls he'd pulled from the case, threw them up in the air, tangled his arms and missed catching them. 'He was in the Navy, a military man. He went missing.'

'Did you ever discover what had become of him?' Unseen by Smith, Joan had taken the ring he'd given her from the pocket of her cardigan, and was turning it over in her fingers.

'No. Everybody thought that he was a traitor, but I don't think that's true.'

'My goodness. And what about Verity, your former fiancée?'

'Former? Does that mean I have one now?'

'Don't count your chickens.'

'I haven't seen her in years. Except… in a dream. She married a teacher – or was it a soldier?'

'You told me it was a sailor.'

'Did I? Perhaps it was. I'm very confused.'

'You do seem to be a trifle perturbed, today. Why, for instance, did you insist that we walk so swiftly away from the end of the field? I nearly dropped my blackberries, you rushed me so.'

'I just thought there might be a storm. Perhaps it's my finger.' He held up the wounded stump. He'd reached the bottom of the suitcase without success. 'Perhaps this is all my finger. Septic, poisoned. Perhaps I'm losing my mind.'

Joan went to him and kissed the top of his head. 'Not at all. But you have been through a terrible adventure. Perhaps you've been a bit too brave. You haven't even told the Head about it, yet.'

'No, I suppose I haven't. Do you think I should take some time off?'

'Perhaps it would help you to think it through. And on that matter, John, while you are so churned up, should I take it that your proposal was merely speculative? I should be glad to do so and await later confirmation.'

'No!' He grabbed her hand. 'No, I'm uncertain about a lot of things, but that's the one thing I am sure of. It was sudden, I know, but it's certain. It's the thing I'm hanging on to.'

Joan released the breath she'd been holding. 'Well, then I shall take you seriously, and you will have my answer. For now, we shall take a look at that finger, and then perhaps have a cup of cocoa.'

Smith stood up to embrace her. 'I was just thinking of cocoa. You always seem to say just the right thing.'

Alexander and Benny were making their way through the streets of town, walking quickly and keeping a lookout for the boy they'd seen. It was good to be free of their metal burden. There was a general sense of tension about the place this Saturday teatime. People were out on their steps, looking at watches and talking to each other excitedly over fences. In the market square, the stallholders were packing up, but one or two of the carts seemed to have returned, and their occupants were conducting hand-waving arguments with those that remained. The gentle rain, the first onset of the storm that was approaching, was making the pavements glisten.

They passed the town telephone box, an ornate red construction with a tiny pagoda-like point on top. A man in a neat tweed suit and bowler was stepping out of it and locking it behind him.

'I say, Horace!' Alexander ran over to him. 'What's going on?'

'Line's down,' explained Horace, whose job it was to sit in the box, make the connection for whoever wanted to make a call, and then stand outside waiting for them to complete it. 'If you want to call anyone, you could ask at the school. At least I get to go home early.'

From somewhere in the distance, there came the crack and boom of an explosion. Horace pricked his ears up. 'Hey-ho, the boiler's blown on the engine!'

'Couldn't it be the OTC at the school again?' Alexander asked.

'No, my old man used to be the fireman on a train. That's the sound of an engine going up. Hope no poor soul was caught in that. See you at the meeting, eh, Alexander?'

'Damn,' whispered Benny when he'd gone. 'You could cut the atmosphere here with a knife.' People were gathering in groups looking to the east, where a plume of smoke was drifting from the direction of the branch line. 'What's this meeting he was talking about, anyway?'

'Oh, the Labour group meets on a Saturday night in the town hall. I'm normally there.'

'Well, if you want to go…'

Alexander sighed and took her by the arm as an old matron passed, flashing the woman a dangerous grin as she glanced disapprovingly at such closeness, such trousers, such a haircut. 'Richard's addressing them.'

'Oh. Sorry.'

151

'Think nothing of it, loved one. Now, shall we go back to school?'

Rocastle sat stock still in his armchair, his hands gripping the antimacassars. He'd hauled himself into the chair after he'd passed out... and of course the child had run away. Couldn't have been long unconscious or the boy would have fetched somebody. Or perhaps he'd been too scared to call anyone.

Rocastle had, after all, slapped him across the face.

His father had never done that to him. He'd put him across his knee and thrashed him with his belt often enough, but he'd never delivered something so direct, so tawdry.

And of course you could never tell a boy you were sorry, that you'd only been frightened of gunning him down. He'd wanted to express somehow that the boy's wildness and difference were almost an invitation to others to do that, that the way to get by was to square your back and join the line. Strong youngster like Dean should have been with the others, behind the gun, not in the line of bloody fire. A better teacher, a better leader, could have told him that, could have impressed it upon him. You make a move out of line, boy, and they gun you down.

And then he'd collapsed. He'd done that when he was at the opera once, with dear Cordelia. They'd been laughing as they walked down the steps outside, and the next thing he'd been rolling, down into the gutter under the full moon. A dozen bright young lads had run to him and got him to sit up, and he'd shied them away, scared to the point of tears by the sudden pain in his abdomen.

That had gone after a few days. He'd got the first symptom on Cordelia's behalf, he'd joked, because she told him she was pregnant that next week. Maybe she had thought she should tell him then, in case he didn't make it. How ironic. He hadn't even seen her body, despite bellowing at the intern that he'd seen men dead three-deep on the Spion Kop, that a woman and a baby

152

were the only two dead he'd ever wanted to see.

He should retire. He should –

His teeth set hard together.

What would be left to do then that was hard enough? If he was still a military soul, he'd be like some bloody German, finding insult in his fellow officers all the time, and demanding duels, just so –

There came a knock at the door.

He opened his mouth, and found that all that was going to come out was an almighty sob.

He slapped himself hard across the cheek.

The pain made him sit up. He opened his eyes and they were clear. He stood as the knock came again and adjusted his tie in the mirror by his desk. 'Enter!'

The bursar, Mr Moffat, a young Scotsman with curly hair and permanently perplexed eyes, entered. 'Excuse me, Headmaster—'

'Ah, Mr Moffat, I've been meaning to have a word with you about Smith. You're both from north of the border. What do you think of him?'

Moffat thought for a moment, surprised by the question. 'I wasn't aware that he was Scottish. He knows as much about Aberdeen as the average Cockney, and seems to have trouble with his accent. Altogether, it's a pretty poor performance.'

'Hmm. And these stories that I've been hearing from town, that a young teacher's romancing a barmaid?'

'Obviously it isn't me, I lodge in the east-wing apartments. You'd know if I was coming and going.'

'Very good. Was that all?'

Moffat stared at him. 'Headmaster, I only came in because there are two visitors to see you. I couldn't find Miss Robertson. Have you given her the weekend off?'

'Eh? Well, no, I don't know what's become of my secretary since she took the day off to visit her parents yesterday. Another tiny drama. Who are these visitors?'

'A man called Shuttleworth who runs the local museum, and a woman by the name of Summerfield.'

'Shuttleworth… oh my God. All right, give me a moment and then show them in.' He sat behind his desk and found some papers to play with.

A moment later, Alexander and Benny entered.

Benny wasn't feeling very confident. She'd rolled up her trouser bottoms and thrown on a skirt and blouse that Alexander's sister had owned. She thought she looked like a scarecrow. But Rocastle barely gave her a second glance. He rose as Alexander entered and shook his hand warmly. 'Mr Shuttleworth, what can I do for you?'

'Well, it's quite a delicate matter, actually.' Alexander and Benny sat down in the comfortable chairs of the study, and Benny was surprised to find that hers was still warm. She studied Rocastle as he moved, this man who the Doctor – who Smith – feared so much. His face was ruddy, like he'd just gone through some emotional crisis, and, despite trying to look interested in what Alex was saying, his eyes kept straying. Benny followed the direction of his glance to a tiny cameo of a woman on the wall.

'So,' Alexander was saying, 'I found that, after this party of schoolboys had toured the museum, a certain item was missing. A red pottery sphere, used for cooking by the Iceni tribe. I'd left a display case open for cleaning that afternoon, and there were no other customers, so I reluctantly have to conclude…'

'This sphere – valuable, was it?'

'Only to an archaeologist.'

'Right.' Rocastle thumped his big palm down on the table and got to his feet. Benny and Alexander did likewise. 'I cannot have this happening. I shall call an assembly instantly, and, if you would be so good as to come with me, we shall discover the culprit.'

'Well, there's no need to—' Benny began.

'There's every need,' Rocastle replied, rather curtly. 'Can't have my boys' reputation suffering. Come along.' He locked the door of the study behind them as they left, and took a moment to grab a passing first-year, who, after a few quick words, ran off in the direction of the big golden bell that stood on a table in an alcove. He began to ring it with all his strength.

After a minute, bells began to sound from all over the echoing old building. Rocastle stood at a slight distance from his visitors, listening to every one of them like he was following the libretto of a favourite opera.

'I think we've done the worst possible thing for him,' Benny whispered to Alexander. 'We've given him just what he needs.'

Smith was wearing his apron, making salad sandwiches for tea, rattling round the inside of a jar of mayonnaise with a knife to extract the last drop. Joan was inspecting his bookcases in the front room. She'd re-bandaged his finger, which seemed to be healing nicely with no sign of infection, and they'd had two cups of cocoa each.

Smith found himself wishing that he could ask her to stay the night. That was an outrageous thought, of course. Just expressing it as an idle fancy would probably make her drop him altogether and run from the room. If she wasn't already scared off by his oddness. Mental note: stop being so odd. At least in front of her. But he was starting to rely on her. And that business about being a soldier or not... he didn't feel particularly positive about the military, but it was something that happened, and if it did, why get in the way of a fact of life? It was because Joan had lost someone, he decided. She didn't like to think of any of the boys going the same way. But they were boys, and they dreamed of adventure and glory. Good for them.

And what would he have done if she did stay? A sort of vaguely defined soft thing that she knew more about than he did, and that wasn't right, was it? He'd had trouble with kissing Verity.

But if girls didn't do this until they were married, and boys did it before, who did the boys do it with? Mental note: ask the boys.

There came a knock on the door. Smith opened it. There stood a schoolboy. 'Tell me—' began Smith, and then stopped. 'No. What?'

'Please, sir, Mr Rocastle sent me to get you, sir. He's called a general assembly in half an hour.'

'Has he? All right. Off you go. We'll… I'll be there.' The boy ran off again. Smith glanced up. The sky was dark with squalls and approaching storm clouds.

Joan wandered into the kitchen and plucked her cardigan from the back of a chair. 'I heard. The man's insane. Shall I go first and you follow in a minute?'

'No.' Smith removed the apron, opened a cupboard and absent-mindedly dropped an umbrella into the crook of his arm. 'We'll go together.'

Joan smiled. 'All right. I'll be brave if you are.' She saw the umbrella and gasped. 'John! Is that what you were looking for?'

'Hmm?' Smith glanced down at the object he was carrying and bounced it off his elbow with his hand. 'My goodness!' The umbrella had a garish red handle in the shape of a question mark, currently reversed in Smith's grip. Smith spun it round the right way and replaced it on his arm. He gazed at Joan. 'Isn't it strange what you find when you're looking for something else?'

9

THE FINE PURPLE, THE PUREST GOLD, THE RED OF THE SACRED HEART, THE GREY OF A GHOST

A cluster of teachers, most of them trying not to appear annoyed, had formed in the little corridor outside the Great Hall. Bernice and Alexander stood at the back, watching over the teachers' shoulders as the hall filled with boys. There was an atmosphere of fear and anticipation in the air.

'Do you really think this is going to work?' asked Alexander.

'What, do I think one of them is going to hold up the sphere and say: "Oh, you mean this?" Not really. I thought the headmaster was going to conduct a search or something.' Benny glanced around the wood-panelled corridor and shivered. 'I can see why people have nightmares about going back to school. I went to a place very like this. Mixed, at least, though. This place is all floor polish and testosterone. Oh my God.'

Smith and Joan had arrived at the end of the corridor, Smith carrying a very familiar umbrella, but now dressed in a teacher's cape and mortarboard. He saw Bernice and wandered over. 'Hello. What are you doing here?'

'We're the reason for the assembly.' Bernice considered mentioning why, but decided against it. 'And this is…?'

'Oh, yes… this is my friend, Joan Redfern.'

Benny curtsied to the woman. 'I'm Bernice Summerfield and this is my friend Alex.' She hoped that she hadn't put too much emphasis on the *my*. The woman who stood beside Smith was surprisingly mature. Attractive, in a horsey sort of way. Nothing special, really. If the Doctor had to go and get involved with somebody, then it ought to have been a classic beauty or a great artist or an academic. 'And what do you do, Miss Redfern?'

'Mrs,' Joan told her, icily. 'I'm a teacher here. Did you assume that I was the dinner lady?'

'Not at all. I've heard a lot about you. I meant what subject do you teach?'

'Science. I've heard a lot about you, also. Aren't you the young lady with the trousers?'

'Often. Don't you find these skirts a problem sometimes?'

'Not at all. But then, I've never had call to do anything where they might get in the way.'

There was an awkward silence. Smith suddenly ruffled Benny's hair, grinned and shrugged when Joan looked at him. 'Are you still trying to find your Holy Grail?' he asked. 'The one that'll turn me into a spaceman?'

Benny sighed. 'I'll explain all that to you one day.'

'Well, perhaps you could start now,' said Joan. 'John was quite disturbed by the whole business.'

'What, erm, happened to your finger?' Alexander asked Smith.

'A burglar chopped it off.' Smith waved the bandaged stub about happily.

From the hall, the general sounds of movement suddenly cut off. Rocastle had taken the stage. The teachers began to shuffle on. Smith and Joan nodded to Benny and Alexander and followed them.

'You know what I was saying about fingers, Alex?' Benny murmured. 'Well, I'm willing to bet I know whose pie that one ended up in…'

'What did you think of her?'

'She's fine.'

'Nice?'

'Fine.'

Timothy was walking through the orchard where he'd found the Pod, tossing the thing from hand to hand. He was seeing all sorts of strange things today, like those two people carrying slabs of metal like tortoises. He was starting to think about sleep and warmth. His night on the tree had certainly changed him, but he still wanted somewhere warm to spend the night. Could he go back to the school dormitory? He had nothing to fear but words, after all, and he'd found out how he could deal with that now. This Pod had done it, changed him to the point where he was like Sherlock Holmes and Jack Harkaway rolled into one. But what was he supposed to do now? Fight crime? Explore the world? Were there others like him?

He noticed an owl sitting on a branch, looking balefully down at him. 'What would you do, Mr Owl?'

The owl leapt from the branch in a flutter of wings. Tim spun on his heel and saw a figure crouched behind a tree trunk. Something made a noise like a catapult.

He grabbed the Pod out of the air where he'd thrown it.

A metal spar bounced off the tree behind him and spun back in the direction it had come.

Tim ran, zig-zagging through the trees. Silent blue lightning struck giddily around his heels, sending clods of earth flying.

A roaring figure burst from the bushes and sprinted after Tim, tearing through the branches as the boy kept just ahead.

Tim glanced over his shoulder, and dived into a thicket.

Greeneye had only lost sight of the boy for a moment when he ran into the clearing. He looked around, astonished. No sign of him.

The others were quick behind him. August stared at the scanner in his hand. 'I don't believe this! The emissions have ceased! The Pod knows we're after it, that's the only explanation!'

'He's here,' Greeneye rumbled, looking slowly around the clearing. 'He's hiding.'

Tim stared at his pursuers from behind a pair of apple trees. It was fortunate for him that the estate let the orchard get so overgrown. These were his enemies, then. Something inside him suggested a dizzy idea, to get captured deliberately, but then he saw the curved knife that one of them, a short, bearded man, was slapping against a leather wrist-band, and repressed the urge.

Aphasia released her balloon. 'Hunt,' she told it. 'Kill. Don't eat.'

The balloon rose into the centre of the clearing and hovered, spinning on its axis.

'We are so close,' whispered Serif. 'We cannot lose him now.'

Tim turned and started to walk slowly away, watching over his shoulder as the balloon started to move across the clearing in his direction. The balloon sped up. Tim sped up. It shot through the trees towards him faster than a real balloon could push through the air.

He sprinted.

The family crashed through the trees after him.

Tim ran, heaving breaths into his lungs. That seemed easier than it had been in the past, as if his body was on his side, breathing just as he wanted it to. He kicked his heels and leapt randomly from side to side as he ran, avoiding the silent blue beams that smashed foliage aside past him.

He ran to a fence and hurdled it, feeling the heat as it dissolved under him, disbelieving his luck. He was on the road now, the curving road which led up past the school gates. Without thinking, he turned automatically towards the school. The ground was open here, though; they were going to be able to shoot him.

A horseless carriage puttered around the bend, the occupant squeezing its horn to tell Tim to get out of the way. It was Mr Condon who owned the Lyons tea house, who would often let boys going into town have an extra iced bun if they were well behaved.

Tim leapt up onto the running board of the car, much to Condon's amazement.

'Hey, you nut! What are you up to?' called the moustachioed man.

'Sir, it's a matter of life and death! You must get me away, quickly!'

Condon yanked up a gear and tightened his gloves on the wheel. 'When you say life and death, young man, I take it you do mean that, and not just a late essay or some such?'

'I do, sir.' Tim glanced over the rear seat of the vehicle and saw the roaring man running out on to the road, obscured in a second by the bend. 'I do.'

Greeneye slapped his thigh. 'A…' He searched his memory for the term. 'Car! Come on, let's get after them, we can catch up if we try.'

'Don't trouble yourself,' said August. 'He was wearing a uniform, that of an educational establishment, and I do believe…' He clicked a few buttons on his scanner. 'Yes, the map shows a suitable building nearby. He doesn't know why we're after him. He'll go back there.'

'Good,' hissed Serif. 'If he does not think that he is followed, he will not hide the Pod.'

'He's a little trickster,' muttered Greeneye. 'Don't you think he was moving a bit fast for a human? Don't you think—'

'He came from a school,' Hoff interrupted. He smiled at Greeneye again. 'Not a cattery.'

*

'I have a very serious matter to report,' Rocastle began. He was standing on the stage, his hands gripping the edges of a wooden lectern. Behind him stood the teachers, listening in a line. At the side of the stage stood Benny and Alexander, looking nervously at the audience of boys. 'This lady and gentleman are in charge of the museum in town. They tell me that a theft has occurred, and it seems that it can only be a Hulton College boy who is responsible. The article stolen is of no value, being a pottery sphere found by archaeologists. I have been assured that the museum does not wish to pursue the matter via the police. If the boy who took this sphere comes forward now, he will not be expelled, nor his parents informed. He will receive six strokes of the cane, and the matter forgotten. I think that's a fair offer that any honest Christian boy would accept, and I hope that you're not going to let the school down in front of our guests.' He gestured to Bernice and Alexander. 'Well then – who's got it?'

There was silence.

Rocastle clicked his tongue against his teeth. 'Very well, one last chance for all of you. Either the thief comes forward now, or he damns his fellows with him.' Silence again. 'Then it is my sad duty to inform you all that the town is out of bounds for the next month, or until the thief confesses. Now—'

There came a shattering explosion from outside the building.

'My God,' Bernice whispered. 'They're here.' She glanced at Smith, who was looking around at his fellow teachers in panic as the boys started to yell and run. 'Who's going to save us this time?'

The family stood in the courtyard of the school buildings. Hoff lowered his gun, nodding proudly at the remains of a statue that he'd atomised. The others stood in a line, watching the windows, weapons held at the ready. Even Aphasia had a gun, a big showy photon rifle that she'd painted orange with black spots, her balloon tied around the end of the muzzle.

August put a black cone-like device to his lips. His voice was amplified and projected by the equipment, winding its way into the school, echoing through every room and gallery. 'Listen to me. My name is August of the Aubertide family Dubraxine. One of the young humans in that building has something we want, a red sphere known as a Biodatapod. You will send it out to us, and we will leave with it. If you do not, then we'll level the building and kill everybody. We're watching every exit.' He put his hand over the mouthpiece for a moment and looked at the others meaningfully. 'I said, we're watching every exit…'

'Sorry.' Greeneye, Hoff and Serif ran off in different directions around the perimeter of the house.

August sighed and spoke into the cone again. 'You have thirty of your Earth minutes.' He switched off the machine and smiled at Aphasia. 'I've always wanted to say that.'

Aphasia aimed her gun at the roof of the school and fired. The recoil sent her flying backwards.

Concerned, August helped her up, glancing over his shoulder at the plume of smoke spiralling from the guttering above. 'Sniper?'

'Gargoyle.' Aphasia explained. 'I hate gargoyles.'

Timothy was watching from a tree in the orchard. He closed his eyes hard as if to banish a dream. So his magical prize wasn't something destiny had given him. It was something mean enough to be struggled over. The people in the courtyard, the Aubertides, natives of the planet Aubis. The Aubertide Queen lays eggs every hundred years, and the King fertilises them in the ground. The new Aubertides bud to reproduce. You have to find out who's the eldest and talk to them. They like citrus fruit, but they can eat anything, and they're usually terribly friendly. Timothy blinked again, it was as if he'd just made up all that about them. The people in the courtyard were going to destroy the school.

Let them. Let it burn. What he had was worth much more.

No, that was a wicked thought. The lives of all his – no, not his friends, his enemies. The lives of his enemies were worth more than his happiness.

He gathered all his resolve together. He had to do something.

At the appropriate moment, that inner voice told him. Timing was everything.

Rocastle shouted again. 'Silence!'

The yelling mass of boys and teachers actually quietened. Rocastle had raised himself to his full height and he was actually looking at them proudly, with a slight smile on his features. 'Very good. Now, does anybody know what that was all about?'

Silence. Benny looked quickly at Smith and was about to say something, but by the time she'd thought of anything that Rocastle would find even remotely reasonable, he'd turned to one of the other masters. 'Thought not. Mr Moffat, you always have a fine white handkerchief about you. Here –' He picked up the cane he'd propped on the lectern and handed it to the teacher. 'Wave it from the window, and tell these… Aubertides… Greeks, I think, that we don't know what they're talking about, but if they're willing, I'll pop out and have a chat and we can sort it out. All right?'

Benny turned to Alexander. 'That's just what I'd have done,' she whispered. 'Rocastle's not as stupid as he looks.'

Rather nervously, the bursar tied his handkerchief to the end of the cane. He walked through the rows of children to the end of the hall, where a triptych of large panel windows looked out on the grounds. He opened the latch on one of them and poked the cane out nervously.

'Damn soft tactics,' Hutchinson whispered to Merryweather. 'Who are they, anyway? Where are the police?'

'Hello,' called Mr Moffat, nervously. He waved the cane gently back and forth, the handkerchief flapping. He was standing a good distance from the window. 'We don't know what you're talking about. But Mr Rocastle wants to meet with you. We can work something out.'

'Until the police get here, anyhow,' Rocastle murmured to Alexander. 'This thing they're after; it isn't the artefact you're missing, by any—'

There came a sound from the window.

The cane and handkerchief had spread across the room in a wash of red light. The bursar was staggering backwards, clutching his chest. He was shouting at something that had fixed itself there, a blazing red spot that he was scrabbling at like it was a stinging insect.

With a great cry, he managed to catch it and throw it at the window. The spot exploded, and the glass shattered into a billion pieces, the window exploding outwards in a sonic boom.

The boys fell to the ground, covering their heads with their hands. The bursar staggered back to them, his palms bleeding.

'Doctor...' hissed Bernice, her hands curling into fists.

Smith was shooing Joan back behind the curtains of the stage, his expression full of panic and confusion.

Rocastle was staring at the stormy light that was flooding through the windows, the first distant strikes of lightning making their way across the distant fields. A slight smile seemed to force its way onto his face, but then he clenched it down and his eyes shone with a determined certainty. 'Farrar, Wolvercote, Trelawny, away from the windows!' he shouted. 'Captain Merryweather, run to my office, call the police! Mrs Redfern, tend to the bursar! Boys, find your house master, and in those units, follow me.' He pulled a set of keys from his pocket. 'We're going to break out the arms and make a show of it until help arrives!'

'Doctor...' Bernice tried to catch Smith's eye as he stared at Rocastle in disbelief.

'Other teachers are to check that doors are locked, board up windows and otherwise provide for a state of siege.' He spun back and called to the boys. 'Get up! Buck up and play the game!' The boys were getting to their feet, the Captains running round their forms, pulling the younger ones to their feet and slapping them on the back. 'We're going to show them that Hulton College boys are made of old English stuff! The stuff that built the Empire, the stuff that doesn't back down to threats and bullying! Who's with me?'

A great cheer came from the boys, who ran to cluster around their form masters, the Captains saluting quickly to Rocastle as they snapped to attention.

'Right!' Rocastle called, his stare fixing on the masses of cheering children before him. 'Let's break out the weapons and fight!'

'Doctor!' Bernice shouted.

He turned, annoyed, from staring after Joan where she'd gone to aid the bursar. 'What?'

'Who!' Benny growled, and grabbed him by the collar, yanking him off behind the curtains at the back of the stage. 'That's the question. Come here, git!' He vanished as Rocastle turned to look for him, the boys of Farrar House clustering around the Head.

Alexander realised that they were all looking at him and shrugged. 'I think he just... popped out for a moment.'

August slapped down the end of Aphasia's gun. 'What was that about? That was a human, not a gargoyle!'

'He was showing me his handkerchief.'

'He was holding out a white flag, a sign of surrender amongst human colonists. You shooting him'll make them a bit tardier in sending out the Pod, don't you think? Well, don't you?'

'Yeah...' Aphasia scuffed her shoes on the gravel.

'Just don't do it again.'

*

Smith and Bernice stumbled through a door that led to a theatrical storeroom behind the stage, the little teacher trying to wrestle out of Bernice's grasp. 'What are you doing?' he shouted. 'I have to get my House in order!'

'I'll say!' Benny slammed the door and advanced on him, prodding him in the chest. 'Gallifrey! The Hoothi! Ace! Come on!'

'I don't know what you're talking about!'

'You're the only person who can turn this situation around. You! The Doctor!'

'Why do you keep using my title?' Smith spread his hands in frustration. 'Why do you think I'm somebody I'm not?'

'Because you're the Doctor, a Time Lord, somebody not of this planet. You created John Smith, like a character in a book. Here, look at this!' He'd half turned away in disbelief as she fumbled for the history unit and thrust it into his hands. 'This is technology beyond this time period, right? And what about that umbrella, where did you find that?'

Smith glanced at the unit and shook his head. 'Very impressive, very advanced, but what does it prove? Bernice, you're my niece, my brother's daughter. I remember him, I remember his wedding, I remember hearing about you being born! Where is there room for all this – Oh, why am I listening to you!' He waved his arms and pushed her aside, heading back for the stage. 'Pull yourself together,' he told her, before hopping out of the door.

'Damn.' Benny slumped against the wall.

Smith emerged into the middle of the boys of Farrar House and found himself bombarded with questions. 'Quiet!' he called. 'We'll go up to the dormitory and set up the fire sandbags around the windows there.'

'Do we get guns, sir?' asked Hutchinson eagerly.

'Yes, I suppose so.' Smith glanced around the hall. Amid the

167

masses of boys heading for the exits he glimpsed Joan, helping the bursar walk. She noticed his concern and returned a smile. 'Come on then,' Smith told the boys. 'Let's see how brave we can be.'

Benny emerged from behind the curtains when the hall was nearly deserted, and made her way to Alexander, who was standing in the centre of the stage, watching as a group of boys piled boxes by the shattered windows. A cold breeze was blowing about the polished room. Alexander glanced at his watch. 'Ten minutes. In twenty minutes' time, they'll start flattening this place. Is there nothing we can do?'

Bernice laid her head on his shoulder for a moment. 'I don't think so. They're getting ready for a battle. The Doctor won't listen to me. Unless we can find the Pod and use it on him before all this starts, then I don't think we have a prayer.'

'So what do we do?'

'Go and be with him, I suppose.' Benny straightened up. 'At least I can get that bit right this time.'

The dorm was a bustle of activity, boys running to and fro with heavy sandbags. The window at the end of the room had been opened and a bed propped against it. Smith was supervising the construction of fortifications.

Rocastle walked in, three boys behind him carrying a series of crates. 'It's good to see you're with us, Smith. I thought you'd come through at the end. I just heard from Merryweather that the telephone line is down. Johnny Foreigner's been spotted all around the school perimeter, but he isn't trying to get in. There's only about six of them, and they're only carrying small arms by the look of it. All the doors have been barricaded. It's up to us to hold them off until the police hear the racket and come to investigate.' He moved closer to Smith and whispered, 'Actually, I reckon we can do better than hold 'em off. If these are the buggers who set off the poison gas at the hospital, then we're quite justified in putting some lead through them. Which is why – ' he indicated the crates that were being unpacked in the aisle between the beds – 'I brought the Vickers gun up here. Good height and angle above the drive. Phipps can take it on; he got to see how it works at close range at practice.'

Phipps looked up from the barricade he was helping to erect and gave a proud salute, despite the momentary fear that had gripped him. 'Reporting for duty, sir!'

'Good lad,' Rocastle beamed. The other boys were taking rifles from the boxes, swinging them excitedly over their shoulders. 'Any questions, Smith?'

Smith's glance had settled briefly on his umbrella, which he'd propped in the corner by the door, but now his attention returned to the Head. 'No,' he decided. 'None at all.'

Benny and Alexander asked directions from one of the boys as he scurried past them, and found the right way to the dorm, climbing a spiral staircase. On the landing they met Joan, also on her way up.

'Mrs Redfern.' Benny stopped her. 'Joan. Can't you do something to stop all this? The Doc – John – doesn't want to get involved in a battle, does he?'

'There's not going to be a battle,' Joan told her. 'Those outside will either realise that they cannot enter, or will encounter the police.' Benny was about to say something else, but she interrupted her. 'Believe me, Miss Summerfield, I'm not happy about this either. I lost somebody dear to this sort of idiocy.'

'Both of us.' Benny put a hand on her arm.

Joan sized her up for a moment. 'Then come on,' she said. 'Let's see if our counsel may avert disaster.'

As the three of them reached the door of the dormitory, there came an ear-splitting blast of noise from inside.

Alexander threw the door open. Phipps was sitting astride the Vickers gun, his teeth clenched together as he fired a withering blast. The weapon had been assembled atop one of the beds beside the window. Smith was standing beside it, the ammunition belt in his hands, his eyes closed. He seemed to be counting or reciting to himself, cut off from what was happening around him. The other boys were standing around, gazing at Phipps with a kind of holy awe, their rifles unslung, ready to take up firing positions.

'Test firing completed!' Phipps reported, sitting back on his haunches. 'Saw a couple of them out there, sir, but they ran off when we got the Vickers going!'

'That's... the idea.' Smith opened his eyes again, and frowned as he saw the new arrivals. 'Joan, I mean, Mrs Redfern. What are you doing here?'

'I'm here with my medical kit,' she said, sitting down determinedly on one of the beds. 'In case anybody gets injured.'

'Oh, that's bad form,' whispered Hutchinson to Merryweather. He'd been pacing the room angrily ever since Phipps had been chosen to man the gun. 'Women on the front line, and talking about injuries!'

'And why are you here?' Smith walked up to Bernice and Alexander and then turned away again, with the air of somebody discovered in a misdeed. 'To tell me more fairy tales? To try and stop me doing my duty? Well, it's impossible! I wish you'd all just let me do what I have to do, be who I have to be!'

'I wouldn't dream of interfering,' Bernice told him. 'You and the boys can get on with your war. We'll just sit here quietly and watch.'

'One minute,' Alexander whispered to her.

Outside the building, Greeneye and Hoff sheltered behind a line of bushes in alabaster pots.

'That was some sort of projectile weapon!' Greeneye was

muttering. 'And this is a school? For cruk's sake, Hoff, when are you going to listen to me?'

'I do not,' Hoff told him, 'believe that there are Interventionists at work here. However, I do object to being shot at.' He pressed a button on his cuff. 'Let's see what August has to say about it.'

August listened intently to the communication, and then looked at his watch. 'Wait until the deadline expires. If one of these humans doesn't come to a window and start talking about the Pod in thirty seconds, then you can retaliate.'

'What's retaliate?' asked Aphasia.

'It means,' August cut the link and flicked the safety catch of his gun off, 'kill most of the enemy and let the survivors apologise.'

'Time,' Alexander whispered.

'Fire that gun thing some more,' Smith told Phipps, almost embarrassed. 'Make sure they stay ducked.'

'Yes, sir.' Phipps squeezed off another burst, Smith letting the oily belt of shells pass through his hands into the body of the gun. There were square bullets in with the round-nosed ones. Those were the ones that tore and splashed, that shattered inside so you became a blundering mass of organs, knowing that you were going to die, able to talk about the when and how of it.

But this was a battle, this was a whole system that swayed and changed on who died, not how. He remembered the books, the songs, the spectacles. Death was at the back of all the poetry, the muse that made it all so tragic and brave.

The rhythm of the gunfire blocked out everything else, and Smith gazed around the room as if it were silent and still. Joan, with her hands clasped over her ears, but her eyes still fixed upon him with a determined protest. Bernice, her anguish much more evident, huddling in the corner with Alexander. Anand was shaking his head. Only Hutchinson was enjoying the spectacle, his smile growing wider and wider as he aimed through the window along the barrel of his rifle.

The burst finished. Silence crashed back in on the room. Phipps turned to seek the approval of his teacher. 'I think that'll give them something to—'

He stopped, looking puzzled. He slapped at something on his neck and twisted his head.

A tiny metal sphere was imbedded in the back of his scalp. The boy turned back to Smith. 'What is it, sir?'

Smith stared. 'I don't—'

Phipps' face turned red.

His lip started to vibrate, as if he was going to burst out crying. 'I'm sorry—' he blurted out.

And then his head exploded.

The blood slapped Smith straight in the face, covering his chest and hands, a fine spray filling the whole room.

The boys yelled and screamed, falling to the ground.

Smith stumbled forward, blinded by the liquid, trying to find Phipps' body.

Joan was screaming for John, and Arthur, and trying frantically to get up over the mass of boys trying to hide.

Benny had pulled Alexander down and thrown herself on top of him. 'Don't look!' she was shouting. She looked up. 'Doctor!'

Smith grabbed for the headless body and clutched it to him, his fingers finding the remains of the neck and the perfect hands as he tried to blink away the blood from his eyes.

He thought he could hear distant laughter ringing through the sound of the gun in his ears.

Everything he could see was red.

A vision was swimming before him in the red, a cat pinned out on a slab.

He was making sounds himself, he realised, as he rocked the body to and fro, the head still fountaining the red stuff. Noises came from the back of his throat without calling, and names.

172

Names that he didn't recognise.

Benny had clambered to her feet, and threw herself across the beds, scrambling to make her way through the screaming children to the Doctor. She grabbed the handle of the umbrella as she went without thinking, perhaps just after a totem, a reminder.

Joan tripped and faltered across the red-sprayed room also. 'John!' she called. 'John!'

Smith was fumbling with the fingers of the corpse, pulling them roughly from the trigger of the gun. The meaty thing fell aside, washing him in more red as it went. He pulled the gun up to his chest and rubbed a red line from his eyes with his sleeve, trying to see through the window. Trying to see the enemy.

There they were, two of them, down there. The ones who'd killed the boy. His fingers tightened on the trigger. There was no need to think.

But he did think.

He thought about Puff the Magic Dragon, who lived by the sea. He thought about Verity, whispering words in his ear on the shingle beach. He couldn't hear the words yet, they were mingled with the sound of the waves on the shore, wearing the pebbles down to sand.

And then Benny was at one shoulder and Joan at the other.

'John,' said Joan.

'Doctor,' said Benny, and swung his umbrella into the line of his bloody vision, offering it to him. The question mark framed the two men down below.

Smith stared at it for a moment, a terrible pain creasing his face. He had to drop his gaze from the question the umbrella asked. Looking down, he found that he was looking at the poppy in his buttonhole, a lighter shade amongst the red all around. A single flower.

Unsteadily, he let one hand drop from the gun and grabbed at the poppy, held it gently in his fist as if it contained the answer.

'I'm not him, not the Doctor,' he told Benny. 'But he's real. I know he's real. He wouldn't kill them, would he?'

'No,' Benny told him. 'He wouldn't.'

'Even though they took first blood. Even though the war had already started?'

'No,' Joan told him, with a glance at Benny. 'You wouldn't.'

Smith nodded. He let go of the gun and grabbed the poppy with both hands, staring at it like it was the most important thing in the world. 'So what would the Doctor do?' he asked Benny.

'He'd find a way to turn this around,' Bernice told him, the words spilling out of her like this was the most certain thing she'd ever said in her life. 'He'd make the villains fall into their own traps, and trick the monsters, and outwit the men with guns. He'd save everybody's life and find a way to win.'

Smith made a decision. His hands enfolded the flower.

He snatched for his umbrella, spun round, and stood up, a frown of terrible concentration on his face. 'There's another way,' he told the boys. He dropped his hat and let the cape fall to the floor. 'Throw away your guns.'

10
WHAT'S BIGGER ON THE INSIDE THAN ON THE OUTSIDE?

Major Wrightson was sitting in the front of the van, trying to compose a cable to HQ as the rain lashed down, visibly bouncing off the dome over the town. His own feeling about the barrier was that it was somehow divine rather than the work of the enemy, but he couldn't put that down. He had already called for reinforcements, without much idea of what they were to reinforce. All he really wanted was a general to come down here, see the barrier and make it into his problem. His men had been turning away civilians all day, and now it was approaching dusk. Tomorrow, they'd probably have the press to deal with. From inside the barrier, around teatime, had come the noise of machine-gun fire. That had dismayed the men. Machine guns were the ultimate taboo for the private soldier, and the thought that they might be being used in there on civilians... Wrightson had walked round the barrier in the last hour, having a word with all the sentries shivering in their oilskins.

There was still, of course, the matter of composing a letter about Torrence.

A new figure appeared on the darkening road, a bicyclist in a long mac. He hopped off as Wrightson looked up, and wandered over to the van. He had a centre-parting and a grin that had been utterly unperturbed by the rain. 'What's going on, Major?'

Wrightson was pleased that somebody had recognised his

rank. 'The area's been sealed off, sir. Nobody in or out, I'm afraid.'

'But I live in Farringham. I'd just cycled over to see my aunt in Shellhampton. Not only that, I'm due to address a meeting in town tonight.'

'Sorry, you'd best make provisions to stay somewhere else for the night. How are you fixed for accommodation?'

'That's all right, I can just go back to my auntie. You can't tell me what this is all about, I suppose?'

Wrightson shook his head. He hadn't been able to think of a story that wouldn't cause a mass panic. 'What's this meeting of yours, anyway?'

'Labour group. I'm Richard Hadleman, hopefully the next MP for this town. Hello.' Hadleman shook Wrightson's hand.

'You'll have some hope, won't you? No cotton mills in there.'

'Plenty of underpaid farm-hands and shop boys, though. Here, have one of our leaflets.' Hadleman reached into his satchel and produced one of the newly printed red pamphlets.

Wrightson smiled at it. 'The Ten Commandments of Socialism? Won't please the clergy, will it?'

'The opiate of the masses, according to Marx.' Hadleman smiled, but, seeing Wrightson's frown, he became serious. 'Anyway, I'm not here to win votes. If you can't tell me what's going on, can you at least tell me when it'll stop?'

'I'm afraid not. Out of my hands, rather.'

'Sure. Tell you what, if you chaps would like it, I can have my aunt send over a pot of stew and some whisky.'

Wrightson nodded. 'Thanks, but hold the whisky.'

'Oh, so it's that sort of—'

From the town, there came the sound of an explosion.

Wrightson leaned out of the van window and called to the soldier standing by the barrier to his left. 'Position and weapon!'

'Position and weapon!' called the soldier to his comrade nearby.

Hadleman listened as the call was repeated into the distance.

'That wasn't a shell or a grenade.'

'No,' Wrightson muttered, and then turned to Hadleman in surprise. 'How did you—'

'My friend Constance has an interest in the military. What the hell's going on in there, Major? Have you engaged an enemy?'

'No, I wish I bloody – sorry, I wish I had.'

'I'll leave you to it, then.' Hadleman started back up the road, hopping onto his bicycle.

Wrightson instantly caught the falseness of the comment. 'Don't do anything rash! There's—' But Hadleman was already out of sight. Wrightson sighed. He wasn't sure what kind of lie he could tell about the barrier anyway.

'Excuse me, sir,' the soldier by the barrier to his right called. 'Do you really want to know the position of Rippon?'

Smith led his class quickly through the corridors of the school to the library.

'But this is mutiny, deserting our post!' Hutchinson was protesting. He was the only one who still carried his rifle. The rest had been left piled in a corner of the dormitory.

'Quiet!' Smith growled. 'I'm trying to save our lives. Bernice, the Doctor, how does he do what he does?'

'It's hard to say. It's rather like judo, or Reversi. The opposition usually thinks they've won, and then he makes them see the situation in a different way, and it turns out he has.'

'Hmm. Tricky.'

'John,' Joan began nervously. 'You aren't labouring under the delusion that you really are this Doctor, are you?'

'Of course not!' Smith held up his hand, and the troupe of boys halted in front of the library. From all over the school, the sound of small-arms fire could be heard. 'It's just a useful mental model. Now, something I've been wondering since I got here.' He gestured with his umbrella at an elaborately carved panel above the library door. 'What did you say that meant?'

'Maius Intra Qua Extra?' Joan laughed. 'You mean you really didn't know what the school motto meant?'

'No,' Smith mumbled, 'it's in a foreign language, isn't it?'

'Bigger on the inside than the outside!' Hutchinson snapped. 'It's about books. Now, don't you think we should—'

There came a vast explosion from one of the floors above. The boys all fell to the ground.

Smith remained standing, tapping his teeth with the umbrella handle. 'Yes. I see. How long's the school been in this building? Twenty years?'

'Yes,' Joan picked herself up and took his arm. 'Eighteen, to be exact.'

'Then how old's that inscription?'

Somewhat self-consciously, Benny took his other arm. 'Older. The arch is needed to support the ceiling here, and you can tell the carving's not been added later, because it extends further out than the edges of the arch. That was planned from the start.'

'So the motto was originally that of the building. Rocastle took it on. Is it a family motto?'

'No coat of arms,' Alexander said.

'It would be Rocastle all over to see it there and appropriate it,' Joan added.

'And, being over a library, it is, as I said, about books!' Something inside Hutchinson snapped. He pulled back the bolt on his rifle and swung it to cover Smith. 'Take us back to our post, you're guilty of mutiny.'

Smith took a step forward, so that the muzzle of the rifle was pressed up against his chest. He held up a hand to stop Benny from making any sudden move on Hutchinson.

The other boys stared at the two of them.

'If you don't return to your post, then I'll be forced—'

'Forced?' Smith's tone was quite mild. 'To do what?'

'To...' Hutchinson looked desperately around the other boys, looking for any sign of support. But all he saw were tired, frightened, sometimes tear-stained faces. Even Merryweather was slowly shaking his head, as if advising Hutchinson that this was a bad move. 'To report you to the Head!'

'Really? Oh.' Smith turned away from the gun and started examining the inscription again. 'Off you go, then.'

Hutchinson looked round his classmates. 'Well, which of you lads are coming with me?' There was a general turning away. Not one of the boys responded to Hutchinson's eager stare. 'Come on! There's adventure happening! A scrap! What sort of boys are you?'

'Living ones,' Anand told him.

'All right!' Hutchinson snarled. 'If you prefer cowardice over honour!' And he ran off.

'Isn't it odd,' opined Alexander, 'how close masculinity is to melodrama?'

'Only in an Irish dictionary,' said Joan.

'Why an Irish one?' asked Benny.

Joan stared at her. 'Why – it's a joke…'

'Is it?'

'Stop, stop, I need you both to think!' Smith put a hand atop each woman's head and turned them to face the inscription, flashing Alexander a mixture of grin and shrug. 'I think *that's* a joke. An architectural one. Let's go inside and see if it's true.' He shooed the boys into the library. 'The walls are marble, too. Very hard. Very sturdy.'

'Doctor,' Benny began.

Smith glanced at the look on Joan's face. 'Call me John. You know, I think that being covered in all that blood did something strange to me. I saw a dead cat. Is that normal?'

'You had a cat. Chick. It died in a very bad way.'

'Chick…' Smith whispered. 'The name means something… something far away. And Gallifrey, you've mentioned that twice to me. I used it in one of my stories. I thought I'd made it up until I remembered—'

'John,' Joan touched his face with her hand, and wiped another tiny patch of blood away, 'you're frightening me. Are you in shock?'

'I'm not sure. It's working, though. Don't worry. I love you.' The last of the boys had been ushered into the library, missing his whisper by a second. Now he shouted to them, 'I want everybody to start combing the walls. Call if you see anything unusual.'

Joan was smiling at him. 'I love you, also.'

Benny took Alexander by the tie and dragged him away, her fists clenched. 'That woman!'

'I think it's wonderful, loved one. Just because you and I have both lost our sweethearts, don't let's get bitter, eh?'

'I am not bitter.' They began to search the bookshelves. 'It's just so obviously going to end in tears. When the Doctor regains his senses, is he going to be pleased to find that he's going out with a wrinkly racist? I think not. Hey, wait a minute, did you say that you'd lost your sweetheart?'

Alexander froze. 'Oh, that was a long time ago…'

The library had an ornate plaster ceiling, which Smith stared up at, pointing his umbrella upwards and extending it at intervals in various directions, as if calculating. The only windows were a series of high panels to let in light. As she calmed down, Benny realised that she did, indeed, feel safer here. A number of small explosions were being heard at intervals throughout the school, hard to discern from the thunder outside. The boys were starting to look very stressed indeed, their little faces pinched up and their shoulders hunched. No wonder they hadn't gone with Hutchinson. Rocastle had hugely overestimated their interest in warfare. They desperately wanted to be rescued.

Despite some bad life decisions he might have made, she felt a surge of pride as she looked at the little man in the middle of the room. He was going to do that. He was going to save the day, again.

Then she caught sight of the look on Joan's face. She was also staring at Smith, unaware that she was being watched, and, caught unawares like that, she was terribly afraid.

Perhaps sometimes you couldn't save everybody.

Serif was walking through the corner of the building, using a molecular redistributor to melt away the brickwork in front of him. From the other sides of the school came the noise of the others using their heavy weapons.

The corner masonry dissolved, and Serif walked into a kitchen area, through the remains of what had once been a stove, kicking aside the melting metal doors. Any staff had long since departed. This would make a good place to begin the search.

Greeneye and Hoff were exchanging fire with a group of boys with rifles on a balcony outside Rocastle's quarters, ducking in and out of a row of ornamental topiary.

'Fun, isn't it?' Greeneye grinned.

'If you like that sort of thing.' Hoff clicked a button on his cuff. 'I'm getting tired of it, though.'

He stepped out in the full view of the boys, and staggered back as a salvo of bullets bounced off the force field he'd erected in front of his chest. 'Good shot!' he called. 'My turn!'

He aimed his gun vaguely in the direction of the balcony and squeezed the trigger. A heavy shell spiralled out of the weapon and landed in the centre of the kneeling boys. Some of them stood up in alarm.

The shell exploded and the balcony tumbled from the front of the building, a fiery mass of screaming, charring bodies. It landed with a crash, leaving a gaping hole in the masonry above it.

'Now,' Hoff turned to Greeneye as the latter emerged from cover, 'that's my idea of fun.'

*

Anand was tapping along a section of wall in the library. He was worried about his friend. Tim had been missing ever since he'd been summoned to the Head's office. In all this trouble, he hadn't been able to ask about him.

While he was thinking, his hand encountered a soft spot on the spine of a book. It was one of a whole panel of fake spines, a Victorian decorative device long-beloved of captains who would tell their bugs to go and fetch a particular non-existent title. The spine in question was that of *Sir Gawain and the Green Knight* and the soft spot was circular, and halfway up the binding. Anand pressed it.

Something made a clunk and then a grind, and the whole panel of books swung open.

The boys cheered and the adults ran over to peer down a flight of dank little stone steps. 'Open sesame,' said Anand.

Serif shot three boys who ran across the end of the corridor he was stalking down, and turned the corner a moment later.

He was in the central hallway where the bursar's office met the foot of the great stairways.

A group of boys looked up from the sandbags they had piled against the great doors, which were secured with heavy bolts. They turned, swinging round their rifles awkwardly.

Serif mowed them all down in a blaze of silent blue light. He broke step only to swing the bodies and the bags away from the doors, which he unbolted and swung open.

'Come on,' he called to August and Aphasia. 'I'm sure I haven't killed the right boy yet.'

Smith's party were running down a narrow brick-lined passageway. Smith himself hung back for a moment, noting that Captain Merryweather was always glancing behind him, biting his lip in panic, and tripping over his feet.

Smith drew level with him. 'What's wrong?'

'They'll come after us. They've got all those guns. They'll kill us.'

'But we're cleverer than they are.'

'That doesn't matter. That never matters. It's who's got the most guns that matters!'

'Trust me,' Smith murmured. 'I won't let you come to any harm. I promise.'

Merryweather looked up at him uncertainly. 'Can you promise that?'

'Of course. You boys may know me as mild-mannered John Smith, history teacher, but secretly I'm the Doctor, universal righter of wrongs and protector of cats.'

'Are you?'

'So I'm told.' Smith smiled at Bernice as she hung back from the gentle jog to join him. 'How are you?'

'I'm fine, I was wondering about you. You've changed your mind.'

'So you say.'

'No, I mean that you've started to act like yourself again.'

'I just got fed up. This is all play-acting. I'm terrified. And mad. Like I'm too mixed up to care who I am. Who is this Doctor, then?'

'A man from another planet who travels through time and space having adventures. He has two hearts.'

'I only have one.'

'That's because of the Pod. When we find it, you put it back to your forehead and you become you again. You grow your other heart back. Or so I assume.'

'So why do the villains want it?'

'They want to be like you.'

'Let me ask you a question. Merryweather, cover your ears, I'm in love with one of your teachers.'

Merryweather blinked and did so. 'That's all right, sir, so am I.'

'Ah, wait, before you ask me the question, look at this.' Benny pulled the list of Things Not To Let Me Do from her jacket and showed it to Smith. At the bottom of the list, she'd added, in hastily scrawled biro, 'Don't let me fall in love.'

'Interesting. My handwriting changes. Ah well, too late on that last point. The question is: if in my original state I've got two hearts and two brains—'

'Just hearts.'

'Well, if I'm so odd that I've got lots of everything, could I still love somebody?'

Benny grimaced. 'I've, erm, never known the Doctor to have any concern for the trouser department. He sometimes gets his snaps out and goes all moody, but I suspect that's more a sort of paternal bit. In short, no, I don't think he normally does that kind of thing.'

'I see, two hearts but no love. Well, that makes our plan easier. One, we get everybody to safety, and that includes going back for the other boys. Two, we find the boy who's got this Pod. And three—'

'You put it to your forehead, become the Doctor again and kick some alien bottom?' Bernice asked hopefully.

'Ah, no. We give it to them and they go away.'

Benny stared at him. 'I think it's becoming one of those days.'

Rocastle stood in the middle of the canteen, his pistol out and ready. The boys of 5B were clustered around him in a nest of sandbags. The explosions that they'd heard earlier seemed to have stopped, as had, worryingly, the Vickers gunfire. Quite a few of the boys who'd been sent out as scouts hadn't returned. Probably run away and hid; there was no indication that the defences had been breached. On a real battlefield, they'd have had the luxury of maps and hills to view it from, but here things would just have to be worked out as they happened.

The only OTC unit to have had actual combat experience. Damn it.

The doors at the end of the canteen burst open. Several of the boys snapped up into firing postures, but Rocastle cut the air with his hands. 'Wait!'

It was Hutchinson, running wildly, his clothes and half his face blackened. 'It's Smith, sir! He's deserted his post! He's taken Farrar down to the library to hide!'

'Get into cover,' Rocastle told him. 'Brave lad. Plucky of you to come here. We'll settle Smith's hash when this is all over. Did you get into a scrape on the way?'

'Yes, sir.' Hutchinson slumped behind the sandbags. 'They're inside the school. One of them pointed a sort of flamethrower at me and I caught the edge of it.'

'Well done, Captain. Did you see where the enemy were going?'

'They were heading for the gymnasium, sir.'

'I see.' Rocastle stood up. 'In that case, I do believe that an exploratory mission is in order. The gymnasium has only one exit, and the southern stairs lead down there. We'll have height and they'll have nowhere to run. We may have a chance of settling the whole matter. Follow me.'

The boys did so, shouldering their arms nervously.

'I like being me,' Smith was insisting to Benny. 'Besides, I'm engaged to be married.'

'You're what!'

'If she says yes.'

'You're marrying… her?'

'She's very nice.' Smith tapped Merryweather on the shoulder and indicated that he could unblock his ears. Benny just glowered at him.

Smith took a deep breath and began a chant matched to the rhythm of the jog. 'Do we want to fight and slay?'

'We should all just run away,' returned Benny, remembering the form from grotty route marches around the Academy.

185

'Do we want to all get shot?'

'If we scarper, no let's not.'

'Do we want to bathe in glory?'

'It's overrated, dull and gory,' Benny continued, with a little grin of pride at that one. The gang of children and adults continued to run down the narrow corridor, repeating the verses.

Smith tried to give Benny a reassuring smile, but the look she returned him was anything but reassured.

The family met outside the gymnasium, August's party almost bumping into Greeneye and Hoff.

'I gather we've come to the same two conclusions,' said August. 'One, a complete holographic scan reveals that the boy we're after isn't in the building, and—'

'Two, there's a dirty great tunnel around here somewhere. Three, shall we get after the little crukker? Please?' demanded Greeneye, and ducked into the gym. Hoff, August and Serif followed.

Aphasia remained outside, her finger in her mouth, pondering something she'd read as the family had marched through the building. 'Maius Intra…'

Rocastle's party rounded the top of the landing, and scattered down the banisters into prearranged firing positions, surprised to find that the only person they were aiming at was a little girl.

'Miss!' Rocastle hissed. 'Miss! Would you please come here?'

Aphasia turned and saw them. She smiled. 'Oh? Why?'

Hoff poked his head out of the gymnasium doors. 'Aphasia, come on, we—'

Then he noticed the boys.

He slapped his weapon up to head height.

The wall exploded with gunfire, splinters bursting everywhere. Hoff ducked back inside.

Aphasia spun as the bullets caught her and slapped her to and fro, her chest and limbs erupting with bloody debris.

'Cease fire!' screamed Rocastle.

The little girl fell to the floor, and struggled to right herself, her balloon lying burst across her shoulder. Only one arm seemed to be working, and her eyes were blinking at a tremendous rate, like a clockwork toy winding down. She put her teeth to her wrist, and pulled open the pouch there.

Rocastle noticed that a couple of his boys were standing up, about to go to her. 'No! Wait for—'

Aphasia gazed at the black capsule inside her wrist, and a sweet smile crossed her face.

Then her head hit the floor, dead.

Hoff stepped out into the corridor, looked down at the body, almost casually, and turned to face Rocastle and his boys.

They were staring at what they'd done, appalled.

Hoff looked for a moment like he was going to say something, but then he just shrugged.

He raised his gun and ran a burst of blue light up the stairs.

A row of boys screamed, dissolved, were blasted sideways, tried to run, cannoned into each other, threw their guns aside, separated, exploded, bled. The banisters before them steamed away into a cloud of ugly smoke.

'Retreat!' screamed Rocastle. 'Retreat!'

Amidst the smoke, a few boys did just that, running to his voice.

Hutchinson collided with him as they both sprinted up the stairs. 'We got one!' the boy laughed, clutching at his headmaster's lapels. 'Did you see, sir, we got one!'

Rocastle could only stare at him as the others bundled past.

'Aphasia!' Hoff stumbled back into the gym, dragging the body with him. 'Aphasia!'

The family had been scanning the floor for the hidden tunnel

187

their earlier scans had revealed. They all ran to the body, Serif shoving the others aside to bend quickly to the child, putting a gloved hand on either side of her face. 'If there's a chance, any neural activity at all—' His expression froze and he let out a long hiss. 'No...' His white teeth clenched and he closed his eyes. 'She is dead.'

'Why didn't she put up her field?' Greeneye howled. 'Kill them all, every single one of them.'

'Close the doors,' August told Hoff. 'Put a field across it. Prepare a fusion bomb. This building will be her memorial. Now, quick as we can, let's be about the ceremony.'

Steaming tears were dropping from Serif's eyes, hissing as they fell on to Aphasia's dress. 'This one who was our mother and daughter, flesh of ours, let her be our flesh again.'

'Let her be our flesh again,' the others chorused.

Together, they bent to the body to feed.

The old wooden door gave way after a couple of shoves.

Benny looked around the cellar. 'Yes, that makes sense.' There were casks of beer, racks of bottles and metal pipes all around. 'It's a secret route to the pub. The Lord of the Manor must have told the missus that he was studying.'

The boys filled the cellar and closed the door after them.

'Fascinating,' Joan said to Alexander. 'I've never been in a pub.'

'It gets better,' he told her, 'the higher up you get.'

Smith hopped up a flight of stone steps and listened to the door at the top of them. Suddenly he took a step backwards and waved at the others to get down.

The door opened.

A surprised-looking landlord stared down at them.

'Thirty-eight lemonades, please,' Smith told him.

'And a pint of bitter,' Benny added.

They marched out into the beer garden with their drinks. It was getting dark now and the storm was passing. The regulars had stared at the parade of schoolboys filing up out of the cellar. 'School outing,' Smith had explained as he paid for the round. It turned out that the landlord was quite aware of the passageway, and that the bursar had been an occasional customer through it.

Several of the locals muttered about the noise from the OTC being loud today, and one who claimed he was a Boer War veteran who'd 'drunk his fill of Bovril' cornered Smith and tried to row with him about it until the little teacher wriggled out.

'Well, what happens now?' Benny asked once they were in the garden. She'd had the awful feeling that she had been getting disapproving looks from locals who remembered her fleeing from Greeneye. 'We can't stay here long.'

'No, you can't.'

'You?'

'I've got to go back and let the others know there's a way out.'

Joan gripped him by the arm. 'Can't we communicate with the school in some way, let them know?'

'No. They've been cut off from the outside world. I have to go back. I'll be careful. The rest of you must search for this Pod thing. Bernice, what did the boy who had it look like?'

'He was quite old, but still a bit small. Fair hair. Looked like he'd been dragged across a field.'

'Tim!' Anand said. 'You saw Tim!'

'Dean?' Smith asked, putting a hand on Anand's shoulder. 'Yes, he fits the description. And he's been very secretive lately. Who saw him last?'

'I saw him running out of school,' Alton murmured. 'He seemed intent on getting away. That was near teatime.'

'We saw him afterwards,' Benny told Smith. 'He's out there in the forest.'

Joan squatted down beside Anand. 'Where does he like to go? What are his favourite hiding-places?'

'There are several. He used to walk on his own quite a lot.

He liked going to the tea-shop, and looking around the library in town. They have better books there than at school. And he always liked the orchard. We used to go picking apples there.'

Alexander nodded. 'As I said. We should send out people in all—'

The skyline suddenly went white.

The shadows stretched negative black and long.

'Oh my God!' Benny shouted, the only one of them that understood it. 'Get—'

The sound cut her off, hitting like an enormous clap of thunder.

The blast knocked Smith's party off their feet, blasting the wooden pub tables into the field beyond the garden. Benny, Joan and Smith grabbed the children and fell in a sprawling mass. Alexander wasn't so lucky, rolling over and over down to the bottom of the garden, finally flattening against the hedge. He looked up and yelled, astonished at what was coming towards him.

Through the blazing sky, a tree trunk was spinning straight at him.

It shot over his head, just clearing the hedge and bouncing off down the field. Splinters flew from it as it hit.

The wind roared past, thousands of tiny objects battering across the humans as they lay there. The hedge became a mass of glasses, foliage and stones. Alexander shielded his face with his arms.

The blast thundered through the town, signs flying from buildings, shop windows disintegrating, the cockerel being torn from the top of the church spire. The market traders, turned back from the roads by the frantic shouts and gestures of the army, had reassembled in the square, and their carts were hurled all over, skidding and smashing across the cobbles.

People ran out of their houses, crying about the end of the

world, and were blown off their feet in the wind, wailing as they skidded down the streets.

Then, just as suddenly as it had started, the sound ceased.

A fine grey dust began to descend.

Joan was curled in Smith's arms. 'What... what was that?' she cried.

'Some sort of explosive,' Alexander called from the hedge, trying to shout over the ringing in his ears.

The boys were all shouting and openly sobbing, finally giving in to the fear that had pursued them for so long.

'A fusion bomb.' Benny spat to get the dust out of her mouth. 'High blast, very low radiation yield.' She stood up, and shivered at the spectre of the mushroom cloud that was rising above the slight valley that had once contained the school. 'I had hoped that I would never get to see one of those.'

Smith got slowly to his feet, pulling Joan up with him. The first people were staggering, shouting and screaming, out from the still-intact pub.

'All those boys...' Joan whispered. 'And the teachers...'

Smith held her tight, marvelling at the terrifying shape in the sky.

Tim had been wandering in the forest, wondering when the time would feel right to do anything. He'd felt suddenly certain when he'd happened upon the barrier and rescued that soldier. That had been like following lines in a play, remembering his cues. Now, he was back in the wings, waiting to be called again, hearing the faint whispers that seemed to come from the Pod in his hand.

He'd been startled by a noise in the bushes and come upon Wolsey, staring up at him from his hiding-place in annoyance.

'Hey, come on, boy, come on.' Tim dropped to his knees and crawled towards the cat, clicking his tongue. Wolsey decided that the smell of the boy was interesting and strange, and not really frightening, and so edged up to him, rubbing his neck against Tim's hand. 'That's a good cat. Now where—'

That was what saved Tim from the explosion. Suddenly, all the trees on the hill were flat, and he was lying under one of them, the weight of its fall broken by the shrubs that Wolsey had been playing in.

As the roar rumbled away, the cat leapt off, jumping from tree trunk to tree trunk very fast.

Timothy clambered out from under his particular tree, holding his ears. He counted the descending note of the sound, wondering what he was doing as he did it, and came to some startling conclusions about distance and explosive force.

'The school!' he whispered to himself. 'What have they done?'

The family opened their eyes, blood still on their lips.

They were standing in a small force dome, in the centre of the school. Beneath their feet was a circle of unharmed tiling.

Above their heads stood the school.

Only now it was made of fused glass.

Patterns of light from the shimmering cloud scattered through it, rainbowing the gym and the library and the kitchens. Multiple lenses twisted the images and magnified them, the fiery brightness flickering through the Upper School and along the dormitories.

Inside the building there were glass statues, boys captured as they were caught in postures of running or hiding, their bones burst into glass and their flesh fused away.

In the silence, silver dust began to fall.

Around the building, the grounds had been flattened by the blast of transforming energy. Trees and bushes had been ripped out of the soil and flung off into the sky. The circle of destruction only stopped at the distant boundary wall, still half upright, and the tree line along the top of the nearby hills. The gate lodge had been torn in half, the struts of its roof opened and the brickwork dashed into the road.

The family had followed the ceremony to the letter, walking out of the gymnasium when they had finished feeding, and locating the precise centre of the building, underneath the old clock tower. Serif had dedicated the transformation to the soul of Aphasia, which had now returned to the place from which it had come, the belly of her family.

They'd set the fusion bomb on top of the force dome and closed their eyes, beginning the litany that they'd only just finished. The actual detonation had been almost unnoticed amongst the emotion of the words.

They looked at each other and licked the blood from their lips. Not a scrap of their daughter and mother remained. The ceremony was over.

'Now,' August said after a moment's appropriate silence. 'Let's find what we're after, shall we?'

'Yes,' Greeneye agreed. 'And along the way, we'll make them pay for Aphasia. Blood for blood.'

'Blood for blood,' the family agreed.

'Not much chance of finding this tunnel,' Hoff noted, looking around.

'No,' August agreed. 'Well, we can always follow the line of it overground. Still, who knows…' He tapped the keypad once more. 'The Pod's transmitting again, it's – ah, no its gone. It was somewhere over there…' He gestured over the hill. 'Why does it keep doing that?'

'It is transmitting information,' Serif hissed. 'Perhaps to the boy who is carrying it, perhaps,' he glanced at Greeneye, 'to others. Perhaps both. We can only detect it when it is processing information.'

'In that case, we'd better treat this more urgently,' August ordered. 'According to Laylock, the Pod's made of pretty strong stuff. So, as soon as one of us sees the boy—'

'We shoot the annoying little crukhead?' Greeneye asked.

'Precisely.'

'Good.' Greeneye slapped the power on his gun up a few notches. 'I was starting to think that we were planning to adopt him.'

11
CASTLING

Amid a crowd of local people who rushed out of the pub, gesturing and shouting at the shape in the sky, Smith gathered his party together. 'Bernice, you know what that was. Did they – the ones who are after the ball – do it?'

'Unless a first-year had an unusually successful day in the physics lab, I think they're a good bet.'

'Then we definitely shouldn't fight them. They're too strong.' He walked back and forth through the huddled boys and adults, his hands clasped ferociously behind his back. 'This is only a war if we make it a war. We need to play a different game. A game like chess.'

'Pawns,' Alexander told him carefully, 'get taken in chess.'

Smith bit his knuckle in concentration. 'Yes. So we cheat. All of you, listen to me, we need to find Tim.' He divided the boys up into groups, and sent each of them out to a particular one of the boy's haunts and gave them the same instructions. 'If you find Tim, with or without the red sphere, bring him back here. Come back here anyway in two hours. If you see the enemy, run and hide. Don't let adults try to protect you, just get out of their way. Benny, Alexander, you two take a few boys and go up onto the hills. Joan and I will try the orchard.'

'Now, wait a minute—' Benny began, but Alexander had grabbed her by the elbow and hauled her away through the gathering crowd before she could finish her sentence. The boys delegated to their party ran after them.

'I don't think your niece likes me very much,' Joan told Smith as she watched them go.

'You're too alike,' Smith told her, leading her away. 'Not that I think either of you appreciate the comparison.'

A few minutes after the couple had left in the direction of the orchard, another commotion added to the one that the crowd were creating. Another group of tired and tattered schoolboys, a vast number this time, threaded their way out of the pub and collapsed in the garden, holding their hands to their bleeding ears.

They'd been in the tunnel when the bomb went off. The explosion had rushed down it as a pressure wave, the air rolling over them and bursting their hearing like a terrible, intangible fist against their temples. They looked like defeated prisoners-of-war and their faces were blank and hollow. Some of the locals started to help them up and a doctor moved from boy to boy. The startled townsfolk began to ask questions of them.

After the last schoolboy had climbed the stairs, Mr Moffat the bursar staggered up out of the cellar behind him. He'd run about the school for half an hour before the explosion, avoiding battles and shepherding schoolboys towards the library.

He collapsed onto the bar and a barmaid ran to him, pressing a glass of brandy to his lips in concern.

'Ah…' he said to her. 'You've saved my life.'

Smith and Joan approached the gate of the orchard, holding hands. They'd been talking about Bernice's bizarre idea that finding the Pod would transform Smith into another person and had even started making jokes about it.

The dark cloud was starting to disperse, and the silver dust had begun to settle across the countryside.

'The size of that explosion…' Joan whispered. 'John, I am beginning to suspect that some of what Bernice says may be true.'

'Some of it,' Smith muttered. 'Not all of it.'

'So, may I ask why you have suddenly steeled yourself so?'

'Once, perhaps, but try asking it five times fast.'

'Don't evade me, John. You've changed.'

'For the better?'

'Yes. I didn't think you could play a soldier for long.'

'You're right, it isn't me.' Smith vaulted the gate and helped Joan climb over. 'I can see why Rocastle thinks that way. It's attractive. Imagine, never having to make any decisions. Because of honour. And etiquette. And patriotism. You could live like a river flowing downhill, hopping from one standard response to the other. Honour this. Defend that.'

'May I add the concept of the waterfall to this gay picture?' Joan asked, enjoying their conversation despite, or perhaps because of, its grim setting.

'Oh, you may. But that's just death, and Rocastle's principles let you get over that in a barrel.'

'Well, the edge of that waterfall looked very close until you decided to paddle against the tide. I can't believe that either of us are still alive, or that we're still active and not shocked into silence.'

'That's because we're doing something. That's why I sent the others off so they wouldn't sit still and get afraid. Tim will be in the orchard. When I was a boy, I used to go and see a man who lived on a hilltop, and on the way there were fruit trees—'

Joan stopped walking, and held Smith's arm harder. 'There was a man who lived on a hilltop? Near Aberdeen? That doesn't sound very likely.'

'Yes!' Smith insisted. 'Near Aberdeen. I can see him. I can remember—' He turned his head to reassure Joan and blinked in astonishment. 'No I can't.' He turned back to the angle he'd been standing at before. 'Yes I can, he was—' He turned back to her and took in a long, frightened breath. 'Joan, my memory of this man seems to depend upon the angle I hold my head. What does that mean?'

Joan struggled with a terrible desire that had boiled up inside her, to hit him or drag him away or just stop this madness from happening.

Because she had a terrible feeling that it was going to happen. To her. Again.

'It means that I can hear another waterfall,' she told him bitterly. 'One all of my own.'

'Sorry?'

'It means, you foolish man, that the thing we're after −' she pointed in the direction they'd been walking − 'is that way.'

Timothy had found the going easier as he walked down the hill. The trees on the other side from the school had been shielded from the blast and were thus still intact. He was vaguely hoping to see the cat again, but it hadn't appeared. He was heading for the orchard, waiting to feel certain about something again.

His eyes narrowed on the sphere, thinking almost that he'd heard it speak again. The demon inside the ball talked in whispers. He squeezed it tightly. That didn't work. He drew it to his face, thinking to look into it like a crystal ball. He'd already tried rubbing it, wondering if a genie would appear and grant him wishes.

And the voice was nearly there, right on the edge of hearing. It got louder as he moved the Pod closer to his forehead. Sparks were dancing in his eyes now, leaving bright trails across his vision. An inch closer and the lightning would leap, the connection would be made. He'd never have to feel pain again, he'd be above missing his dead mother and his father abroad who'd wanted him to be a soldier. But it was terrifying, the things he'd started to see, a great river of information pouring into his head, as if from the lip of a cup that was about to overflow. The responsibility of taking on all that… It would fill him to bursting.

He felt like the young Arthur, the sword standing in the stone before him. All he had to do was grasp it, free it, take on his destiny.

His destiny?

He lowered the sphere from his head, panting. 'I can't do it,' he said bitterly. 'You're not mine.' Then his expression hardened. 'You're right. I must find who you belong to, and give you back to them.'

Smith and Joan were picking their way through the orchard, Smith turning his head every now and then like a bloodhound on the trail. 'I don't understand this any more than you do,' he told her, 'but it seems to be working.'

'If you find this artefact that everybody seems so desperate to acquire, what do you intend to do with it?'

'Make a bargain. I give it to them, they go away. This battle's about a thing. A round red thing that represents nothing. A thing that's made them kill many times, that made me feel that I could take a life.' His growl receded to a mutter. 'They're welcome to it.'

Joan squeezed his hand tightly, heartened by his words. 'John, let me play devil's advocate for a moment. What if Bernice is right, and the sphere contains something of great value to you? Are you sure that you should give it away? I just want you to be certain of what you're doing.'

Smith shook his head, certain. 'What is there that I could have that I'm not aware of? I can hear and see, I have life and intelligence. Even if she is right, and the Doctor is some advanced being that I'm just the shadow of, I won't feel the loss. I've gained so much, being human. I know I have.'

'How can you be sure?'

'Because I have you.' He took her in his arms and kissed her again. 'And the Doctor didn't.'

Joan enjoyed the kiss, holding on to him gladly. If she was being honest, desperately. When the kiss was over, she whispered: 'This may be a bad time to mention it, but in the last few hours, have you noticed anything different about me?'

'Different? Apart from ragged, burnt and charmingly tousled? No.'

'Rather more specific than that...' said Joan. She tapped her chin with a finger.

Smith glanced down and saw his ring on it. 'You've—'

'Accepted, yes. Do you think that we should make an official announcement now, or wait until the remains of our workplace have been cleared away?'

'I...' Smith grabbed her and spun her round in a joyful, random dance. 'Whatever you think best. Or let's just get married. Tomorrow. Yesterday. Tonight!'

'I think that your head was pointing in the wrong direction then,' she laughed, holding on to her hat. 'But there are vast, lately unexplored stretches of me that would quite appreciate being married this evening.'

'Shall we just pretend?' said Smith, his eyes sparkling.

'Don't tempt me.' They fell against a tree and several apples fell from it, one bouncing off the top of Smith's skull. 'Oh, any new thoughts?'

'Nothing Newtonian. I never liked him. He was always very bad-tempered and completely...' His eyes narrowed, and he turned from Joan, fixing his gaze on the figure that had just appeared at the other end of the orchard.

It was Tim, clutching the Pod in his hand and staring at the teachers in wonder.

'Obsessed with death,' Smith finished.

'Damn,' whispered Joan.

The family came to the edge of the forest at a run. August activated the scanner and clicked his tongue approvingly. 'There it is, a clear signal! Something's happening.'

'I wonder what?' Greeneye muttered suspiciously.

'We'll approach them slowly and carefully.'

'Why can't we just run at them?'

'Because when we run at them, they get away. We need to be more subtle.'

'They get away when Greeneye's being subtle, too,' Hoff muttered.

August sighed. 'The idea is, we spread out a bit and try and cut off all their exits. The Pod may be singing away now, but we can't guarantee that it won't have stopped by the time we get there. All right?'

'All right!' Greeneye grabbed the second scanner and marched off determinedly.

'Sometimes,' August opined, 'I wish someone else was the oldest.' He checked the scanner. 'Come on, then, let's finish this.'

'Hello, Tim!' Smith called brightly. 'Please, don't run away, we've been looking for you.'

Tim stepped forward uncertainly. 'Dr Smith, Mrs Redfern... What happened to the school?'

'It was blown up,' Smith told him, walking towards him. 'In other circumstances, we'd have a party, but—'

'No you wouldn't. You liked the place. You liked everything about it.' Tim began to back away. 'You've come to get me because I ran away. When I was bullied, you told me to put up with it.'

'Yes. I did.' Smith stopped and considered. 'I did that because I was trying very hard. To fit in. To be one of the gang. I wanted to have a place so much that I did things I didn't really want to do.' He glanced at Joan. 'I've got a place now, I know who I want to be. I've grown up. I'm sorry that I gave you the wrong advice.'

'So it's all right that I ran away from school?'

'If you don't like a place, you shouldn't stay there.'

'And what about the bullies?'

'They're the worst thing in the world. It's a big circle. They hurt people. The people they hurt feel powerless and go on to hurt other people when they're able to. And the original bullies were once hurt themselves. The wheel keeps on turning. Unless you step off.'

'That's what I'm going to do,' said Tim firmly. 'That's what's in this sphere, you know, the things you need to know so that you don't have to cause harm.'

Joan spoke up. 'John knows all about that, now.'

'Well, that's good. For myself, I know I shall never hurt anybody again.' Tim paused for a moment. 'Were you ever bullied, Dr Smith?'

Smith took a deep breath. 'That depends on what you call me. I remember running through the streets of Aberdeen, with a gang of boys behind me. I remember a lot of military louts shouting at me, and I remember girls hating and excluding me. That's in here.' He tapped his head. 'But in there –' he gestured towards the Pod – 'I remember other kinds of bullying. A boy in my class who so hated and loved me that he kept upsetting my experiments. I made myself forget it, thought that I was an adult and could leave it behind. But if you ignore that, you ignore yourself.' He closed his eyes, concentrating on what the sphere was telling him. 'Recently, I thought I had become wiser than him, but found that I was still hurting people terribly.' He opened his eyes again, an expression of excited discovery on his face. 'I'd climbed back on the wheel. Become a bully. Which is why I decided to stop.'

'Being a bully?'

'Being me.'

Joan put a hand on Smith's shoulder. 'So it's all true? This man I've got to know isn't the real you?'

Smith took her hand. 'He is now. Tim, I know what you're carrying. It's mine, though I didn't know it until now.'

'Then I should give it back to you.' He was frowning, something in his head shouting to him about context and consequences.

'Yes.' Smith held out his hand.

Tim paused, looking at the Pod. 'If I put it to my head, I'd change, wouldn't I?'

'You'd become the Doctor, I suppose. Do you want to?'

'He's the one in the Pod?'

'Apparently.' Smith concentrated on what he was feeling from the Pod. 'He's like me, only inhuman. Dangerous. Loving greatly but not small-ly. He's Merlin. You know the sort of thing.'

'You were him?'

'I took that part of me out and put it in there.'

'Do you want to be him again?'

'No,' Smith said firmly. 'I don't think he's quite me any more.'

'I feel like I should tell them to form a crocodile,' Benny muttered. She and Alexander were leading a group of four boys down the track that led on to the hills. They'd spent the last half hour wandering about the hummocks and dells of the hillsides in the dark, the boys occasionally gazing down at the moonlit glass palace that had once been their school. 'I mean, why did we do this? Was Tim really fond of coming up here?'

'He did go up there sometimes, miss,' Merryweather said.

'Call me Bernice or Benny, I really don't like being reminded of my marital status every sentence, particularly at the moment.'

'You're thinking about Dr Smith's engagement?' asked Alexander. 'Oh dear.' He glanced at the startled boys. 'That's let the cat out of the bag.'

'To Mrs Redfern, I gather?' said Alton. 'Everybody knows that those two are sweet on each other.'

'Bleh,' said Merryweather.

'My thoughts exactly.' Benny patted him on the head. 'I mean, she's so old…'

'Don't you think that you're being a bit jealous, loved one?' said Alexander.

'Jealous? No, no, I don't think it's jealousy to hope that the man who's been transporting you about the place won't settle down in one small country and… oh yarbles.'

'Yarbles?'

'It's terribly rude, but they won't understand that either.'

'Interesting,' Alton began, 'that we're old enough to be shot at, but not to hear wicked words.'

Benny ignored him. 'The only reason he sent us off to do this was so that he could spend some time alone with Mrs Redfern. And in the middle of a crisis! I ask you!'

'Well, we've got a few minutes to kill before we get back to the pub,' Alexander said soothingly. 'I don't suppose we could go and have a look at what's happened to the school?'

'Oh, could we, miss?' the boys started to call. 'Could we?'

'Stop! Stop!' Benny waved her arms for quiet. 'I don't believe this! There are people out there who are trying to shoot us, but you want to go sightseeing.'

'We could just take a look from a distance. If anybody's there, we'll sneak off again. Benny, it's made of glass, where are they going to hide?'

'All right,' Benny agreed. 'But we just pop our heads up, say ooh, and pop them down again. OK?'

'Thank you, miss.' Merryweather gave her a little hug.

Benny shrugged him off. 'And no hugging.'

They crept up to the remains of the boundary hedge between the school and the forest.

'Ready?' Benny asked. 'One, two, three!'

They all stuck their heads up over the hedge.

'Ooh,' said Merryweather.

The glass school shone in the moonlight, casting a fabulously complex shadow of intersecting silver.

'There's somebody inside,' said Alton.

And indeed there was. Two dark shapes moved through the building, randomly like ghosts.

'Is it them?' Alexander asked.

'No,' Alton replied. 'One of them's wearing a Hulton uniform.'

'It might still be them. I'll go and take a closer look,' Benny told them. 'And no, Merryweather, you can't come too.' She hopped through a gap in the hedge.

The two figures resolved themselves as Bernice got closer to the spectral building.

It was Rocastle, with that awful boy Hutchinson behind him, wandering from room to room, a large book in his hands. Benny stepped through an open window, wondering as she did so about the incongruity of the dull panes of glass in the gleaming walls, and approached them. The aliens would never do anything so trivial and English as whatever these two were doing.

Rocastle turned from inspecting one of the glass statues that the bomb had made of the boys. 'Ah, Miss Summerfield. I'm glad to see that you survived. Are any of the boys with you?'

Benny found herself chilled by his matter-of-fact tone. 'Dr Smith got most of his House out. Apart from that, I don't know.'

'He ran away, you mean!' Hutchinson snarled. 'If he'd stayed at his post, this might not have happened! How many lives do you think his cowardice cost?'

With a great effort, Bernice ignored him. 'I wouldn't recommend staying around here. The aliens might be back.'

'Oh, do we know for certain that they're aliens?' Rocastle asked, making a tick in his book. 'They sounded almost English to me.'

'What are you doing here, anyway?'

'I staged a retreat, took a number of my boys out through the dormitory windows and onto the roof of the sheds. Then

205

the explosion happened. Like magic, isn't it? Quite like magic. Anyhow, after it had all died down, I thought it'd be best to ascertain the casualties. I'm going to have to answer for the life of every one of these boys, Miss Summerfield. The least I can do is identify them.'

Benny couldn't help asking, 'What's the difference between a retreat and running away, exactly?'

'The difference is, he's in charge!' Hutchinson told her. 'He gives the orders, which Smith disobeyed.'

'I wouldn't get so touchy about it. What's past is past.' Rocastle waved a hand airily. 'Smith has some good sides to him. Knock off a few corners and he'd be a solid chap. What he has to do is to concentrate on what's best, eliminate the negative.'

Benny followed as the teacher and pupil wandered into another glass room, this one full of small statues. Some of them were throwing their hands into the air, some had intensely pained expressions on their faces. The light creaking of the glass suggested somehow that the pain continued, even in death. 'So what are you going to do after you've finished this?'

Rocastle looked up from the register and tapped his teeth with his pen. 'Oh, I think I shall have to eliminate the negative altogether. Do my duty. I have no future, madam.'

Bernice shook her head. 'Look, there are other ways to go about these things. We've got a party of boys together. Come with us.'

Rocastle seemed to consider it with the same gentle dislocation that had rolled over all his decisions. 'All right. When we've finished this.'

'If you don't want to use it,' Timothy asked, 'what do you want it for?'

Smith slowly withdrew his hand.

Joan glanced between them and decided to break the deadlock. Her poor old heart had been filled with joy at Smith's

206

declaration. Astonishing as it was that he really had once been some kind of cosmological wizard, his decision not to take it all up again had been vast. A grand sacrifice for her, a big gesture that, in her emotions now, made him every inch her husband.

'I say,' she began, 'could I have a go with this magic object?'

Smith looked at Tim. 'What do you think?'

'Just don't put it too close to your head.' Tim handed Joan the Pod slowly and suspiciously, shivering slightly as he let go of it.

Joan took the Pod in her hand. 'Don't worry, I won't run away with it.' She felt it react, in some odd way, to the new touch. Then she closed her fist round it and closed her eyes. 'Arthur,' she whispered. 'Oh my God, Arthur.' Then, with a cry, she let go of it.

The Pod fell to the ground. Joan took a step back from it. 'I saw Arthur, my husband, as he died. And then I felt the Doctor in the sphere. His opinion of it. He was so distant, so... cold. It was as if he was watching that death in my mind, but from such a height. Oh, John, I'm afraid of him, I'm so afraid of him.'

John held her, patting her arm. 'I'm quite scared of him myself. It's odd that you saw Arthur. On the way here, I kept seeing images of Verity. It's like she's in the Pod's memories, but also in my own. I remember our courtship, how we kissed on the rocks in the moonlight. But she's in the glimpses I get of my other past. Why should that be?'

Tim picked up the Pod again. 'I don't know. But, please, answer my question. If you don't want to use the Pod, why do you want it back?'

Smith decided to tell the truth. 'I want to give the Pod to those attacking us, since it's all they want. We don't need it. Then they'll go away and stop killing people.'

Tim stared at him, his expression pained. 'I wish – I wish I could agree –' he suddenly stuffed the Pod into his blazer pocket – 'but I can't. I won't let you do that. It isn't right.'

'Timothy, let's talk about it, work it out.' Smith grabbed the boy's shoulders urgently.

A blast of blue light silently exploded the ground between them. Timothy and Smith stumbled backwards, both looking in horror in the direction of the blast.

August and Hoff stood at the end of the orchard, their weapons trained on the humans. 'We have cut off your retreat,' August advised them. 'There is no escape. Now, let's put an end to all this destruction, shall we? We know that the boy has the Pod. Give it to us.'

'What do you want it for, exactly?' Smith asked.

'We've already been through all this with Professor Summerfield,' August began.

'Professor? I didn't know she was a professor,' Smith grinned. 'Do you know what of?'

'John, don't antagonise them!' Joan hissed.

'Oh, I'll antagonise.' Smith took a step forward. 'I'll antagonise like I've never antagonised before. After all, these two bullies, these two blundering butchers, are going to get what they want.' He waved his hands in the air, glaring at the two aliens. 'They've wiped out hundreds of lives, traumatised a whole community and now they're just going to take what they're after and go.' He fixed August with a piercing gaze. 'Aren't you?'

'That is so,' August assured him. 'We have no wish to – hey!'

Tim, noticing that Hoff's gaze had wandered off him for a moment, had dived off towards the trees.

The two aliens had time to take careful aim before they fired.

But Timothy leapt high in the air, then jumped left right left, and the bolts kicked up the earth around him, shattered tree branches, blasted holes through bark and leaves, until the young boy was lost in the darkness of the orchard.

Smith gazed after him and then sheepishly raised his hands to August and Hoff. 'That, erm, wasn't actually part of the plan.'

Hoff had made to run after the boy but August put a hand on his arm. 'No.'

'No? Do you think I'm going to wait for Greeneye to get here and—'

'There's a much easier way. Serif's analysis indicated that Dr Smith here has a particular weakness.' August pulled a device from his pocket and pointed it at Joan. 'That's her.'

'Wait!' Smith yelled. 'Don't—'

But August had already fired. A tiny dart embedded itself in Joan's chest. Her expression froze, and she started to walk, unsteadily, towards the aliens. Smith grabbed her wrist and tried to pull her back, but with sudden strength, she threw him aside.

August took Joan by the hand and looked down at Smith. 'She's coming with us.'

'If you hurt her—'

'We won't. You have my word. That is, unless you don't bring the Pod to our base in the forest before dawn. In that case, I'll let Greeneye vent his frustrations on her.'

Smith was about to bellow something, but he made it come out as a whisper. 'Where is your base?'

August raised an eyebrow. 'You'll find it. Well, you'd better, hadn't you?'

And, with that, the two of them walked off into the night, taking Joan with them.

Smith waited until they were gone, and then dropped his head to the ground in despair.

12
KNOCK KNOCK

Tim ran through the orchard, cursing himself, the Pod, everything.

It was all falling apart. That stupid man Smith had wanted to give their enemies the Pod. That couldn't be allowed to happen. He didn't know why, it just couldn't. The timing wasn't right.

So he was running pointlessly again.

Or so he thought.

Ahead, some of the apple trees which had been felled by the blast had fallen across the top of some large object.

Some large blue object.

Timothy cautiously walked around the obstruction, until he could see what it was.

A police box.

Not much like the ordinary kind, but recognisable none the less. He rubbed the grey dust away from the notice on the front: *Call here for help.*

'What's a police box doing in the forest?' he asked the Pod. The thing felt… special. Full of possibilities. It reminded Timothy of October teatimes, while his mother had still been alive, eager walks through leafy fields, back for tea and bread with condensed milk. It reminded him of being read to, of being safe.

Gingerly, he touched the surface of the box. It was vibrating gently, humming even.

He knew what the box was then. It was somewhere to run to, somewhere that would always be there, no matter what else was spoilt.

It was magic in a corner of a cold world.

It was home.

Timothy put his arms around the box and hugged it.

And then a telephone began to ring.

Timothy looked around incredulously, trying to find the source of the sound. It seemed to be coming from the box, from behind the sign.

He fumbled with the edge of the plaque and it swung open on a very rusty hinge. Inside was a blue telephone, and that was what was ringing. The Pod was vibrating in time with the sound.

Timothy had never answered a telephone before. He picked up the receiver. 'Hello?' Then, a moment later: 'If that's where I have to go. Why do you want me to show him that? All right. Who is this?'

He shook the telephone, and found that it was dead.

Bernice, Alexander, Rocastle and the boys were taking a careful route back towards the pub, walking slowly down the forest slope rather than risk the school road.

Rocastle was dawdling in the middle of the group, smiling at the boys sadly and walking with his hands in his pockets. That was a posture Bernice had never seen the Head use before. He was certainly in some sort of shock.

'What are you going to do when we get back?' she asked him.

'Oh, I don't know. I can't think of anything further than—'

'Oh my God, look out!' Alexander shouted.

August and Hoff were approaching through the forest, Joan walking stiffly ahead of them.

The party scattered, diving behind the fallen trees.

The two Aubertides wandered by, Hoff checking a dial on his wrist to adjust Joan's direction of movement slightly. 'Serif and

Greeneye will still be sealing off the orchard,' August was saying. 'Think we should leave them to it?'

'They'll eventually get bored,' Hoff muttered. And they moved on, still talking.

After they'd passed, Bernice's party broke cover.

'Mrs Redfern,' Merryweather gasped. 'What are they going to do to her?'

'She's a hostage.' Alton rubbed his chin thoughtfully. 'Or they'd have already harmed her.'

'Well, if the other two are down there in the orchard,' Alexander said, 'I don't fancy running into them.'

'We could go round the line of the hill,' Benny began.

'Excuse me,' Rocastle said. The others looked at him automatically, surprised by his quiet tone of voice. 'Joan – Mrs Redfern – she's also my responsibility, and somebody who might have been a friend. I'm going to rescue her.' He looked slowly around the group. 'Would anybody be willing to help?'

Smith knelt on the ground, staring at his fists.

He was only human. He could walk through the forest shouting, but Tim could hide from him. The boy didn't know the stakes now, didn't know that the most precious thing in Smith's life was now at risk.

What were his principles beside that?

Now that both the sphere and Joan were gone, he felt impotent and lost once more. He was only a small Scottish schoolteacher. He didn't have any heroics to save Joan. All he could do was what any human could: bargain. Bargain ethics against everyday life, the image of how life should be against how it really was.

He closed his eyes, and put his hands together. 'Our Father, who art in heaven, hallowed be thy name. Thy kingdom come. Thy will be done, on Earth as it is in heaven. Give us this day our daily bread, and forgive us our trespasses as we –' he clenched his teeth, and realised that he was crying – 'forgive those that trespass against us. Give us this day our daily bread and deliver us from evil. For thine is the kingdom, the power and the glory. For ever and ever. Amen.'

He curled his knees up to his chin and hugged them.

Gradually, the tension ebbed from him and his body began to realise how late at night it was. The light of the moon overhead reflected off the silver dust all around and made the orchard shine.

He couldn't sleep now. He had to save her. He promised that he'd save everybody.

But on the edge of his mind, he could see her, that other, older her, now, standing with him on those silver rocks in the light of the moon. She put her lips to his ear and whispered something, but still he couldn't quite hear it.

On the branches of the trees around the glade, a circle of owls had landed, standing guard at all points of the compass.

Or perhaps that was in the dream, too.

She was beautiful. 'Verity…' His lips formed the word.

'I say, are you all right?' A voice interrupted him.

He sat bolt upright. 'No!' he yelled at the newcomer. He scrambled to his feet and stared manically at a young man with a centre-parting, who backed away from the madman that he'd woken up. 'She would have told me! She would have told me what I need to know. If I'm a bully or a victim or a coward or a hero. She would have said.'

The man raised his hands in pacification. 'All right, old chap. All right. I'll leave you to sleep.'

Smith rubbed a hand through his hair, realising how wild it had become. 'No. Stay. Bad dreams. What are you doing here?'

'I'm looking for a chum of mine. I met a young lad and—'

'You did? Where?'

'Down by this barrier thing. He let me through. Sent me this way, but it doesn't seem—'

'He can do that?' The question was almost to himself.

'Apparently, yes. What's happened to the school? Do you know what's going on?'

'Less than you do. Can you take me there? To the barrier?'

'Why, yes, of course. Look, who are you?'

'Doctor.'

'Doctor who?'

'We'll see. Who are you?'

'Richard. Richard Hadleman. Soon to be this constituency's MP, hopefully.' Hadleman extended his hand to the ragged figure, who shook it distractedly and grabbed his umbrella from the ground.

'Well,' Smith muttered, 'you won't need much of a majority. This constituency's getting smaller all the time.'

They walked through the forest, Hadleman staring at the silver dust around them. 'It's like *A Midsummer Night's Dream*,' he whispered.

'More like *Hamlet*. Tell me, do you believe in God?'

Hadleman, looking around him, was caught off guard by the question. 'Eh? Oh, no, not at all, actually. I believe in dialectical materialism, the force of history and the revolution. Two ideas collide, form a new idea, a synthesis, and that new idea is naturally revolutionary. History's like a big hill, and we're all rolling down it towards the inevitable. Towards the revolution.' He stopped. 'Of course, that needn't necessarily be a violent revolution. What, ah, are your politics, Doctor?'

Smith considered. 'I don't know if I have any. Not yet. I'll let you know when my own synthesis happens.'

They came to the other edge of the forest, where a tiny stream flowed along, a wooden bridge over it. The bridge was connected to a stile, and the odd haze of the barrier shimmered halfway across the water. The moonlight gave the scene an eerie quality, like it was just a film set.

Smith hopped over the stile and wandered up to the barrier.

215

'Yes, I've seen this before. It's… dangerous. You say Tim brought you through?'

'Yes, I was standing there on the opposite bank, just out of sight of a soldier who's on guard a few hundred yards down there. They'd told me that there was something dangerous going on. Thing is, I heard an explosion, and then, not very long ago, the big one that was probably the school. I was afraid for my friend. I had to get inside. The barrier feels disturbing. I don't know why, but I had a feeling of dread as I approached it, a terrible fear of dying. I was just plucking up the courage to take a run at it when I saw this youngster wandering down the path. He seemed quite surprised to see me, but when I called out to him, he walked up to this… barrier, well, whatever it is, took my hands, and pulled me through. It was like ducking through something very hot and there was a muddy taste. But here I am.'

'Yes…' Smith stretched out his umbrella until it connected with the barrier and then stepped back, as if he'd got an electric shock. 'Very nasty.' He turned back to Hadleman. 'I need to find the boy. We have to talk.'

'We certainly do.' Timothy stepped from behind a tree on the other side of the river. He walked onto the bridge and halted halfway, one hand holding the Pod, the other playing with the air of the barrier like he was idly plucking a harp. 'I had to do this, to put this between us. This way you can't grab the Pod from me and give it to them.'

'I wouldn't just grab it,' Smith said. 'You know I wouldn't.'

'Do I? They have the person you hold most precious in the world.'

'You know about that?'

'I was told.'

'Then why won't you give me the Pod, let me give it to them in exchange for her?'

'Because it doesn't stop there. There's more to it than that one deal. That's why I brought you here. I sent him to find you.' Tim indicated Hadleman.

'Did you?' Hadleman frowned.

'Hmm. Rather manipulative of you,' Smith muttered.

'Perhaps. Come and join me, Dr Smith.'

Hadleman glanced between the two participants, feeling even more that he was in a play. 'We can't cross like you can. He'll be—'

'No.' Smith handed Hadleman his umbrella. 'Take this. If it kills me, give it to Bernice, tell her to carry on.'

'But who's she?'

Smith didn't answer. He stepped onto the bridge and walked forward, his hands reaching out to grasp Timothy's.

Through the barrier.

The fires stretched all the way to the horizon. The ground was blackened and steaming. In the distance stood a vast statue, a little girl with a balloon, made of crystal. Its head stood amongst the slight grey clouds.

Smith looked up at the burnt orange of the sky. 'I know this place,' he said.

'While you're with me, you do,' Timothy told him. They were standing amongst the flames. 'The barrier is two perceived frames of time, different ones, put next to each other. I'm not sure what that means, I was just told it. But a sort of... rubbing between them, that's what hurts people who go through it. Unless they're something called a Time Lord. They can just walk straight through. That rubbing is also what lets us do this.'

'What is this place? Is it hell?'

'It's one possible future. This is the Doctor's home. This is Gallifrey.'

A great singing was echoing across the landscape. Smith watched as a parade passed by down a narrow valley, a series of robed individuals hanging from poles, strung between a row of marching figures. The captors were all different, of many races, some humanoid and some not, of many sexes and sometimes both. They were all clad in fine costumes, with exotic weapons hanging from their belts. They sang a gorgeous, complex song as they hauled their captives between the burnt canyons, towards the foot of the statue. 'Who are they?' asked Smith.

'The children of the Aubertides, the ones who took on the biology of the Gallifreyans. Every regeneration buds, every new individual can regenerate twelve times. They're a vast army now, united and loyal to their family. They used the Doctor's TARDIS to land on the planet, and did what nobody else had managed to do: took the Citadel by force. The Time Lords on the poles are the High Council, the ones in charge of the place. Does this make sense to you?'

'No. Yes. I don't know.' Smith shook his head furiously, as if to clear it. 'They can do this because they got the Pod?'

'Yes.'

'But this is a distant world, nothing to do with me, or Earth, or anything I know. And you said this was one possible future. These Time Lords might fight them off, or perhaps we could warn them, or perhaps—'

'Look closer.' Timothy gave the Pod a squeeze, and they were suddenly at the foot of the statue. An old woman in the robes of a Time Lord was looking imperiously up at August, who held in his hands a wire crown. A much younger Time Lady stood beside them, her straight blonde hair incongruous against her high collar. Behind the two Gallifreyans stood Greeneye, a long curved sword in his hands.

'We found this,' said August. 'It's one of the links to the Matrix, isn't it? How do I access it?'

The old woman pursed her lips. 'You will find no Time Lord willing to give you that information.'

'No, Lady Flavia, I'm sure you're right. I'm sure that this is the impulse that comes over most invading races. The locals won't show them how to preserve certain aspects of their culture, so they destroy everything and, as they rebuild the place in their own image, have to face the indignity of being called barbarians. Flavia, you know how petty and amoral this whole process is. In a century, if that, we will be the Gallifreyans and you will be history. Our descendants may regret this carnage, but they will be secure and happy and here. Don't you wish to preserve some slight details of your civilisation by telling us about them? It is, as you must know, the only possible morality on the grandest scale of things. To have a few pieces on the right side. To win a little. What do you say?'

Flavia thought for a moment and then smiled. 'I like the thought of you being called barbarians for a century or two. Let that be my little victory.'

'Oh.' August nodded to Greeneye imperceptibly. The Aubertide swung the sword back and swept it through Flavia's collar. He halted the swing precisely as the elderly Time Lady fell forward, her neck half severed. Blood poured from the wound and she weakly tried to put her hands to her neck, writhing on the ground. 'Well, I'm sorry, Flavia, but this is for history too. We'll let you regenerate each time and then keep on chopping. It could be worse, believe me.' August turned to the other Time Lady. 'Now, you're the one called Romana, aren't you? Will you tell me how to use this crown?'

Smith flexed his hands into fists. 'Can't we stop them? Can't we interfere?'

'No,' Tim replied. 'We mustn't be seen to be here.'

'I want to go home. I want to go back to Earth, I don't want to see this.'

'Fine, we'll go back to Earth. If you don't care about this—'

'It's too big for me to care about. I can't care about everything. What he said was true, nothing lasts, everything changes. Why should I worry about anything but what I can see, what I can touch?' Smith raised his hands, agonised.

'Why indeed?'

Romana had evidently said something insulting. Greeneye had forced her to her knees in front of him.

'Why won't she just tell them what they want to hear?' Smith demanded. 'It can't be more important than her life, can it?'

Timothy was silent.

'All that they said about history, it's true,' said Smith, his eyes on the twitching Flavia. 'Time doesn't care. But I keep thinking about a school playground. They must have been hurt by somebody. As a family. Hurt as a species. So they hurt back. So they don't change. So nothing changes. Do I really have to hurt them again to stop them? And if I wanted to, could I? All I want is for me and Joan to be left alone.'

The blade scythed up into the air and the young woman looked at it, a slight curl of contempt on her lip.

Smith thought about a dying flutterwing. He could think about it. That was another piece of him that was about to die down in the valley. 'Take me home,' he told Timothy. 'I won't give them the Pod. I'll think of another way. Even if it kills me.'

The man and the boy were standing across the bridge again.

Smith let his hands drop to his sides. Timothy walked forward, the barrier shimmering around him, and joined Smith on his side of it. Hadleman was still watching, entranced.

'Here.' Timothy held up the Pod to Smith. 'Take it. It belongs to you. I know you'll do the right thing with it now. Just as I was told you would.'

Smith held out his hand and took the sphere with a sigh. 'Damn it. Why is everything always so complicated?'

Timothy thought for a moment, his posture slumping back into that of a frightened youth. 'That's life?'

Joan was manacled to an upright post in the family's dome. Hoff had sunk a deep bore into the soil and secured it with magnetic pegs before pulling the dart from her skin. The Aubertides had reassembled at the dome a few minutes earlier.

'So it's unlikely she'll get away?' Greeneye murmured. 'Unlike the other two?'

Hoff only grunted in reply.

'I do not see why we didn't just pursue the boy,' Serif hissed. 'He may be fast, but we would have caught him eventually.'

'Oh yes,' August agreed. 'But consider, if he's starting to be able to leap and hop like a young Time Lord, then the Pod's started to communicate with him. We've seen the information transfer on our scanners. If it's doing that, then it might be—'

'Trying to persuade him to put it to his forehead?!' Greeneye shook his head in frustration. 'Crukking cruk.'

'Exactly. We don't want a little Time Lord on our hands. That would be going back to square one. Therefore, I don't want the boy to feel that he's in danger. Smith will get the Pod from him and bring it to us. Simple.'

'He was quite prepared to, you know.' Joan spoke up. 'Until you captured me. Now I hope that you don't get what you want.'

'Very noble. Any idea what you're being noble about? What this object we're after is?' August plucked a hair from her head and chewed on it thoughtfully.

'I've experienced it. It felt rather terrible and rather wonderful at the same time, like a bottle with a demon in it. It's very powerful.'

'Indeed it is. With it, we could multiply endlessly, conquer half the galaxy, start venturing through time, turn almost everything in the cosmos to our advantage.'

'Why? Aren't you happy with what you've got?'

'No,' Greeneye sighed. 'As I've often said, our whole motive in life is to find something to do. And once you've done that, you have to find something better to do next.'

Joan managed to smile at him. 'I felt like that after Arthur died. But then I found myself involved in teaching. And then I fell in love again. Love really does make you feel satisfied. Have you never known that emotion?'

'I suppose… I keep trying.' Greeneye looked at her seriously. 'Though the others laugh at me for it. I reach out to people, want to touch them, get involved in their reproductive processes. But they always see that as something negative.'

'If you mean what I think you do,' said Joan, 'then I am not surprised. Is that your only definition of love?'

Greeneye shrugged. 'We love each other, us six, us five now. That ought to be enough, oughtn't it?'

'If it is, why do you want to multiply so much?'

Greeneye thought for a moment, then shook his head slowly, pulling a sword from his harness. 'If you say anything else to me, anything at all, I'll cut your head off.'

Joan pursed her lips and smiled sadly again, looking almost sorry for the alien.

'We are unused to such discussions,' Serif hissed. 'If Aphasia still lived, then I might—'

'Look! Greeneye shouted.

Outside the dome, between two trees, stood Bernice Summerfield, a pistol in her hand. The gun was pointed at the dome, but her eyes had just fixed on Greeneye staring at her and her mouth had formed a single dismayed syllable.

She turned and ran.

Greeneye grabbed the nearest member of his family, which happened to be Serif, by the sleeve. 'It's her!' he yelled. 'The one who got away! Come on!'

And he pulled Serif out of the door with him.

'Now, wait—' August found that he was talking to nobody. He sighed and turned to Hoff. 'Do you think that Greeneye would care that that was obviously a trap?'

'No.' Hoff produced his pistol and stuck it under Joan's chin. 'But it's best to be ready. Just in case he can't chop his way out of it.'

*

Benny ran frantically through the forest, uphill along the track that led up on to the downs. She had intended to fire off a couple of rounds against the dome's surface, but the intended effect had been achieved, they were chasing her anyway.

Great. The good bit was that the shattered forest was full of cover. The bad bit was that it was correspondingly hard to run through, even though Benny had carefully selected her path beforehand.

Behind her, Greeneye and Serif were crashing through the undergrowth, trying to bring their weapons to bear on her. If they stopped for a minute and thought about why they were pursuing her, then this was all going to fall apart. She glanced back and saw the look on Greeneye's face. No, actually, he seemed to know exactly why he was doing this.

She hurdled the stile that led up on to the hills, the chalky path shining slightly in the moonlight, and, struggling for breath, sprinted uphill. She had to be over the ridge in, oh, two minutes, otherwise they'd get a clear shot.

Laying this out had seemed so simple compared to actually doing it. At least Rocastle seemed to have lost a lot of his bullishness. Alton had come into his own, too, working out the timings. It had come down to which one of them could best achieve them. Rocastle had wanted to, but that was ridiculous, and in all conscience, Bernice couldn't send one of the boys to do this, not even Hutchinson. Even with her beer belly, which she was personally rather fond of and of which Guy had been terribly enamoured, she was going to be faster than any of the other adults.

She made it over the ridge in one minute fifty, and no energy bolts whizzed past her. She was under cover for the next five minutes.

Then it was a sprint up to the monument.

'Why,' hissed Serif, 'are we doing this?'

'Because of her, because of Aphasia, just because!' Greeneye growled. The two Aubertides were pounding their way uphill, burdened by their heavy weapons.

'Having sexual congress with one more human will not bring Aphasia back!'

'Maybe not, but it will make me feel better!' The aliens skidded down the chalk slopes into the long ridge that led around the lip of the downs, and saw Bernice vanishing around the curve ahead of them in the darkness.

'These are ancient fortifications,' Serif reported. 'I saw in the notes that this area was the scene of a dramatic slaughter. These are earthen walls built by the Iceni against the Romans.'

'Who?' Greeneye had nothing but red rage in his face.

Serif took a deep breath and kept running. 'If you don't learn the lessons of history...' he whispered.

Bernice saw the stone features of Old Meg looming up on the hillock above her and doubled her speed. Her two pursuers would round the end of the channel down below in a minute or so, maybe more if they thought they were about to be fired upon.

Alexander popped up from behind the monument and called to her. 'Turn to your right, don't run ahead!'

She swerved and took a curving route round to the monument. She dived behind it, panting. 'Wonderful diet. The Pursued By Aliens Plan. I can recommend it.'

'How many did you get?' asked Rocastle. There was no sign of the boys.

'Two.'

'One would have been better for a hostage.'

'I'm terribly sorry. Did you manage to do anything with—'

'Too dangerous. I think we managed to put those wonderful tools of yours to good use, though. Now, off to the flint pit with you two. I'll wait here.' He took his pistol back from Bernice with a wry little smile.

Alexander and Benny dashed down the hillside behind the monument. Ancient flint diggings provided useful cover there. The two of them leapt in, to find the boys lying there, an assortment of rocks and rough wooden stakes in their hands.

'Oh, Bernice!' said Anand. 'Merryweather here has been fretting terribly about you.'

Merryweather glared at him.

'Maybe we could have dinner when this is all over?' Bernice winked at the embarrassed boy.

'I, ah, beg your pardon?' Merryweather squeaked.

Alexander patted him on the head. 'I do believe she's teasing you.'

Greeneye and Serif ran out on to the light slope where the monument stood and looked around. 'Where is she?' Greeneye muttered, pulling both his swords from his harness.

They split up, fanning out in different directions. Rocastle peered out from behind Old Meg and winced. They were supposed to assume that the statue was the obvious cover and run straight for it.

Greeneye indeed was wandering towards him, but Serif was some distance away, slowly turning as if smelling the air.

Rocastle took a deep breath, poked his head out again and shouted. 'Oh my God, they're here!'

Greeneye spun. He ran at the monument.

And fell straight through the ground.

Before she'd left, Bernice had shown the boys how to use her excavation probe, a gravitic device that could, at its highest setting, create a large pit. Over that pit, they'd put a film of resin created by her ion bonder. Then they'd just thrown a light covering of the soil and grass from the pit back over it.

Greeneye dropped straight through the resin, bellowing as he went. His swords had gone flying as he tripped over the edge.

But Serif stopped just short of the pit's edge, his arms spiralling.

He balanced himself and stepped back. 'You did this?' he hissed at Rocastle, who stepped out from behind the monument.

'I did,' Rocastle said. 'And my lads killed your girl.'

He jumped back behind the monument as an energy bolt hissed past his head.

Serif glanced down at the pit beneath his feet. Greeneye was staring up at him angrily from about twenty feet below, his face a mass of blood, one eye caked shut. 'Throw both of them down here,' he bellowed, 'and I'll toss you the scraps!'

Serif nodded and stalked towards the monument, firing energy bolts at intervals into the ground in front of him.

Hutchinson scrambled to climb over the edge of the flint workings, but Alexander grabbed him by the collar and pulled him back.

'Not yet!' Benny whispered. 'If I let any of you get into danger, Rocastle will kill me.'

'But he's—'

'He's armed. We're not.'

Serif had reached Old Meg. He stepped slowly around it, anticipating an attack at any second.

Rocastle stepped out behind him and raised his gun. 'Now—'

Serif spun and knocked the gun from his hand. 'You should not have warned me.' He swung his own pistol up.

Rocastle lunged forward and slammed the alien against the stone. 'You destroyed all my dreams, you know,' he told him as they struggled, almost conversationally. 'But, strangely, I feel almost as if I ought to say—'

Serif spun him round, smashing the human against the base of the statue. Rocastle fell, winded, and looked up as Serif aimed his pistol at his head.

'Thank you.'

*

The force of the explosion threw Hutchinson and Alexander back off the edge of the flint diggings. The others threw their hands over their heads as debris rained down, small lumps of the stone that had made up Old Meg.

Benny peered up over the edge. The monument was a crater in the ground, at its centre a mass of flaming debris that was sparking up into the sky, small detonations still going off.

She climbed out and walked over to the flaming pyre, Alexander and the boys following her.

'He knew that it would explode,' Hutchinson said. 'It was the only way.'

'No it bloody wasn't,' Benny whispered.

There might have been an argument then, but Merryweather had turned to look in the direction of the pit. 'Look!' he yelled.

A hand had gripped the rim of the pit, and was scrambling against the crumbling earth, trying for a solid hold. As they watched, Greeneye slapped another hand after the first and began to haul himself over the edge, his face a mask of rage and sorrow. 'Serif!' he was bellowing. 'You animals! I'll cover this hill with your blood!'

Hutchinson started to say something, but it came out as a roar. He sprinted towards the pit and the other boys followed, yelling shrill cries.

Hutchinson grabbed one of Greeneye's swords from the ground where it lay and Merryweather grabbed another. The rest of the boys formed a rough circle around the pit as the alien climbed out of it, clutching their rocks and clubs.

Only Anand stayed back, beside Alexander. 'Are you going to help them?' he asked Bernice.

Benny realised that she'd just been staring at the scene, absolutely useless to everybody. She was feeling sick inside. It took her a moment to realise why.

She'd seen this before.

She started forward. 'Wait—'

Greeneye was now fully emerged from the pit. 'Well then?' he shouted. 'Who's first!' He grabbed for his gun.

Hutchinson lashed out and Greeneye clutched at his upper arm, the gun tumbling from his numbed fingers.

Merryweather ran in and struck him across the leg, the ultra-sharp blade bursting a line of blood from Greeneye's thigh. He roared and lashed out, knocking Merryweather to the ground. He stumbled forward, felling boys to the left and right with his fists. Hutchinson went flying too, dropping his sword.

But the boys still closed in, swinging their rocks and clubs.

Benny shoved her way through the crowd, pushing them aside to get to the man.

Lashing out all around him, he was blindly groping to get a hand into his boot.

He pulled out a small black capsule.

Benny leapt through the boys, straight at him. She knocked him over, landing on his chest, blows still falling randomly around her.

'You can't stop us!' Greeneye was roaring. 'I – will – see you all die…'

His fingers squeezed the end of the capsule. It was about to burst.

Benny felt something give inside her, an internal explosion of some vast rage she'd never known. 'Nobody else dies!' she shouted.

And she punched him.

Very hard.

The body slumped back onto the ground, unconscious.

The capsule fell from his hand.

The boys fell back.

Hutchinson swayed into view amongst them, having recovered the sword. He swung it up overhead, about to behead the alien.

But Benny threw herself onto the body, clutching him tightly

228

to her, slamming her head against his. 'Nobody else dies! Do you hear me?' She glared up at Hutchinson. 'Do you understand?'

'She's hysterical.' Alton stepped forward. 'Let's get you—'

'I am not bloody hysterical, I'm not the one trying to kill the hostage!'

There was a general mumble of agreement. The boys started to drop their improvised weapons.

Hutchinson placed the sword on the ground, visibly controlling his anger.

Alexander helped Benny to her feet. She was shivering. 'Busy day.' She flapped her hand, wincing. 'Ow, I think I've broken my knuckle.'

Alton spoke up. He was crouching by Greeneye's neck, his hand on the alien's pulse. 'This man's going to come round soon. Can't we secure him somehow?'

'Schoolboys who don't have any string?' a familiar voice called from behind them. Smith was standing against the burning crater on the skyline, leaning on his umbrella. 'That's unusual.'

13
LET ME TELL YOU
SOMETHING THAT'S TRUE

'Doctor!' Bernice cried, and ran to him.

Smith disengaged himself from the hug. 'Smith. Still.' He pulled the Pod from his pocket and spun it in the air thoughtfully. 'I haven't yet applied for my honorary doctorate. I saw how you saved him, by the way.' He pointed to Greeneye, who was even now being bound in miles of schoolboy string. 'Well done.'

'We need him as a hostage.'

'I doubt that would work. Anyhow, that wasn't why you did it.'

Benny resumed the hug and this time he allowed it. 'No,' she whispered. 'It wasn't. I think I've developed this phobia about letting people get surrounded by men with swords. Hey, how did you know about that?'

'This.' Smith rubbed the Pod on his elbow. 'It lets me know little bits. At random, I think. Oh, by the way, I brought some friends.'

Up the hill behind him had appeared Hadleman and Tim.

Anand ran to Tim and shook him warmly by the hand. 'I thought you were dead!' he laughed.

'So did I,' said Tim.

Alexander had been helping the boys secure Greeneye. Now the curator looked up. For an instant, he closed his eyes. Then he made himself smile and stood up, waving. 'Richard!'

Hadleman ran forward, and the two men stood at a distance from each other, their hands forming restrained spirals before them.

'Alex, old chap, what are you doing here?' Hadleman grinned.

'I could say the same. Come and, erm, see what's happened to the monument.' Alexander glanced at Smith and the boys, and the two men wandered around to the other side of the destroyed statue.

Benny was still holding on to Smith. 'So, you're finally convinced that you weren't always human?'

'I am. What an odd thing to find out.'

'Well, this might be a good time to consider what species you'd like to be. You know about Joan?'

'Yes. They've told me I have until dawn to give them this, or they kill her.' Smith gazed at the brightness that was starting to redden the eastern horizon. 'I had thought of just making the swap, but Timothy showed me what would happen if I did. I was tempted to go through with it anyway, because I do love her, Benny.' His eyes sought hers. 'But I don't think the Doctor would like it.'

'You mean you're still going to stay as Smith? You don't want to be the real you, despite all this?' Benny sat down heavily on the grass. 'The Doctor would have some plan worked out in two seconds. One, if we had a chessboard handy.'

He sat down beside her. 'John Smith is the real me. And it's because of all this, not despite it. You don't know what you really want in life until it's taken from you.'

'You mean Joan?'

'Yes. She agreed to marry me. I have to save her. And I have to do it as me.'

Benny looked at him for a moment, and then resignedly laid her head on his shoulder. 'If there's one thing I've learnt in the past few weeks, it's that we don't get second chances. Do you need a bridesmaid? I've always wanted to be one, but everybody I've ever known has been scared to death of altars.'

'You mean you think I should?'

'I think you ought to go for whatever you think will work. I might even start to like her.'

Smith nodded solemnly. 'So we have to win, if only so you can expand your wardrobe. But we're going to do it as you and me. Smith and Summerfield. Will you come with me?'

Benny carefully planted a kiss on top of his head. 'You're beautiful,' she told him. 'Of course I will.'

Smith grinned, frowned and bit his lip at the same time. 'Erm, thank you.'

'You know, I think Rocastle got a bit of Doctorishness off of you before he died. It must be catching.'

'Perhaps. But does the Doctor have to sacrifice himself to win?'

'Sometimes.' Benny shivered, not knowing why. 'So,' she asked, 'shall we go and have this adventure?'

'The last adventure. Before I retire.'

'And do you have a plan?'

'Oh yes. Tell me, have you ever played poker?'

August checked the controls on the vortex tunnel. 'We can be ready to depart as soon as we have the Pod.' He glanced at the approaching dawn. 'If, that is, Serif and Greeneye get back.'

'I'm worried,' Hoff muttered. He was still squatting by the post, his gun jammed under Joan's chin. 'They're taking too long. And we heard an explosion.'

'That'll just be Greeneye overreacting. Still, if they don't appear before Smith does, then I'll just use the Pod before we go to search for them. We'd be able to locate them in a moment with the services of a TARDIS at our command.'

'You're certain he'll bring the Pod?'

'Of course. We have the thing he holds most precious in the world.' August patted Joan's head.

'I'm not a thing,' Joan told him.

'Oh, in this game you are. We're all things when it comes to war. You see—' August realised that Hoff was staring out of the dome in surprise. He followed his gaze.

Smith and Bernice were wandering unconcernedly towards the dome, Smith wearing his white evening gloves. The two of them walked straight in through the open doorway.

Hoff pressed his gun closer into Joan's face. 'John!' she cried. 'I hadn't dared hope—'

'What?' hissed Smith. 'Oh, of course – she thinks that I am Dr Smith. Greeneye and I succeeded in cornering his fleeing companion on the hillside. She and some of the boys had mounted a trap for us. We fooled them through my assumption of this form. That finger I consumed proved to be... very useful.'

'And I had some fun afterwards. Professor Summerfield put up quite a fight.' Bernice wiped the back of her hand across her mouth, her other hand on her hip. 'Delicious memories, almost as good as that Auregan.' She wandered over to Joan and ran a hand through her hair.

Joan shivered. 'Does this mean that... Is John dead? Please tell me.'

'No. He wasn't about. Lucky for him.' Bernice looked up at August. 'Can I have some of this? It's always that way with humanoids: you have one and ten minutes later you want another.' She pulled a strand of hair from Joan's head and chewed on it thoughtfully.

Hoff relaxed, standing up and dropping his gun back into its holster.

August smiled at Bernice. 'Yes, of course, but don't do her too much damage, we need something to give to Smith. This Auregan you mention, do you mean Sula?'

Bernice glanced up from where she'd knelt down, starting to tap Joan's sides with her fingers like a skilled butcher. 'No, not him. Didn't I tell you about Kuala? Or was it Tuola? I just fancy some kidneys...'

Joan began to sob uncontrollably. 'Oh God, somebody save me, please…'

August turned back to Smith. 'You don't have the Pod, I take it?'

'No.' Smith shook his head. 'Smith must still be searching for it.'

August absently picked up a scanner and checked a reading. 'So why keep his form?'

'I can search for the boy like this, also. He will trust me.'

Joan gave a shriek. Bernice was working at something behind her. 'Finger,' she explained. 'That won't annoy Smith too much, will it? They'll be a matching pair.'

Smith idly picked up the control dart-gun from one of the benches and inspected the muzzle. 'Ready?' he asked.

'For what?' August frowned.

'Yes,' Bernice called cheerfully.

Smith spun the gun round and fired darts into August and Hoff.

Bernice threw aside the manacles she'd been cutting through and pulled Joan to her feet. She dropped the laser cutter back into her pocket. 'Sorry I burnt you,' she told Joan, 'but it added a touch of realism.'

August plucked the dart from his chest. 'I'm astonished,' he said. 'But those darts don't affect us.' He snatched his gun from its holster and pointed it at Bernice.

A question mark umbrella handle plucked it from his hand and sent it spinning across the dome.

Hoff grabbed for Joan's shoulder, but she was already running, Bernice pulling her bodily out into the forest.

August swung a blow at Smith's head, but the little man ducked, rolled over and popped up again in time to trip Hoff as he dived for the door. He gave a quick bow and hopped over the sprawled alien, dashing off into the trees.

'No!' August shouted. He slapped a control on the wall.

*

Smith, Benny and Joan sprinted through the lightening undergrowth, Joan being virtually carried along between the other two. 'John!' she panted. 'You rescued me!'

'We're not out of the woods yet,' Smith gasped. 'Still—'

'Is it me, or are we slowing down?' Bernice asked.

They all looked down. Beneath them, the humus was slipping away from their feet. A great wind rose against them, and suddenly they were pushing to make headway, the air around them as thick as treacle. A buffeting hurricane of leaves and twigs thundered by.

Smith swung his umbrella in a slow arc and the handle caught around a tree branch a few feet ahead. He pulled on the umbrella itself and managed to haul them forward a little way, the wood stretching and creaking with the effort.

Bernice got a hand on the umbrella, too, and helped to pull.

'They've got us again, John.' Joan's voice was calm and strong. 'Promise me one thing. Don't give them what they want, even if it means my life. They've told me what they intend to do with it. Do you understand? Don't be unfaithful to who you are. Promise me.'

'They're not going to—'

'Promise me!'

'Yes, I promise. I love you.'

'I love you. Thank you for coming back for me.'

The umbrella started to stretch.

Bernice made a mighty effort. She slapped a hand forward, and worked her way up the shaft, hand over hand.

She managed to get hold of the tree itself and hauled herself past it.

She tumbled down a slope on the other side, free of the force. She scrambled quickly back up the bank. Supporting herself against the tree, she poked her head over the ridge.

It was like being hit on the back of the head with a hammer. The force grabbed her skull and tried to haul it off her shoulders.

'Doctor!' she called. 'Get down here!' She reached out a hand, but Smith and Joan were still clinging on to the umbrella and each other. Joan began to slip from Smith's arms and his fingers grew white on the umbrella handle.

'No…' he said, despairing.

And then he was torn from the umbrella.

Smith and Joan shot off backwards towards the dome, the umbrella spinning after them.

Bernice watched as they went. Hoff and August caught them neatly by the dome and threw them inside. Then the force that had captured them was switched off, and all was quiet again in the forest.

'Do you think you're dealing with children?' August pulled Smith to his feet.

'Children would be better behaved,' Joan told him. She smiled proudly at the aliens. 'John came to rescue me, against all the odds.'

'We have similar ethics, then.' August let go of Smith and motioned to Hoff. The gruff alien grabbed Joan and secured her to one of the benches. 'We both look after our own. Where are Serif and Greeneye?'

Smith glared at him. 'The first is dead. The second we've taken prisoner. I'll swap him for—'

'No. If you had the stomach to harm him, that would have been your initial strategy.' He picked up the scanner again and checked the readings. 'You're swamped with the kind of radiation we've learnt to associate with the Pod. It's not on you, but you do have it hidden somewhere.' He pointed to Joan. 'Our offer still stands. Give us the Pod and she lives. Go and get it.'

Smith looked into August's eyes. 'If she's hurt, there will be nowhere in the cosmos that you can hide from me.'

August inclined his head. 'I believe you. One hour.'

As Smith left the dome, he caught sight of the expression

on Joan's face. Pride and quiet determination. He paused for a moment, then, imperceptibly, he nodded to her.

When he'd left, Hoff turned to August, his eyes closed in grief. 'Serif too…' he whispered. 'This trip has been costly.'

'They'll both be avenged.' August patted his shoulder. 'Before we go, we'll reduce this world to ashes.'

The others were waiting in the forest, sitting in a great circle in a clearing, too shocked or nervous to make their way home. Alton had started a fire and Hutchinson was staring into it morosely. Anand and Tim were talking in whispers, going over Tim's adventures.

'The thing is,' Tim was saying, 'I thought that I knew how Rocastle was going to die. The Pod told me. But he blew himself up to kill Serif.'

'Then that means that the future's wide open. We can change it,' Anand whispered. 'Isn't that wonderful?'

The other boys were huddled together, some of them sobbing, others just slowly calming down, ridding themselves of the tension and the fear of death that had been with them for the last few hours. It didn't help that Greeneye was tied to a tree nearby, under the watchful gaze of Alexander and Hadleman. After he woke up, the prisoner had started shouting threats and curses, but after a while, these had changed into pleas and requests for food. Once it was certain that he wasn't going to get any, he slumped into an angry silence.

The sky overhead was getting lighter. It had been a warm night, but they were all ready to welcome the dawn.

'So,' Alexander broke the silence. He'd been looking at Richard and wondering if he should tell him. He mustn't do that. The only thing he could do was to enjoy every moment they had left. 'Does anybody know any good stories?'

'Oh, shut up,' muttered Hutchinson.

'You shut up,' Tim told him.

'You can't tell me that, bug.'

'Yes I can, and don't call me bug.'

'Who thinks –' Hadleman raised his voice – 'that Tim should shut up? Raise your hand.'

No hands appeared.

'And who thinks that Hutchinson should shut up?'

A lot of hands appeared.

'There. Tell us a story, Tim.'

'It doesn't work like that,' Hutchinson sighed wearily. 'I'm his Captain, so I can tell him to shut up.' There was a murmur of discontent around the circle. Hutchinson looked up, suddenly bemused. 'What?'

'I think…' Hadleman picked up the red sphere that Smith had left with him and stood up. Alexander watched him worriedly. He'd advised Richard not to hold on to the Pod, to leave it by the fire. Now he was throwing it lightly from hand to hand. 'I think that democracy will soon be everything. You lads just got your first vote. If the balloon goes up this year, or the next, maybe the generals will finally realise that, in the end, a soldier fights for his conscience. He isn't an animal to be herded to the slaughter.'

'Wouldn't you fight, then?' Hutchinson glared at him. 'Would you be a coward?'

Alexander watched a distant expression wash over Hadleman's face. Finally, he put the Pod back down on the ground and met Hutchinson's gaze. 'I would fight if I thought the cause was just, as far as any of us can tell that sort of thing. And, believe me, there will be plenty of cowards on the battlefield, and plenty of heroes who make the decision not to go there.' Rather embarrassed by his eloquence, he shrugged and sat down.

Alexander stared at him sadly. 'I love you,' he mouthed, though Hadleman couldn't see.

Hutchinson probably wouldn't have let the matter rest there, but into the clearing walked Smith and Benny.

Smith glanced around the group. 'I'm sorry,' he told them.

'We failed. They still have Mrs Redfern.'

'Well then, there are enough of us!' Hutchinson gestured to the boys once more. 'There are only two of them. Never mind all this anarchist bunkum—'

'Socialist bunkum,' said Alexander.

'It's time for some good old British grit. Play up and play the game, chaps! We've nearly done it, we've knocked out three-fifths of their force! Listen, I have a plan…'

Smith stared at the young man as he started to make the words again, to spread his hands in grand gestures. Unseen, he wandered around the campfire to where Alexander and Hadleman were sitting. Smith bent down and picked up the Pod. 'Mine, I think.'

Alexander looked up at him. 'Is it?'

'Oh yes.'

'Take care.'

'I will.'

Bernice was standing with Tim and Anand's group, much to Merryweather's delight. The Captain had discreetly moved around the fire to sit by them. Benny was making loud coughs and trying to start other conversations as Hutchinson went through the motions of his speech. Every now and then she looked at what Smith was doing, desperate for him, yet not knowing what advice she could possibly give.

Still, she was surprised when he appeared behind her and put a hand on her shoulder. 'It was good to know you.'

'Doctor, you're not—'

'Smith. Dr Smith. Call me that now, at least.'

Benny carefully adjusted his tie, whispering so that Tim couldn't hear her. 'You're not planning on—'

Smith patted her gently on the arm. 'Walk with me a little way, I don't want to listen to that.' He indicated Hutchinson, walking around the campfire, pointing in the air.

*

They wandered through the forest until they came to a dark glade, where the rising sun stretched the shadows of the trees into long, spectral shapes. Benny rubbed a hand across her face. She was so tired that she felt like she might fall asleep any moment. The sensation had come over her in the last few minutes.

'I've discovered a lot in the last few weeks,' Smith began. 'I've found out that being the Doctor… it's not about having special knowledge or abilities. It's about not being cruel. It's about not being afraid.' He walked into the middle of the clearing, searching for the right words. 'There are monsters out there, yes. Terrible things. But you don't have to become one in order to defeat them. You can be peaceful in the face of their cruelty. You can win by being cleverer than they are.' He turned back to Bernice. 'I tried to give up so much – my responsibilities, my past, my guilt. But others kept these things safe for me. Now, for one last time, I, John Smith, will be the Doctor again, and go on an adventure, and defeat the monsters. It doesn't take an object to let you do that. It takes determination. And hope for humanity. And love.'

Benny went to him and held him. 'What you said about sacrifice, John. It doesn't have to be like that. There's always another way.'

'Not this time.'

'I just don't want anybody to have to die. Hadleman, my old Guy, Rocastle. Poor Constance. But especially you. Both of you.'

'Then let me do this, before more children get killed.' His words seemed quieter somehow, as if they were coming from a distance, part of the whole distance of the glade. When she came to write this section of the narrative up for her diary, Benny felt that she was somehow writing fiction.

Especially considering what happened next.

She stepped out from the trees, a beautiful dark-haired woman. 'John…' she called.

Smith and Benny turned and stared at her.

'Verity,' said Smith.

August stood by the door of the dome, gazing out into the darkness. 'It is quite a beautiful world, don't you think, son? I like the trees particularly.'

Hoff ducked his head outside and looked. 'Hm. Trees are trees. I'm worried about Greeneye. Don't you think we should have bargained?'

'And gone back to square one? No. Once we've got the Pod, we'll rescue him. Oh, and talking of which—'

A small, shadowy figure was making his way slowly through the forest.

Hoff picked up his gun and went to stand beside Joan. She had been sleeping fitfully, but now she'd woken once more.

'You know, you really could come to some kind of accord with John,' she said. 'He's a good man. We all feel for our own kind. Perhaps—'

'Shut her up,' August snapped.

Hoff slapped a dart into Joan's neck and the woman froze, breathing shallowly.

The figure in the darkness approached the dome. To the east, the sky was blue, and a prickly expectation was settling on the forest, the calls of waking birds mingling with the departing sounds of night hunters as the sun rose.

August stepped forward. 'Dr Smith. Have you brought the Pod?'

'Yes.' The figure stepped forward, his left hand in his pocket, his right holding the red sphere. 'Where's Joan?'

'Here.' Hoff activated a control and Joan stood up. He took a key and loosed her from her chains.

August studied the little man before him. 'You've finally given up, then? No last-minute tricks? No desperate gambits?'

'Only a request. Reconsider. What's in that sphere is vast and terrible. It's a tremendous responsibility. Do you really want to take it on?'

'I've thought about it long and hard, believe me.' August reached out, and, with an anticipatory pause, took the Pod from the other man's palm. 'I've prepared for this transformation. I've had psionic blockers placed in my brain to filter Time Lord personality data and stop it replacing my own. What I'll get is all the information, all the memories, but none of the compulsions or traits that made the Doctor what he was. He will, in effect, die, but in so doing he will create a new species. A very strong one. Now.'

He slowly raised the Pod to his forehead. Blue sparks began to dance between the two surfaces.

They touched.

August screamed in pain and doubled over, his hand clutching the Pod in determined agony. Hoff stared at the scene, covering the others with his gun.

Suddenly, August jumped to his feet again and spun to look at Hoff, his arms extended. His pupils were shining silver, information spiralling across them. 'Hoff, I can feel it, it's wonderful!'

He spasmed again, twisting into a crouch, his hand still wrapped tight around the Pod.

His eyes met those of the little man in the shadows.

A look of horror passed across the silver pupils.

And then it was gone.

August slowly straightened up and tossed the Pod from hand to hand. He smiled a satisfied smile and stretched. 'Let her go, Hoff. We've got what we wanted.'

Hoff stared. 'It worked? You're a Time Lord?'

'Yes! I feel as if I could fly!' He walked up to Joan, and waved a hand before her sightless eyes. 'I want her to see me.' He plucked the dart from her neck and she jerked back to life, staring at the man who stood before her.

The smile was enough to tell her what had happened. 'You…' Her eyes narrowed, and she glanced between the three men in the dome. Then she said carefully: 'You gave him what he wanted.'

'No.' The man with the umbrella stepped forward. 'I didn't.'

August touched Joan's chin, extremely tenderly. 'He's right.'

Hoff frowned, realising that something was happening that he didn't understand.

He grabbed Joan, pulling her away from August, and pressed his gun into her neck. 'Wait!'

'Hoff…' August spread his hands, amazed. 'What's wrong?'

'I want to see his hand. The one he's got in his pocket. Then I decide what I do next.'

'Well, you could always…' The man in the shadows revealed his left hand, and flexed his little finger. His calm expression darkened into a stormy frown, and he growled: 'Run.'

August lunged at Hoff.

Hoff threw Joan aside and brought up his gun.

The blast went straight through August's side.

But the force of August's run sent both men tumbling backwards towards the wall of the dome.

The Doctor threw the Pod across the room. It slapped against a control on a distant instrument bank. He jumped at a closer panel, and, faster than the eye could follow, clattered hundreds of switches into new positions.

Hoff threw the gasping body of August aside and swung up his gun towards the Doctor.

But the Time Lord had already spun the final dial.

The first time barrier swept into the room through the wall of the dome and into the sphere atop the control panel that the Doctor was working on. Hoff shouted as the shimmering wall went through him. 'No!' he bellowed. 'Don't!' He dived at Joan and held on to her like a lifejacket. 'You'll kill her too!'

'I'll kill no one,' the Doctor snarled.

The second timeframe arrived a moment later.

The two walls collided, with all of them between them.

Hoff fell from Aphasia's wrist, a tiny newborn trailing blood.

Greeneye caught the baby and dropped him into a vat of liquid nutrients. 'Isn't he wonderful?' he said.

Hoff had never known he'd heard that before.

Serif was busy dabbing at Aphasia's wrist as she sobbed. August looked proudly down into the vat and smiled. 'Well, that's the last one. What shall we do now?'

Laylock was standing by the door of the dome they'd erected. Every now and then, he'd glance out at the burning fields in the distance. 'What indeed?' he whispered.

Hoff lay back in the liquid and luxuriated in it. He was at peace, for the first time in his life. And the last.

The Doctor watched the image of the scene spiral away, replaying itself time after time between the shimmering membranes of the timeframe. He was watching with his eyes closed, because he knew that if he opened them, he'd really be just standing in the dome.

And it was good to be able to watch with his eyes closed again.

Good to be the Doctor.

August stood before him in the timeless time. He held out his hand. 'The Doctor, I presume?'

'Good to meet you, Dr Smith.' The Doctor shook the hand of the being who used to be August, marvelling at how familiar the new expression on the alien's face was. 'I got you killed. I'm sorry.'

'Don't be. Joan would never have accepted me like this, in this body. Does she know?'

'I don't know.'

'Then don't tell her. Do I call you Father?'

'If you want. I haven't heard that for a while.'

245

'It doesn't seem appropriate.'

'No.' The Doctor looked past August's, or rather, Smith's, shoulder.

Verity was standing there. 'Doctor. Dr Smith.'

Smith spun round and gazed at her. 'Verity. My dear.'

The woman smiled. 'I'm flattered, John, that you regard me as an old flame. That was your interpretation of what I was doing in your memories. But I think you're on rather dangerous ground. I'm one of the Doctor's dreams, an icon, a female custodian of something that's deep inside him. I was the only piece of himself that he left behind in his head. I'm important to him. He hardly listens to me, mind you. And he never returns my telephone calls.'

'Do you want to tell me what you told John in the glade this morning?' the Doctor asked. 'What you were trying to whisper in his ear for so long?'

'You still don't know? I don't see why I should tell you now. You employed me, after all, to defend and take care of your deepest memories, and then you failed to take heed of any of my warnings.'

'I didn't, you mean,' Smith interjected.

'There are things down there in my unconscious that even I don't know about, memories from before I was born,' the Doctor explained. 'I couldn't get rid of all of them and Smith was certain to start accessing some of it. I just thought that there ought to be somebody in there who knew who I was.'

'Couldn't she have appeared earlier and saved me all that bother?' Smith asked.

Verity patted him on the shoulder. 'I wasn't allowed to. That was the frustrating thing. I couldn't intrude into your consciousness. I could only appear when you'd got it sorted out for yourself.'

'So what did you say to him?' the Doctor asked.

'That he believes in good and fights evil. That, with violence all around him, he's a man of peace. That he's never cruel, or cowardly. That he is a hero.'

Smith closed his eyes for a moment. 'It felt good to hear it confirmed. Of course, that's not a definition of me. That's you, Doctor.'

The Doctor reached out and touched him on the shoulder. 'As I believe you said, being me is a state of mind. Six other people apart from you and I have had a go. You were rather good at it.'

Smith looked at him again and managed a smile. 'Perhaps I taught a few more would-be Doctors how to do it.'

'Perhaps. But I wonder how many will remember when they grow up?'

Verity waved a hand between them. 'Sorry to interrupt. Look who's here.'

Death looked at them all, sniffily. 'You deal with me again, raven Time Lord, possibly for the last time.' She put a hand on Smith's shoulder. 'This one belongs to me, now. I told you long ago, Doctor, that I would take a life from you in return for that of your companion. Our business is now concluded.'

Smith shivered at her touch. 'What's going to happen to me?' he asked.

'Another owl for Lord Rassilon?' the Doctor asked.

'That is not for you to ask,' Death replied.

Verity kissed Smith's forehead. 'It'll be fine. Bloody Eternals think they own the universe. They don't know everything.'

Death began to fade, and Smith with her, the man looking around himself in wonder.

'Give my love to Time and Pain,' said the Doctor.

'If it wasn't for Time, I would never entertain you.' Death glared at him. 'But you cannot let family down.'

She clicked her fingers.

The Doctor opened his eyes.

Joan was standing in front of him, staring at the ring on her

247

finger. 'When – whatever that was – happened, the ring saved me. I could feel it, protecting me, holding me here like a sort of anchor.'

'Good.' The Doctor went to the bank of controls, and pulled a long electrical cord from it. He peered at the globe where the two timeframes spun around each other, then hopped over to where the Pod lay, still in August's dead fingers.

'That poor man,' Joan whispered. 'He must have turned against his fellows at the last moment. He gave his life for his conscience.'

The Doctor bit his lip, pulling the Pod from the cold hand. 'Yes…' He connected the Pod to one end of the cable, and the timeframes to the other, then hit a few switches. The timeframes faded and he spun the Pod in triumph. 'Good, that's Hoff in the Pod as well. Now…' He pulled the cloth from the vortex disc, and reset the controls, so the butterfly tunnel spun off in another direction. 'The Monks of Felsecar guard some of the most dangerous artefacts in the universe. I'm sure they'll appreciate another item for their collection. Who knows, maybe one day they'll let those two out.'

'Why, John, what do you mean?'

The Doctor winced again, secretly. 'Nothing. I'm still confused.' He tossed the Pod into the vortex, and watched it spin away into the distance. Then he switched off the cabinet. 'Shall we go?'

'Where?'

'About three hundred yards away. Out of range of the self-destruct mechanism.'

'Oh,' said Joan.

From the diary of Prof. Bernice Summerfield
In the clearing in the forest, I watched as the woman walked up to John Smith and whispered something in his ear.

She vanished soon afterwards and Smith turned and walked away into the darkness.

I think. When I came to write this all up… Listen, if you're a historian, you know you can't trust a diary, right?

Well, it felt like the woman was just a character I'd made up. Perhaps I'll just start this whole account with the words: 'Long ago and far away.'

I got back to the campfire and walked round and round it, hugging myself.

Hutchinson was still in mid-rant when the time barriers hit us.

We got to our feet after they'd passed, feeling as if a ghost had gone by, or that we'd just missed a fast aircraft at an air display.

Tim blinked. 'I feel like – like I've just woken from a dream,' he said. 'Goodness, Anand, what a strange few days this has been.'

Hutchinson stopped talking, tried to pick up his place and started to flounder. I have a feeling, if my own experience was anything to go by, that he has a smell of mud and iron in his nostrils.

Hadleman and Alexander clutched each other. Alexander looked at the other man and I saw a strange, hopeful, smile on his face. 'I don't know why,' he said, 'but I suddenly feel quite hopeful.'

While I was doing all this observing, and the sun was coming up too – by the way, I'm really quite thorough about background – I realised that I'd started to cry. Or laugh. Or something.

What a strange life this is.

At any rate, by the time the Doctor got there, I was smiling.

Diary Entry Ends

14
CAT HEAVEN

The Doctor stepped into the circle of boys. 'Hello. I'm the Doctor.'

'Are you?' Bernice leapt to her feet and grabbed him, looking joyfully into his eyes. 'So—'

'I used the Pod before I got to the dome. August didn't know that. He was prepared to fight off Time Lord bio-data, not human nature. Smith took over his body. August and Hoff are now in the Pod themselves, off to safekeeping.'

'And what about Joan?'

The Doctor's face clouded. 'Smith died saving her. I think he was fond of her. I sent her back to her house.'

Tim ran forward and beamed up at the Doctor. 'So you beat them?'

'Yes. And I didn't kill them. So I won. Talking of which...' He wandered around the tree and smiled gawkily up at the naked Greeneye. 'What are we going to do with you?'

'I don't care. You can torture me—'

'No. I think I'll have you locked up. I did that once to an immensely powerful other-dimensional sorceress. She got out immediately, but the experience left her feeling sheepish.'

'But we can't have him getting away,' Hutchinson objected. 'He ought to be bloody well hung!'

Bernice raised an eyebrow and Alexander burst out laughing.

Alton wandered up. 'I appreciate how you feel, but don't you think that this man's powers go beyond the army's ability to hold him? We could just shoot him and bury him here.'

'Don't be barbarous. Oh, he might get away –' the Doctor tapped his umbrella handle against his chin – 'but what will he do? He's got no weapons, no technology, and a life span of, what, ten more years at the most? That's the thing about such powerful biosystems. They burn themselves out.' His face darkened. 'I think killing him would be far too merciful.'

'You dog!' Greeneye spat. 'You took away our last chance!'

'Did I? I only just got here.'

Hadleman tapped the Doctor's shoulder. 'Erm, Doctor?'

The Doctor turned, suddenly beamed and pumped Hadleman's hand with two of his. 'Richard Hadleman! Pleased to meet you!'

'We've, ah, already met.'

'Yes.' The Doctor's face fell. 'But you shouldn't know about that. Oh, you mean Smith. He wasn't me. Much. If at all. What?'

Hadleman laughed, bombarded by the Doctor's swift collection of thoughts and postures. 'I just wanted to tell you, there's an army convoy outside the village. We could give him to them.'

'Yes, now the barrier's down, that's very apt. Very neat.'

Hutchinson had been watching the conversation, his hands on his hips. 'I'm just wondering, Smith, or Doctor, or whatever you're calling yourself, how you're going to answer to that same convoy for what you did to the school.'

'Me? I'm going to answer in the same way I answer every message that I don't want to hear. I'm not going to be at home.' He flipped up a finger and pressed a spot above the boy's nose. 'Now fall over.'

Hutchinson did, out cold. Anand and Merryweather looked down at the body, then shook hands.

Smith glanced around the group. 'Well, I'll leave it to you two –'

he indicated Alexander and Hadleman – 'to hand our villain over to the authorities; tell them he mustn't eat meat, by the way. And you boys can take yourselves down to the bakery in town.' He threw a bagful of coins onto the ground. 'That's a train fare home, a bun and probably a hug each… Then we can go home.'

Bernice peered at him, but decided not to mention it at the moment. She went to Alexander and Hadleman. 'I hope you'll be very happy,' she told them. 'If Alex's womanising doesn't get in the way.'

'Your what?' Hadleman frowned.

'My protestations…' the bearded man muttered. 'They may have been a little too successful.'

'And have you considered an American holiday?' asked Bernice. 'Very soon?'

Alexander kissed her cheek. 'We won't run away, loved one. Give my regards to the future.'

Hadleman shook her by the hand. 'Am I going to understand any of this?' he asked.

'Quite possibly.'

Merryweather approached Bernice cautiously. 'Will we meet again?' he asked hopefully.

Bernice framed an uneasy smile. 'Time will tell.'

The Doctor was shaking Tim's hand earnestly. 'Thank you for keeping things safe for me.'

'Thank you for being brave. I've decided that I'm going to be brave too.'

'So what are you going to be when you grow up?'

Tim glanced down at Hutchinson's body. 'Not a soldier.'

They finished their goodbyes, and Benny handed the Doctor the TARDIS key. She wasn't sure just what his intentions were, but, when he began twirling it around his finger and whistling as they walked away, she thought she had a pretty good idea.

When they'd walked far enough from the clearing not to be

heard, she disengaged herself from the Doctor's arm. 'Right,' she said.

'What?' The Doctor stopped. 'Is there one thing you don't understand?'

'I'll say. You said that you "sent Mrs Redfern home". Are you leaving it at that?'

The Doctor frowned. 'I thought we'd slip away. It's usually best.'

'Usually, but not when you've promised to go and see somebody and explain everything to her.'

The Doctor stared at her. 'How did you know that?'

'Because if you hadn't, she wouldn't have let you out of her sight.'

He glared down at the ground, his hands describing awkward little circles. 'She doesn't know... She thinks I'm... It'd be difficult.'

'Not half as much for you as for her. Doctor, you owe her an explanation. Your experiment in being human has hurt—'

'Hurt? I'm a Time Lord. Smith was a human.' He gazed at Bernice vacantly. 'I can't love her. I don't feel that way about her.'

'So she's lost the man she loved.'

'Then how can I help her?'

Bernice looked at him sadly. Distantly, she thought that she might have felt angry, but he looked so lost. 'What, you didn't find that out? What was this all for, then, this holiday in the human condition?'

'I thought it would be peaceful—'

'I'm not talking about the aliens. You're not responsible for them. I'm talking about the heart that you would have broken, battle or no battle. Doctor, please, go and talk to her.'

He looked at her for a moment. Then he nodded. 'Yes.'

Joan was tidying her house as the sun rose over the battered town. The military had arrived in force in the market square and fire brigades from the whole county had been going from house to house, helping to repair the damage. All that had happened to her own place, thankfully, was that a few pictures needed straightening and a bit of that silver dust that was everywhere needed brushing out of the carpet.

She glanced at the ring on her finger and smiled. It was quite a motif, that the sign of his love had spared her. And now he would be a hero, when the story got round, the schoolteacher who had saved everybody. It was quite a shock to discover that there were hostile creatures from other worlds. But there was also her own fallen angel. And he was, perhaps, representative of a gentler humanity that existed in the stars.

She sat down and let Wolsey leap into her lap. 'You're going to have to get used to a new householder,' she told him. 'But you like him, don't you?'

There was a knock on the door. She leapt up, much to Wolsey's disgust, and ran to it.

Her fiancé stood there, wearing a hat and a jacket that she'd never seen him in before.

Joan folded him into her arms and kissed him.

Then she withdrew, staring at him in surprise.

She picked her way back through the hall and into the sitting room, supporting herself on the furniture as she went. She finally sat down. 'John…' she murmured. 'Do come in. I'm sorry to be so… forward.'

'It's not that.' The Doctor closed the door and stepped into the centre of the sitting room, not quite looking at her. 'You know what's happened, don't you?'

'No.' She looked up at him, terrified. 'Please tell me.'

'I had to change back. To save you. You asked Smith not to give August the Pod. He didn't. I did. I'm the Doctor.'

'Oh…' Joan closed her eyes for a long, hard, instant. Then she opened them. 'I'm very pleased to meet you. Doctor. Is there nothing about you that's like the man to whom I've become engaged?'

'I think we believed in the same things. In the end. We're the same shape of person, using different memories. You made him more like me. He was willing to give his life—'

'Don't tell me that, I didn't want him to give his life. I didn't want to go through that again! My God, I don't think I can go through—' She forcibly stopped herself 'You don't love me, then? You have his form, his habits – and you move like him. But you don't love me?'

'No. I can't.'

'Why? Is he not a part of you? The human part?'

'There is no human part. I'm a Time Lord. A different species. He was a character I created, a fiction.'

'Rubbish. I don't give my heart to fictions. When his spirit inhabited you, you were not so different to the way you are now. John, if you're simply lying to me, there's no need, you can take my heart and go—'

'No!' The Doctor grabbed her forearms and made her rise. 'He loved you, he loved you so much that he was willing to become me again to save you. Feel.'

He took her hands and put them over one of his hearts. Then the other.

'And is one of them his?'

For the first time since he'd come here, he allowed himself a moment's uncertainty. 'I think that both my hearts are mine. That was one of the things I wanted to learn, where one part of me ends, where the next begins. Many of his attitudes and ideas, his ways of acting, were mine. But he's a different person, a role I created in order to learn things.'

'So you remember everything?'

The Doctor paused, then decided to tell the truth. 'Yes. What would be the point otherwise?'

Joan gave a short, bitter, laugh. 'You haven't learned how to love.'

'A fish can't learn to—'

'Walk?'

'Not that. A better metaphor. Whatever it is, I'm incapable of it.'

'Could you not become John Smith again?'

'If I could find another Pod. But such horror followed me. Such—' He dropped his head. 'That's not true. I might become a man again, but it wouldn't be John. And I wouldn't want to do it. I know everything I am, and that includes the knowledge that I want to be me.'

'Well…' Joan let go of his hands, and moved off a little way. 'I believe that you're a good man. You didn't know that your human self would fall in love.'

'It seems obvious now. What else do humans do?'

'Go to war.'

'I did both, then. And I was half successful.'

She smiled, sadly. 'Oh, more than half.' She plucked the ring from her finger. 'Do you want this back?'

'No. Keep it. Please.'

Wolsey, oblivious to what was happening, was rubbing himself up against the Doctor's legs. Joan glanced down at the cat. 'I shall have to move, of course. There's no school here for me to work at, now. I gained Wolsey through chance, when I arrived here, and I doubt that he would want to follow me to some other earthly destination.' She paused and took a sharp breath. 'I would like to think that you have a companion to guard you, besides Miss Summerfield. Would you be willing to take him on?'

The Doctor bent and picked up the cat, who curled up in his arms. 'Won't you miss him?'

'Miss him? I'll miss – No, no I'll get myself a litter of kittens and teach them all how to be good cats for good homes. May I keep those stories that you – that John wrote?'

The Doctor felt a heavy weight in his chest. 'If you wish.'

'Very well, then,' she said brightly. 'It's all decided. Was there anything else?'

'Joan... don't...'

'Don't what?'

'Don't...' The Doctor stared down at the cat in his arms. It jerked about, wanting to move, and then hopped up to lie along his shoulders. 'No. You must do what you have to.'

'Of course.' She quickly walked to the door and held it open for him. 'We both must. It was good of you to come and tell me. Thank you for saving us all.'

He paused for a moment at the door and gazed at her face. 'I hope that one day, when I'm old, when my travels are over, and history has no more need of me, then I can be just a man again. And then, perhaps I'll find those things in me that I'd need to love, also. Not love like I do, a big love for big things, but that more dangerous love. The one that makes and kills human beings.' He stretched out a finger to touch her face, but suspended it, an inch from her skin. 'It's a dream I have.'

He turned away and walked down the road.

He didn't look back.

Joan closed the door and sat down, not feeling anything. 'I should go to bed,' she said. Then she stood up suddenly, seized by the idea that she should run after him and grab Wolsey back.

She made herself stand by the door, not opening it.

And she stayed there for a very long time.

Laylock looked up at a sound from outside the tent. It was night, but he'd been pacing for hours, checking to see if the signal had been picked up by the vortex cabinet again.

The sound wasn't repeated, so he glanced at the dial once more.

'Good evening, Laylock.'

He spun round.

Alton was standing there, in a black robe now, rather than his school uniform. The robe carried no seal or insignia, but the cut of it suggested, as it was meant to, that the wearer was equally used to the darkened corridors of the Capitol as to alien fields and foxholes. Besides, an owl sat on his shoulder. Alton was pointing a gun at Laylock.

'Are they… Did they…' The old Aubertide took a step back.

Alton reached into a pouch at his belt. He produced a small bag of coins and handed it to the alien. 'Greetings from Aberdeen.'

He turned and left.

Laylock held the bag in his hand and sighed in relief. Then he went and switched off the vortex cabinet.

That night, Major Wrightson, who'd set up a detail of his men in the market square, was surprised to take custody of a prisoner. Hadleman and Alexander handed Greeneye over, together with statements about Rocastle and the hospital. They gave lengthy warnings about the prisoner, but still they seemed to want to be away. Alexander finally led Richard from all the camouflage and khaki, the younger man still calling things to Wrightson.

The major put his prisoner in a police station cell, to be transferred to a military lock-up first thing. Greeneye was quite passive. As Wrightson bid him goodnight he gave a wink and asked: 'Any chance of a corned-beef sandwich?'

Wolsey licked at the butter they'd put on his paws.

This new place was huge, with big white corridors leading off everywhere and an amazing range of interesting smells to follow. There had been another cat here, once, but it had gone now, so the territory was his. He'd already been shown a whole roomful of cat litter, and another with sunshine, climbing bars and a lot of different and challenging cushions to lie on. Cat heaven.

The two new people were sitting in chairs in the room with the thing that moved up and down. It was warm, so Wolsey was curled on top of it. The two people were drinking from cups. Every once in a while the woman would reach out and hold the man's hand. She'd held on to him for ages when he'd first come through the door, then they'd made the drink together, hardly letting go of each other.

Odd things, people. Still, Wolsey thought that he was going to like it here. It already felt like home.

Then the smooth motion lulled him to sleep.

He was woken only once that night, as his new owner reached down, late and alone, to gently smooth the fur on his head.

The cat could see that the man was weeping.

But there was nobody he could tell.

Epilogue

In June 1914, Archduke Ferdinand, the heir to the Austrian throne, was assassinated by Gavrilo Prinzip, a Serbian terrorist, while parading through Sarajevo. That city was the capital of Bosnia, then under Austrian control. The Serbians also claimed Bosnia.

The Austrians, angered by the killing and seeing an excuse to invade and conquer Serbia, sent the Serbians a list of demands. Some of these demands being completely unreasonable, the Serbians declined to meet them, offering instead to take the matter to the International Court at the Hague. Austria refused, and made preparations to invade Serbia.

Russia was allied to Serbia. It started mustering men on its borders. The great nations, bound by treaty, saw their rivals arming. Germany, allied to the Austrians, knew that France was allied to the Serbians. And the French wanted the German-held provinces of Alsace-Lorraine back. Therefore the Germans attacked France first. To do that, they marched through Luxemburg and Belgium.

And Britain had a treaty to protect Belgium.

Which is how the Ninth battalion of the Norfolk Regiment ended up on the Somme in July 1916, Captain Richard Hadleman with them. He had in his pocket some letters from Alexander, who, to his delight, had been spared his great decision by being judged too old and unfit to go. His life back in Farringham was much the same, bar the blackout at night and the very occasional sight of a zeppelin.

Richard had spoken up at a Labour Group meeting in October 1914, declaring, for some reason, that it was the duty of every good Socialist to enlist and protect the workers of Belgium. He'd seen the effect that battle had had on those children huddling about the fire – though that whole time seemed like a dream now – but he'd thought that he was a man, that he could make a sober decision to go to war and fight to his own specifications. Alexander had seemed very wise on the matter, in bed that evening. He'd said that, though Richard might be killed, it was his life to risk, just as it was a conscientious objector's right to risk hatred and ignorance at home. The government didn't possess the soul of either man, he'd said. Only that of the man who found himself forced or jollied into joining up because it was the only thing he could imagine doing.

Even then, Richard hadn't been comfortable with that.

Now he looked up at the absolute darkness above him and tried to scream, but it came out as a long, rattling choke.

Next time he'd stay home.

Next time. As if there were wars in Heaven or Hell, as if there was another battlefield he'd find himself on. The letters he held would have been enough, at any point, to have had him sent home. In disgrace, yes, but home, and what was disgrace compared to that? But he'd never shown them to anyone.

It was 14 July, just past eleven o'clock at night, and Richard had been lying in the cornfield since the early hours of that morning, coughing up blood and liquids of other colours that disturbed him far more. It was taking him a long time to die. He had, oddly, been part of one of the few successful military actions of the war.

At 3.25 that morning, 20,000 British troops had rushed across No Man's Land in the first-ever night attack, following only five minutes' bombardment. The Germans, used to the regular pattern of meaningless daylight sorties and endless night barrages, had actually been surprised. Five miles of their frontline had been overrun, the Norfolks firing as they ran along German trenches, bayoneting men as they woke from sleep. It had felt like a great victory, a breakthrough that might have brought this all to an end.

After the day looked won, towards late afternoon, Hadleman and his platoon had been sent to support a group of engineers running a telephone line from the Norfolks' incredibly advanced position all along this new frontline. They'd formed a marching group, making their way through the overgrown fields between the trenches as the engineers spun their big reel of wire on a cart behind them, looking around them warily. They had to take cover and creep on some occasions when it became clear that they were in sight of the new German frontline.

The soldiers of Hadleman's unit had been taken, as was the policy, from neighbouring towns and villages, and their associated OTCs, so it was hardly a surprise that he'd found himself commanding one Lieutenant Hutchinson. The young man was a good soldier, as Hadleman quickly found, having had a lot of the bile knocked out of him in his first actions. He still occasionally seemed to look upon Hadleman with contempt, but he never showed it to the men, who seemed to understand his distance and coolness more than Hadleman's own frustrated efforts to muster or befriend them. There were few others of those boys who'd been at Rocastle's academy. Perhaps it was because they were all to be officers, and were thus with other units, or perhaps, Hadleman liked to think, their experiences really had changed them. There had been some stink about Merryweather refusing to embark his platoon at the rail station, and them being forced onto the troop train at gunpoint. Alexander had reported a fine letter from Anand, now back home in his father's kingdom. A troop of his father's infantry had been sent to secure British supplies in the Gulf, but otherwise the war had not touched him and he remained wary of it.

So, it was thus that, towards the end of the day, Hadleman finally found the point that he'd evaded forced upon him, in circumstances where he thought he'd finally won.

There had been no great surge of relieved soldiers running past them up to the new positions. They'd passed a few reconnaissance patrols, who all indicated that some swift new offensive was about to happen. The sound of occasional battle was far ahead of them now, as the sun sank towards the horizon. They'd complete their work in an hour, the engineers assured him. Surely they wouldn't be asked to go forward again then? Whatever attack was being organised to dive into the break in the German line and open it up wide enough for a conclusive push, it was already overdue. Surely, the mass march would be on before they'd got back?

Then on the horizon to the west, silhouetted against the sun, Hadleman saw the cavalry. Three divisions of them, tiredly organising themselves into formation squares on the other side of the great fields of corn that were growing wild out here in the wastes. The engineers laughed and made expressions of amazement. Hadleman's own troops started to speculate that this must be some kind of diversion, until Hutchinson quietened them. He and Hadleman realised the truth at once, that this was the crucial attack they'd been waiting for. It had taken all day to bring the horsemen up to the line. This offensive had been seen as the one opportunity this war had offered for an old-fashioned set-piece action, and those in charge had leapt at it.

There came the sound of a distant bugle and the horses formed up. A sabre was raised, then dropped, and they accelerated forward.

The Norfolks watched in awe as the hundreds of horsemen raced through the corn, a great cry erupting from them. 'They must think that they've got a chance,' Hutchinson whispered. 'Maybe they can see something we can't.'

The noise made them all wince as it started up, the regular clatter of machine guns. At first, it seemed that maybe it was only an isolated post, that perhaps the German line ahead that the cavalry were supposed to over-run contained an isolated weapon.

But then the rattle became a great roar and the air around the cavalry darkened with metal.

The first line of horses crumpled, their riders flying off their backs as they fell, some of them riding them down into a crumbling mass of man, animal and corn. The second, third, fourth lines fell as the guns scythed back and forth across the field. The momentum of the charge continued, hundreds of men spinning off the backs of their mounts, the bodies of those in front tripping and hindering the ones who came behind until the whole field was a mist of noise and metal and flying blood.

'Retreat, for Christ's sake,' Hutchinson was whispering. 'Why does nobody give the order? Why don't they—'

The first whistle sounded overhead and the soldiers threw themselves to the ground, their hands grabbing their metal helmets.

'Christ!' screamed Hutchinson. 'This is the one! This is the one Dean – Christ!'

The shell landed noiselessly, for Hadleman, the sound too loud and close for him to hear. At least, that was his memory of it.

Hutchinson died instantly.

When the noise ended, Hadleman was lying in a pile of dead people, his head ringing from something distant.

He pushed his way out, shouldering corpses off of him, and immediately choked on the air, his eyes streaming. He slapped for the gasmask at his neck, and found that, along with half his pack, it had been dragged off him.

So, under nothing but instinct, he burrowed down into the men again, pulling their warmth back around him, until he was concealed in a dark burrow of flesh, with a little air.

He stayed that way for maybe ten minutes, then had to surface. He lay there amongst the limbs of those he knew, for some time, taking one full breath in three and coughing, aware that he was getting the end of the gas as it drifted away. That, and there was some bleeding in his jacket, a wound the pain of which rose and fell with his lungs.

He didn't even think of trying to get back to the line. He wasn't sure where it was any more, or even in which direction. If it wasn't for Alexander, he would be quite satisfied to die, knowing that the war he was fighting in was utterly futile. It was almost as if he'd proved a point of politics to himself. In this place, upwards of 400,000 British men were going to be killed. They'd lost 20,000 just the other day. He sucked a grim smile. It was like rich countries deliberately killing themselves, leaving their battered remains ready for the revolution that would surely come, for who could return home without wanting to face those who had wasted good men thus?

He raised his hand, and tried to sing 'The Red Flag'.

But he was unconscious before he'd got past the bit about cowards.

He woke again in the night to a noise. He tried not to make a noise, though he heard many distant cries, oddly hoping that it wasn't a German come to rob him.

A face appeared over the low ridge above him, a muddied blond lad in a dull grey uniform. 'Good Lord,' he whispered. 'I knew there were some Norfolks out here. Richard Hadleman, isn't it?'

Hadleman blinked, the face wobbling in and out of vision. He tried to remember the name. 'Timothy? What regiment are you—'

'None, actually. Red Cross. A few of us are having a sniff about out here, because nobody quite knows who owns this bit at the moment, and we kept hearing shouts. Now, if you can move, I don't want to get my arse shot off doing field dressings. Mind taking the hand of a filthy conchie?'

Hadleman reached up and felt everything give as Timothy Dean hauled him out of the pile of bodies. He stifled a shout.

Timothy supported him by his shoulder and the two of them picked their way off towards the British line. Hadleman glimpsed familiar shapes a few hundred yards away. 'Got any jobs going?' he whispered.

'You don't need to worry,' Timothy replied. 'You're going home.'

The bells of Norwich Cathedral rang clear and sharp on an April morning in 1995. Snowflakes were falling steadily. Above the cathedral blew great billows of them, whipping around the corners of the dark building as if to emphasise the structure's harsh lines.

From out of the building trooped a handful of very old men in uniform, supported by their relatives and children. The Norfolks who'd fought in the Great War had a yearly reunion in the city, though their numbers grew smaller every time. This might well be the last one.

By the door of the cathedral, at some distance from the marching men, another old man sat in a wheelchair, surrounded by his family.

'I don't know why you come here every year, Grandad,' said Richard Dean, leaning on the wheelchair's handles. 'What's there to see?'

'Old friends ...' the pensioner whispered. 'Not from the war. From before.'

'So why do you never talk to them?' Richard's wife Jane tucked in the blanket that had come loose about his legs once more. She ignored a glare from her husband. 'It might help if you didn't insist on wearing that.' She tapped the white poppy that Timothy wore on his coat. 'It's not as if it's even Remembrance Day.'

'I wear it because it stands for what I am. I can't ignore that for their friendship. Besides, I always hoped that I'd meet...' His gaze wandered from his words again, lost in time.

'Great Grandad! Don't go to sleep now!' A girl of eleven stood beside the wheelchair. 'Listen to this. I read that they once found a cow in an army cell. A cow! Where they'd had a prisoner! And when they took it off to be slaughtered with the other cows, it kicked and kicked and they had to force it to go in. Isn't that amazing?'

'What have you been reading now?' her father sighed. The girl had become a vegetarian last summer, just in time for Christmas, and seemed to see old Timothy as some kind of role model.

'You let her read what she likes.' The old man came to life again, and put his hand on the girl's arm. 'She's going to be a great scientist. Or an astronaut, or... or all sorts of things.'

'I'm going to be just like you,' the girl told him.

'Then you'll never kill anybody, even when everyone else is?'

'Never.' The girl was looking up at him, hushed, as if she was receiving a benediction.

'And you will never be cruel or cowardly?

'Never.'

'Then you'll live to be as old and as happy as my friends Alexander and Richard, who managed to avoid time's attention for...' His own gaze wandered off again, but this time it found a focus. Two figures were standing on the corner by the cathedral grounds. Two figures that old Tim recognised from somewhere, maybe from a dream. They met the old man's eyes, then smiled satisfied smiles. Timothy started to laugh. 'For that's the thing about time, you see! That's the thing about time! It's like a big story, and it's never over! I remember, when I was very young, and Mother used to read to me in bed, I'd fall asleep before she'd stop reading. But the next night, she'd know where we'd been. She'd never lose her place.'

And Timothy laid his head back against his grandson's hand, his cheek warm against the man's skin. He breathed deeply, and fell into what would turn out to be his final sleep.

The white poppy had fallen from his lapel in his exertions, and was left, unnoticed, on the pavement as the Dean family went on their way.

Just before they turned the corner, the little girl looked over her shoulder and saw the Doctor bending down to pick the poppy up. She looked at him curiously and he gave her a smile.

Then she was gone.

The Doctor slipped the white poppy into his buttonhole.

'So, where do you want to go?' he asked Bernice, who was shivering in her duffle-coat. Earlier in the day, she'd consulted her Portable History Unit again, and discovered that, inexplicably, the casualty list for the Somme had changed. But then the thing had gone on the blink. The Doctor had refused to mend it again.

'Somewhere that sells hot chocolate and crumpets.'

'After that.'

'Perhaps we could go and do something good. Help somebody.'

'We could go back to Guy.'

'We could go back to Joan.'

They looked at each other, and they might have looked sad.

But instead they smiled.

The Doctor took Bernice's arm. 'There's a place that springs to mind. A planet called Oolis. A few things need sorting out there. But it might be dangerous.'

'Oh, will there be monsters?' They started to walk away.

'Of course. The Oolians have wings, and beaks, and armoured battlesuits.'

'And will there be villains? And deadly danger?'

'Oh yes. And probably death, with or without a capital D.'

'Then we should go there immediately. Who else is there to sort these things out?'

'Who indeed?'

Benny shivered again. 'There's only one thing that I wouldn't want to face again in a hurry.'

'What's that?'

'Snow. Does Oolis have any?'

The Doctor glanced up at the snowflakes that sped by, and frowned. 'But if it wasn't for the snow, how could we believe in the immortality of the soul?'

'What on earth do you mean?'

The frown faded from the Doctor's face and he grinned again. 'Do you know, I haven't the slightest idea.'

The two friends wandered off into the city to find tea and crumpets and warmth.

And somewhere in the sky overhead, for an instant before they dissolved into mist, two snowflakes were the same.

Long ago in an English spring.

ACKNOWLEDGEMENTS

With thanks to:

Kate Orman – Kate and I wrote the initial plot for this book together, because I couldn't make my initial idea work on my own. Many elements have changed since then, but quite a lot of the good bits are still hers. 'From a plot by Paul and Kate' would describe it, except then she'd be held responsible for my later errors. Cheers, Kate.

Andy Lane, Steven Moffat, Helen Reilly – Criticism and structural advice. (Steven also plotted Dr Smith's fantasy story.)

Jim Barrett, Nathan Bottomley, Esther Page, Jac Rayner – Research.

Penny List – Moral support.

The NSCT – Fraternity.

Caroline Minall – Owner of the real Wolsey.

Bean, Medge, Rob and the House of Yoyodyne in Adelaide, Sean-Paul, Kelly, Ellie and the House of Gallifrey in Melbourne and the House of the Shameless in Sydney – Hospitality and ideas.

Rebecca, Peter, Andy, and John – 'Every old sock meets an old shoe.'

And to all my friends, for their love and patience. And thanks to Mum and Dad, for Bread and Butter and Honey.

The quotes at the start are from *Paisley Pattern* issue 48, an article by David John Darlington, and from *Melody Maker* 27/7/94, Paul Mathur's review of The Prodigy in concert. The line Smith quotes to Fiona in the bakery was originally Richard Feynman's.

(Thank you… hope we passed the audition)

Also available in the Doctor Who History Collection:

THE STONE ROSE

JACQUELINE RAYNER

ISBN 978 1 849 90906 8

A 2,000 year old statue of Rose Tyler is a mystery that the Doctor and Rose can only solve by travelling back to the time when it was made. But when they do, they find the mystery is deeper and more complicated than they ever imagined.

While the Doctor searches for a missing boy, Rose befriends a girl who it seems can accurately predict the future. But when the Doctor stumbles on the terrible truth behind the statue, Rose herself learns that you have to be very careful what you wish for.

An adventure set in Roman times, featuring the Tenth Doctor, as played by David Tennant, and his companion Rose Tyler.

Also available in the Doctor Who *History Collection:*

THE ROUNDHEADS

MARK GATISS

ISBN 978 1 849 90903 7

With the Civil War won, the Parliamentarians are struggling
to hang on to power. But plans are being made to rescue the
defeated King Charles from his prison…

With Ben press-ganged and put on board a mysterious ship
bound for Amsterdam, Polly becomes an unwitting accomplice
in the plot to rescue the King. The Doctor can't help because he
and Jamie have been arrested and sent to the Tower of London,
charged with conspiracy.

Can the Doctor and Jamie escape, find Ben and rescue Polly –
while making sure that history remains on its proper course?

*An adventure set in the aftermath of the English Civil War, featuring the
Second Doctor, as played by Patrick Troughton, and his companions Ben,
Polly and Jamie.*

Also available in the Doctor Who History Collection:

DEAD OF WINTER
JAMES GOSS
ISBN 978 1 849 90907 5

In a remote clinic in eighteenth-century Italy, a lonely girl writes to her mother. She tells of pale English aristocrats and mysterious Russian nobles. She tells of intrigues and secrets, and strange faceless figures that rise up from the sea. And she tells about the enigmatic Mrs Pond, who arrives with her husband and her trusted physician.

What the girl doesn't tell her mother is the truth that everyone at the clinic knows and no one says – that the only people who come here do so to die.

An adventure set in eighteenth-century Italy, featuring the Eleventh Doctor, as played by Matt Smith, and his companions Amy and Rory.

Also available in the Doctor Who History *Collection:*

THE ENGLISH WAY OF DEATH
GARETH ROBERTS
ISBN 978 1 849 90908 2

The Doctor, Romana and K-9 are hoping for a holiday in
London in the sweltering summer of 1930. But the TARDIS is
warning of time pollution. And that's not the only problem.

What connects the isolated Sussex resort of Nutchurch with
the secret society run by the eccentric Percy Closed? Why
has millionaire Hepworth Stackhouse dismissed his staff and
hired assassin Julia Orlostro? And what is the truth behind the
infernal vapour known only as Zodaal?

With the heat building, the Doctor and his friends set out to
solve the mysteries.

*An adventure set in 1930s London, featuring the Fourth Doctor, as
played by Tom Baker, and his companions Romana and K-9.*

Also available in the Doctor Who *History Collection:*

THE SHADOW IN THE GLASS
JUSTIN RICHARDS AND STEPHEN COLE
ISBN 978 1 849 90905 1

When a squadron of RAF Hurricanes shoots down an
unidentified aircraft over Turelhampton, the village is
immediately evacuated. But why is the village still guarded by
troops in 2001? When a television documentary crew break
through the cordon looking for a story, they find they've
recorded more than they'd bargained for.

Caught up in both a deadly conspiracy and a historical mystery,
retired Brigadier Lethbridge-Stewart calls upon his old friend
the Doctor. Half-glimpsed demons watch from the shadows as
the Doctor and the Brigadier travel back in time to discover the
last, and deadliest, secret of the Second World War.

*An adventure set partly in the Second Wold War, featuring the Sixth
Doctor, as played by Colin Baker, and Brigadier Lethbridge-Stewart.*

Also available in the Doctor Who *History Collection:*

AMORALITY TALE
DAVID BISHOP
ISBN 978 1 849 90904 4

When gangster Tommy Ramsey is released from prison,
he is determined to retake control of his East End territory.
But new arrivals threaten his grip on illegal activity in the
area. An evangelical minister is persuading people to seek
redemption for their sins. A new gang is claiming the streets.
And a watchmender called Smith is leading a revolt against the
Ramsey Mob's protection racket.

When Tommy strikes back at his enemies, a far more terrifying
threat is revealed. Within hours the city's air turns into nerve
gas and thousands succumb to the choking fumes. London is
dying…

*An adventure set in 1950s London, featuring the Third Doctor, as played
by Jon Pertwee, and his companion Sarah Jane Smith.*